VERITY REVEALED

This is a work of fiction. Any similarities to people or instances, past or present, are strictly coincidental. The constitutionally protected opinions and beliefs expressed herein concerning President Lyndon Johnson and the Vietnam War are the author's own.

VERITY REVEALED

FIRST EDITION

Copyright @2019 Jeanette Joyce

ISBN 978-0-578-50602-9

Cover Design by Suzette Vaughn

Edited by Andrea Berryman and Patty Joyce

First Printing – 2019

Printed in the United States

Distributed by Autumn Glow Productions, LLC

All rights to this book are reserved by the copyright and trademark holders including the right of reproduction in whole or in part. No part of VERITY REVEALED may be produced in any manner without the written consent of the author.

autumnglowbooks@gmail.com

DEDICATION

This book is dedicated to Joseph M. Joyce, an unassuming man of prayer and faith-filled wisdom; the kind that comes when one has spent a lifetime in the Word. I am blessed to have had the privilege of calling this man my dad. And to my sister, Loretta Poss, who never ceased to encourage me to move forward with my dream of writing books.

I have adjusted to their absence; in large measure due to a **VERITY** that fills my spirit with hope in a heavenly reunion, when death can no longer separate us from our loved ones.

ACKNOWLEDGEMENTS

To my sister, Patty Joyce, thank you! You were the one constant I counted on and you never let me down. This book would not have seen publication without you. You are the best.

To Michael Walton, former Chief of Police, Springfield, Illinois, for your invaluable assistance in helping me to understand police practices in 1969, I thank you. As a Vietnam veteran, I thank you most of all. Our soldiers are blessed with respect and appreciation today, as a direct result of the disrespect and lack of appreciation that you and your comrades bore; even as you carried out your military duties. I am so proud of you and all of our Vietnam veterans. Thank you! You are a true American hero.

Mary Ann Paulis, Bonnie Pritchard, Bob Cowles, Charlie Cusumano, and to my relatives from down under, Jennifer Ireland and Pam and Clem Mulcahy, thank you for your constructive critique of the manuscript. It made the story better.

Andrea Berryman, thank you for your editing expertise.

To my fellow author and friend, Terry Castleman, thank you for sharing your knowledge and experience with me.

To Mary Ellen Creighton, you are priceless. Thank you, my friend.

To Andy Hegele, thank you. I'd still be pulling my hair out if you hadn't come to my rescue.

To my nephew, Stuart Poss, I thought of you as I prepared the manuscript for publication; remembering with fondness our poolside talks. Yes, it is about time.

Most especially to Don DeHeve, there are no words that can adequately express my gratitude. I can only promise to pay your kindness forward. Rest in peace, my friend.

A NOTE FROM THE AUTHOR
May, 2019

The story you are about to read began with a dream I had in 1987. It seemed to come out of nowhere, although it must have been predicated in part on the death of my brother in Vietnam. Like most dreams, it didn't make much sense. But I couldn't shake this one from my memory. Over time, as I strived to understand its meaning, a picture began to take shape in my head.

VERITY REVEALED is my interpretation of that dream and the fictional story that came forth from it. I tell that dream in Chapter 1 as speaking to you directly, in order to set the stage for what that dream has come to mean to me.

For those who have suffered a grievous loss, I wish you peace and comfort. I hope also, that **VERITY REVEALED** opens your heart and mind to the eternal truth that I found that summer night so very long ago.

VERITY REVEALED

By

Jeanette Joyce

"O death, where is thy sting? Oh grave, where is thy victory?"

1 Corinthians 15:55

CHAPTER 1
The Dream

On a warm summer night, I laid down on my bed, pajama clad under a top sheet, and waited for sleep to overtake me. The alarm clock was set for 5:30 a.m. Before long I found myself dreaming. The experience was one I would not likely forget.

I found myself sitting all alone on a street curb with no one else in sight. It was dark and although the light standards were on, they didn't seem to give out much illumination.

I had no idea why I was sitting there. I would never be able to recall the particular street or where it was located. I only knew I felt no fear but felt completely safe and secure.

I looked to my right and suddenly saw two young men with their backs toward me, walking up the street, away from me. Somehow, that street was elevated from the one that I was on, although it was directly connected to my own.

I saw their back sides clearly as there was illumination all around them. The light, a bright gold tone, seemed to permeate from the street on which they walked. There was beauty all around them, something not recognizable in the place where I was now standing, less than one city-block away. It appeared unearthly.

It looked as if the two young men might well be touring the world's most beautiful spot on earth except there's nothing even remotely like that anywhere I have ever been.

Its beauty reached beyond my feeble ability to describe it accurately. The street shone of gold; the gate located just at the edge of the light sparkled with ruby, amethyst and a multitude of other precious gems.

A river, clear and glistening from the illumination, ran just to the right side of the road. Lions and lambs alike were mingling together in peace and harmony.

This place was as alluring to me as any place I had ever known. Strangely, it felt like home. Not the physical house one lives in, but rather that safe haven where you're loved and accepted unconditionally, sheltered and protected by the strong arms of a loving father and mother.

That's the way my childhood home was, and I am richly blessed for having been reared in my father's house. But my father's house seemed to pale in comparison to the place where the two young men were.

There was an awesome presence in that place. I could feel Him watching over, although I never saw His face. That presence conveyed a gentleness as soft as a baby's breath, but at the same time, exuded power and strength beyond my wildest imagination.

His aura was awesome. I was awestruck and began to tremble, although I never saw the Keeper of this place. I trembled at the thought that He was watching me as well as the two young travelers on the road.

I realized then, that the two young men and I, separated by a mere city block, were in reality worlds apart.

But neither the breathtaking beauty nor the warm alluring light that surrounded the men, or the presence of the gentle, powerful One watching over was attracting me so much at this moment.

I looked seriously at one of the young men, -- the one on the left, -- and my heart started pounding as it had never done before. I recognized him through his walk -- that swift, swinging trait so familiar to a large number of my family members.

"Tommy. Tommy!" I hollered as I began to run as fast as I could toward him. Oddly, as I ran in the direction of the two young men, I made no progress. The distance between us seemed to remain the same. So, I pushed harder, ran faster to catch them, but to no avail.

The light moved with them and I was continually in the dark. Still, I refused to quit. I ran, calling my brother's name, for what seemed to be hours, but was probably only seconds.

I felt hot and sweaty from my labors to catch up to them. Still, they never stopped to wait for me. Eventually, I had to cease from running, as my sides were hurting, and I was struggling to catch my breath.

I began to cry hysterically, so fearful that my much-loved brother would leave without so much as a hello. I fell to my knees on the street in sheer frustration and exhaustion.

"Tommy, stop!" I pleaded hysterically; with the last

remaining strength I could muster. Still, neither young man turned to look at the poor, pathetic young woman now lying prostrate on a darkened, dirty street.

I pulled myself up, back onto my knees, tears streaming down my face.

I screamed at Tom in blood-curdling fashion. "How can you do this to me?" Had this not been a dream, the sleeping people in the homes along the street would have awakened and called the police. "Someone sounds like they're being murdered," they would have reported. But that didn't matter. I was desperate.

I hollered at Tom, still walking away from me. "I told you once that I would never forget you." But my voice was weak from the hysterical sobbing. Maybe he just didn't hear me.

I was heartbroken but unwilling to give up my plight to reach him. In a whimpering half-whisper but with all of the ability within me, I continued my efforts to capture his attention.

"Have you forgotten me already? Don't you remember who I am?" Tears streamed down my face.

"Please stop and talk with me. I'm your sister!" My heart was breaking, completely devastated by the apparent lack of recognition.

I stretched out prostrate on the asphalt road. All of my efforts had been to no avail. He wasn't going to stop for me, I began to believe. I rested my head on the street, my spirit completely broken.

I had no more strength within me. I lay there sobbing for what seemed to be hours, unable and unwilling to move from the spot where I last saw my brother, Tom.

Eventually, I looked up again to watch him walk down the gold-illuminated street that he and his companion traveled. I sorely accepted the fact they weren't going to stop for me, but I wanted to feast my eyes on my brother for as long as I could before he disappeared and I wouldn't see him again.

It had been twenty-seven years since the last time I looked upon him and I longed to savor the moment I now had.

Yet, to my absolute amazement, I saw they weren't walking away anymore. Indeed, they had stopped, turned around and were gazing at me as I lay on the street. I raised myself to my knees quickly, not wanting to take my eyes off them.

And for the first time I saw their faces and knew without a doubt I was seeing my beloved brother, and something else; his companion looked familiar to me also, although at the moment I couldn't seem to place him.

Who is he? I pondered.

The two young men appeared as if they could have been brothers, although I knew they never were, at least not in the world that I was presently occupying. It wasn't so much a physical likeness they shared but rather a common Spirit within them that seemed to tie them together in brotherhood.

It was the way they looked at me. There was something about their eyes that attracted me equally to both of them. They seemed to be filled with such a perfect love, the likes of which I had never experienced before. Their faces radiated peace, their countenance exuded joy. There were no stress lines etched in their faces, no pain or toil.

They appeared wise beyond their earthly years. It was as if they knew so much more than me, although today, I was the oldest amongst us.

For a moment, I felt foolish for my hysterical outburst but their compassionate faces dispelled all that. There was no ridicule; only a love that surpassed human understanding. Tom knew me and somehow so did the young stranger equally.

I felt myself being drawn to that stranger with the same intensity that drew me to my own brother.

Who is he? I struggled internally. I kept trying to place him, trying to recall when it was that I had known him. Somewhere in my past, he had been there. I could feel it but I couldn't recall where.

As they stood looking at me with warm compassionate smiles on their faces, neither said a word but they didn't have to. Their silence spoke volumes. I felt my lifetime flash before me as I stood looking into their faces.

All the pain and sorrow of my brother's untimely death evaporated in the balmy air of that silent summer's night. The pain of loss was gone.

I had found Tom again, looked on his face and somehow knew that my tears were being turned to joy. He was safe, completely happy and appeared absolutely confident that no evil would ever touch him again.

Somehow, seeing the place where he now was, I knew that had to be true. I could sense that he was telling me these things. They both were, although neither spoke a word.

Now, I wondered if their compassion toward me was due to any future painful events that I would have to endure throughout the remaining years of my life, whatever those events might be.

Somehow, they were aware of those things, things my future held in store, but neither appeared troubled by them. They seemed to desire that I be of good cheer.

They knew the struggles of life were nothing in comparison to the joy that awaited me down the road that I traveled; the road directly connected to their own.

I could almost hear them telling me that I would walk with them someday in that beautiful place. Still neither had spoken a word. I felt so happy inside that my spirit leaped within me. For that moment in time, I knew it desperately wanted out of the skin and bones that trapped it.

I looked at the young man traveling with my brother and I smiled, hoping he wouldn't recognize that I was struggling to identify him. Yet, deep down I knew he was aware of my toil.

He didn't appear concerned but rather showed a confidence that it would come to me eventually. He cared for me deeply. I could see it in his eyes and at that moment I loved him as much as I loved my own brother; as much as I had ever loved anyone. Somehow, I realized he truly was a brother after all -- a brother in spirit. But what was his name?

As we stood peering at one another a change came over me. It was a change I would never have accepted before this summer night. From the darkened street on which I knelt I began to realize that life truly goes on eternally. I always had a head smart about that, but suddenly that knowledge was seeping into my very soul.

It was all true, the teachings of my childhood. My brother wasn't dead but was alive; more now than he had ever been on this earth. Logically, while he lived here, each breath he took brought him that much closer to his death; something all the living must experience. But now, that was all behind him. He'd never have to experience anything like that again.

It didn't matter, all the brutality he'd experienced in his short life. Somehow that pain was dissipated in the joy that now filled him completely. In fact, he appeared as if he didn't recall any of the injustices that he experienced fighting a war that shouldn't have been or by losing his life by the design of an incompetent leader. Somehow, I sensed the mere thought of hatred or anger had no place in his world today.

Tom was looking at me and I knew he was witnessing the anger and rage I harbored within myself toward Lyndon Johnson. I could sense it, and began to feel ashamed. The two young men didn't seem to have an understanding of those hardened feelings. They were so foreign to them now.

I didn't want them for myself anymore, either. Quickly I prayed for forgiveness. I realized the wasted energy I had expended over all these years. Suddenly, I only wanted the best for Lyndon Johnson and hoped he was sharing in the serenity of that place where Tom and the stranger with him were.

But who is he? I toiled to place him, for I knew he had been a part of my past.

As I stood there watching, the two young men turned away from me and continued on their journey. Although I didn't want to see them go, I didn't struggle. I was completely filled; satisfied by the time we spent together.

The weight of grief and sorrow over my brother's passing had somehow lifted from me. I stood there staring for the longest time as the space between us widened, and that's when it happened. A light bulb turned on in my head.

I hollered as loudly as I could. "I've got it. I know who you are. You're Daniel. Daniel Sycamore!"

The young man glanced back over his shoulder and smiled warmly at me.

I was so delighted at my eventual recollection that I jumped up gleefully and spun myself around in a circle. When I stopped, I searched for them but they were gone. The place where they once stood had darkened and the street was lined with similar houses to the ones that were located on the block where I now stood.

For a moment I lingered, savoring every last instant I could, before turning to make my way back home again. And as I did, I saw the darkness being overtaken by the light of the rising sun.

When I awakened, I was back in my bed where it all started. Words cannot describe the joy that shrouded me that morning or the lightness that my body felt, like a feather swaying in the wind.

Truly, it wasn't pounds I shed throughout that unforgettable summer night but rather the weighty bonds of hate, anger and bitterness. I was freed at last. Paroled from the albatross that weighted around my neck for almost thirty years. Truths had been deposited in my heart that time could no longer assail. It was settled. I had achieved unshakeable confidence in an everlasting verity.

CHAPTER 2
The Guy Back There is Dead
1969

Brian Redmond was traveling to Chesterfield, Missouri from his home in Racine, Wisconsin. The twenty-two-year-old was a junior at Gateway Technical College in Racine. But this was Christmas break, and he was going to visit friends he'd met while attending a junior college in Missouri the year before.

The young man glanced at his speedometer, not wanting to get a ticket as he traveled U. S. Route 66 southward in his 1969 green Pontiac Custom S. As he journeyed through Sturnus County, Illinois, the time was almost 3 a.m. on the morning of December 19, 1969.

The moon offered little light to the blackened wintery sky. The temperature had dropped well below freezing at a bone-chilling 23 degrees. A strong wind was blowing, and the overpasses were glazing over with frost and becoming slippery.

Brian was traveling through unfamiliar territory. Early on, he decided to keep an eye on the fuel gauge, not wanting it to drop any lower than a quarter of a tank. Checking it now, he noticed it had reached that point and he certainly didn't want to run out of gas on that dark stretch of pavement and have to wait for help to arrive. A Texaco Station, looming in the distance, was a welcome sight for sore eyes.

Brian turned off the highway onto the county road that led into the full-service station. He noticed a blue Chevy II making a right turn onto Route 66, heading south toward St. Louis at a high rate of speed.

He thought the car looked familiar; similar to one that passed him on the highway awhile back. Pulling up to the fuel pumps closest to the entrance, he drove over the air hose attached to a bell on the inside. As he did, he heard the buzzer that should have alerted the night attendant to his arrival.

The station was illuminated inside and out, displaying the

small cardboard sign hanging on the front door that read 'Open.' Credence Clearwater Revival's "Proud Mary" was playing on the radio, and Brian's fingers tapped to the beat on the steering wheel.

He was anxious to get fueled up and back on the highway. Earlier, he took the Culver Street exit at Starling and drove onto the parking area surrounding the St. Peter Catholic Church. There he was able to sleep for a few hours. Now, however, he was wide awake and looking to make up for lost time.

Once again, he glanced to see if he could spot the guy from where he was parked at the pump, but to no avail. He turned the car off and walked to the front of the automobile, raised the hood and checked the oil. Still, no one came outside. As he looked around, he wondered what could be taking the attendant so long.

Brian began to think he might be inside sleeping. Leaving the hood up, he made his way into the station. Entering the main room, he saw no one but noticed an open door that led into a storage room. *Maybe the attendant is sleeping back here,* he thought as he stepped through the doorway.

What he saw was worse than any horror movie he'd ever seen as a kid. The body was lying on the floor and blood had stained the concrete over to the drain. "Oh, my God, my God!" he shrieked. He reeled and ran back into the main room.

A blood-curdling scream rose from his gut, and his lower jaw dropped wide open. "Oh Jesus, help me. Help me, Lord, help me."

He wondered if whoever was responsible for this might be lurking somewhere just watching him. He could feel the hair on the back of his neck rising and was seized with chills running up and down his spine.

Terror gripped Brian from all around. The silence at the station was deafening and shattered only by his heavy breathing. He could hear his heart pounding in his chest and could feel his entire body trembling. He wanted desperately to run as far away as possible. Instead, he saw a pay phone hanging on the wall over by the entryway.

"Just keep calm and get some help," he commanded himself as he reached for the phone receiver.

His hands were shaking as he rifled through his pants pocket to come up with the dime required to use the telephone. Steadying

19

himself, he deposited the coin into the slot and noticed a list of emergency numbers written on the wall. His intention was to call the police, but in his excitement, he dialed the emergency number for fire instead.

The call went to another service station on the outskirts of Piedmont, located a few miles southeast on Route 114. Piedmont is a small farming community and in the late and early morning hours, the Sully Standard Station overlapped as the fire reporting center for that area.

Walter (Wally) Williams was working the midnight to 7 a.m. shift. A steel worker by trade, he worked part time at Sully's. It was 3:06 a.m., when he answered the call from a frightened Brian Redmond.

Brian was breathing fast and heavy. "Is this the police?"

"No, it isn't. What's the problem?"

"I'm at a gas station on Route 66 and someone has been shot here. I found your number on a list hanging on the wall, but I thought I was calling the police. I've got to get 'um out here fast man, I'm really scared!"

Wally felt his own adrenalin kick in. "Whoa! I need you to take a deep breath, calm down and tell me where you are."

Brian's voice shrieked with fear. "I don't know, I don't know!"

Wally spoke softly to the distraught caller. "It's all right. If you found my number on an emergency list, you can't be far away. I'll call the police if you can give me a clue to your whereabouts."

Brian took a deep breath to calm his nerves. "All I know is I'm at a Texaco on Route 66. I'm not from around here, man. I just stopped for gas, and now I wish to God I never had!" Brian was close to tears but struggled valiantly to maintain his composure.

Wally's concern mounted as Brian's shaky voice pierced his ear. "Calm down, it's going to be okay. Can you look for an address? Is there any mail lying on the desk?" Both men struggled to remain focused and clear headed.

"No, there's nothing like that lying around. Hold on, I've got an idea." Brian put the phone down and went outside to look for a landmark. He noticed a sign above the outside door that read 'Harlan Vernon's Texaco' and returned to relay the information.

It was all Wally needed. He knew the station well. He told

Brian he would call the police for him.

Before hanging up Brian pleaded with Wally in a cracking, fearful voice, "I'm really scared, man. I'm all alone. Please get the police out here as fast as you can!"

Brian felt unnerved by the eerie silence, and now wished he was back in the safe haven of his mother's loving home.

Wally was born and reared in Piedmont. He knew there were shootings and bad things happening in cities like Chicago and places like Starling, with a population of about 95,000 people. But here, almost 15 minutes outside Starling, things like that just didn't happen. Everybody knew everybody else, and folks were friendly.

Walter assumed an accident must have occurred while one of the boys was cleaning the 12-gauge shotgun known to be kept at Vernon's. Still, he never received a call like this one, and he found himself feeling extremely nervous and uneasy about it.

Wally quickly placed the phone's handset into its cradle, disconnecting the line with Brian, and immediately drew it back to his ear. He steadied his trembling hand and dialed '0' on the rotary phone. The operator immediately connected him to the State Police.

Corporal Darryl Heath, a sixteen-year veteran, was working the desk at police headquarters, located five miles south of Starling at Route 66 and East Haven Drive. Heath logged the call in at 3:08 a.m.

Walter anxiously relayed his conversation with the traveler. "The attendant at the Vernon Texaco on Highway 66 at Glenrose has been shot!" Heath immediately passed the information to the radio room where it was dispatched to the State Police car working that area. Then he called the Sturnus County Sheriff's Department under whose jurisdiction the station was located.

After talking with Corporal Heath, Walter took a few moments to gain his composure. His mind was racing as fast as his heart was pounding. He wondered which one of the boys was working at Vernon's that night. Of course, he knew most of them. Some even lived right there in Piedmont.

They're just kids, -- all of them just working to make a little extra spending money. What the devil is going on over there? he thought to himself.

The night stillness burrowed beneath Wally's skin, gnawing on every nerve ending until his thoughts centered on his neighbor.

"Harlan!" He found himself saying the name aloud. "Somebody ought to let Harlan know."

Wally knew Harlan Vernon, the proprietor, well. For almost twenty years, the two friends shared an annual outing to Adams County, Illinois during deer hunting season. Once again, Wally picked up the telephone.

The ring raised Harlan from a sound sleep. Reaching for the receiver, he drowsily said, "Hello."

"Harlan, this is Wally. I just received a call from your station. A traveler pulled in for gas and said there'd been a shooting!"

"What?" Harlan shook the last remnants of sleep from his head, threw the covers back, swung his legs to the floor and sat on the edge of the bed. Now, he was completely conscious.

"Is this some kind of a joke?" But Harlan didn't mean it. He knew Wally would never be a party to anything so cruel.

"All I know is what the guy said, and he sure sounded sincere to me."

Harlan was stunned. Still clutching the receiver, he reached for his pants lying over a chair and hurriedly began putting them on. "Well, what on earth happened?"

"All I know is the caller reported the attendant had been shot! Harlan, who've you got working over there tonight?"

Harlan knew Wally wasn't asking to be nosy. He knew the people in their small town genuinely cared about each other, usually knowing one another all their lives.

"Daniel Sycamore," Harlan responded.

Wally gasped. "Oh, no. I just saw him the other day. He dropped by Sully's to say hello."

"Yeah, he was home from college on Christmas break, back working for me now for a couple of weeks."

Harlan breathed heavily as the news seeped into his brain. "Oh, God, I hope he wasn't playing with that shotgun. I told those boys to be careful with that thing. Is he going to be alright, Wally?"

Harlan was unwilling to consider the worst possible scenario. He hoped he was dreaming, a nightmare from which he would awaken. He began to feel nauseated and his brain was spinning like a top. It seemed so surreal. He couldn't believe, didn't want to believe what he was hearing.

Wally regretted he hadn't asked the traveler that question. "I don't know his condition."

"Well, has anyone called an ambulance yet?" Harlan hoped to be assured that none was needed.

"I called the police, but I didn't think about an ambulance. I'll find out for you, and I'll call for one if that hasn't already been done."

"Thanks, Wally, that'll save me from having to take the time. I really need to get over there to find out what's going on!"

As the two men said goodbye, Harlan felt his blood run cold as menacing thoughts of doom gripped his mind. He could feel himself trembling as his concern for Daniel mounted with every passing minute.

Swiftly, he finished dressing and headed for the station. The information on the shooting was sketchy. He'd known Daniel for four years since he first applied for a job and was fond of the bright youth he hired on the spot.

Harlan found himself hoping Daniel had been taken to a hospital by now and that he would be okay. That hope would remain, but only for the fifteen-minute drive to the station.

Meanwhile, Brian went outside to wait for the police. "I just wanted to get away from there," he later said.

While talking to Wally, Brian noticed money on the floor and a candy bar just inside the doorway. And now, outside, he saw a bill on the apron close to the pumps. Picking up an empty soda bottle, he placed it on the bill so it wouldn't blow away in the whistling frigid air.

As he waited for the police, a car pulled into the station for gas. Brian told the officers he informed the customer that "there has been a robbery and the station is temporarily closed."

After hanging up from Harlan, Wally called back to the station. Brian came from outside to answer the phone. After identifying himself, Wally assured the traveler he called the police and they were on their way.

"Do I need to call for an ambulance?" A vestige of hope resonated in Wally's voice. But with the last remnants of his composure dissipating into the frosty air, Brian began to weep aloud. "I don't think so. The guy back there is already dead!"

CHAPTER 3
On a Wing and a Prayer
1996

Driving rain pounded the windshield of Echo Middleton's Prelude that Tuesday morning in March as she traveled Interstate 55 north from Starling. Thunder rumbled in raucous waves as bolts of lightning lit the darkened sky like a disco ball. Still, she barely noticed. Her mind was much too preoccupied.

The petite blonde with honey-colored eyes and a welcoming smile was traveling to the Logan Correctional Center in Lincoln, to visit a man she hadn't seen in over thirty years. Russell James, seventy, has been in prison for almost twenty-seven years, spending the first two and a half years of incarceration on death row.

As Echo proceeded down the highway, her mind revisited a time in her childhood when his family and hers were neighbors.

She remembered him as a kindly man who would load up sacks filled with hamburgers and French fries from the Broiler Restaurant for her brother, Tom, and his friends to enjoy on their fishing expeditions. Russell's eldest son, Steve, was the night manager, and Russell helped him balance the registers and close for the night.

Tom was two years older than Steve James and didn't run in the same circles. But Russell coached Tom's youth baseball team and they remained friendly in the ensuing years.

Echo recalled what prompted this odyssey she was on; a simple phone call she received in January from Geoff James, Russell's second-born son.

She hadn't seen Geoff since her family moved from the old neighborhood and was surprised by his call, because although they attended the same Catholic grade school, the two were never classmates.

Geoff said there was going to be a clemency hearing regarding his father's 1970 murder conviction. He asked if she might be willing to share a memory in a letter to the Governor of

Illinois on his father's behalf. That was easy. It only took a moment to recall a kindness Russell extended to Tom when Echo was twelve years of age.

Tom enlisted in the United States Marine Corp and received orders that sent him to Vietnam. He was there for six months before he returned stateside. Then, in June 1969, he was being sent back to Vietnam after a furlough.

Tom was just twenty-years-of-age, and having previously experienced the 'hell' over there was much afraid. Consequently, he was absent without leave (AWOL) for about ten days.

During this time, Russell counselled Tom to return in order to avoid any trouble with the military authorities. His aspirations for the young soldier included a good future with an honorable discharge. Eventually, Russell came to the Middleton's house to alert Tom's parents to his AWOL status. Tom was afraid to tell his parents for fear of disappointing them.

The Middleton's understood Tom needed to complete what he started when he enlisted. They knew for Tom it was the only honorable thing to do. They understood also, he just needed someone to talk to.

And who better than Russell James, a man who could empathize with the quandary the twenty-year-old was in? He had firsthand knowledge of the ramifications of being AWOL, as he had been in Tom's shoes twenty-three years earlier, for approximately twenty-one days during his military service.

Eventually, Tom would board a bus in Starling for the ride to St. Louis, Missouri, where he turned himself over to the Marine Sergeant there.

Tom never made it back from Southeast Asia. The next time Echo saw his handsome face he was in full-dress uniform, encased in a casket for burial, and accompanied by a military escort. Shrapnel from a Viet Cong grenade and automatic weapon fire at Quang Tri Province felled him on October 26, 1969.

Echo understood Tom's passing made Russell's kindness all the more important to her. Had Tom lived, the incident may have long been erased from her memory. But that's not what happened.

Russell's kindness to Tom had occurred in June and Echo couldn't forget his cruel and contradictory behavior in what occurred six months later to nineteen-year-old Daniel Sycamore at his hands and the hands of his eldest son.

So, in her letter to the Governor, Echo wrote that the murder of Daniel was so cruel and final that nothing could be added or detracted from the horror of it. She did not wish to minimize the severity of the crime or the immense loss suffered by the victim and his family. She acknowledged their lifetime as one filled with emptiness, grief, unrealized plans and lost dreams. She did not presume she could influence the Governor one way nor the other; neither did she try. She strove to remain impartial and do only what she was asked.

After the Middletons moved from the old neighborhood in 1968, they lost track of the Jameses. That is until January, 1970, when their faces were plastered all over the 6 p.m. and 10 p.m. news programs.

As Echo bypassed the little town of Williamsville, she began to think about the James' victim. As fate would have it, he, too, was an acquaintance of hers. When her parents sold their home in the old neighborhood, they moved the family to rural Avery. The Middleton's new home was located approximately three miles west of the Vernon Texaco Station.

Echo used to wait for her mom at that station when she and her mother's sister attended the stage performances at the Little Sullivan Theatre. Her aunt did the driving, and Vernon's Texaco acted as a pick-up point, so her aunt could head back home without having to travel that dark, three-mile stretch of county road alone. Echo would wait for them at the designated time for their arrival.

She met Daniel Sycamore, the night attendant and freshman at Indiana University, in Bloomington, when he noticed her car parked on the station's apron close to the county road that ran in front of it. He came to ask if she needed help.

Echo explained she was waiting for her mother to return from an outing. The two talked for about ten minutes before Daniel left to pump gasoline for a customer. When her aunt's car pulled up next to Echo's, Mariah Middleton exited the car and climbed into her daughter's Prelude. They said their goodbyes and watched as her aunt navigated north to Starling on Route 66.

Daniel looked over just as Echo started up the car. She and her mother waved to him as they pulled off the apron and turned west down the darkened, remote county road. Daniel smiled and nodded their way.

Echo looked over at her mother as they rounded a curve in the road that ran alongside a large dairy cattle ranch. "Daniel told me his Aunt Mavis is a sister to Aunt Maybelle."

"Yes, that's true. And did he also tell you that Maybelle and Mavis are twins? Small world, isn't it?"

Echo began to feel nervous and uneasy as the first Lincoln exit loomed just ahead, bringing the guard towers of the prison into view. "What am I doing here," she questioned aloud? In her whole life, she had never been to a prison before. Yet she was the one who asked for this meeting in the first place.

Echo felt confident when she wrote to the governor that she did what her brother would have wanted her to do; to speak about the decency of Russell as he had known him, before the downfall. After she mailed the letter; however, she felt compelled to know what happened.

She went to the office of the Sturnus County Circuit Clerk and read through the volumes of documents pertaining to the case. She contacted the court reporter who gave his permission for her to receive a copy of the trial transcript.

What she read was chilling and enlightening. It confirmed what she suspected. Russell and Steve James did commit the brutal murder of Daniel Sycamore. She now knew what happened. Her trip today, she hoped, would be the first of many on her journey to find out 'why' and 'how' he allowed it to happen.

Echo wondered if Russell would share with her the antecedents that he felt were paramount in leading him to commit the crime. She hoped to write his story, proffering a platform through which he might tender moral accountability along with his legal debt, and apologize to those he harmed. She knew if something could be learned from this tragedy, then good might still come from it.

She didn't think it would be easy, but she hoped Russell would be willing to try. She was not looking for excuses nor was she willing to be used as a tool through which he could offer any.

Echo's father always encouraged her to try her hand at writing. He lived by the adage, 'nothing beats a failure but a try.' Marshall would ask his daughter, "When will you get started on that book of yours? There's at least one good story inside everyone, you know."

"I guess when I find something worth writing about, Dad," was always her reply. Still, the whole idea lay dormant until Echo received that call from Geoff James. And that's when it came to her that this might be the book that she always had a hankering to write.

Echo turned onto the curving road that led to the prison grounds. Her thoughts wandered to Don DeLario, Chief Investigator for the Sturnus County Sheriff's Department at the time of the murder, now retired.

She recalled phoning his home, not knowing whether he would consider rehashing an old case with a total stranger. She said she was interested in talking about a murder he investigated twenty-seven earlier.

She told him about being a neighbor to the James family and later moving close to the Vernon Texaco, where she met Daniel Sycamore. She mentioned one other fact. When her parents sold their home in Avery, it was purchased by Harlan Vernon and his wife.

"There's going to be a clemency hearing," she told Don. "I'll be attending to gather information for a possible book. I have no notion of what direction it may take, yet I feel drawn to walk the path where it leads." Don agreed to a meeting, and they set up an appointment for noon the next day.

Echo had no idea when she made that call to Don DeLario, that he would open doors for her that surpassed her ambition of authorship, or that a wonderful and lasting bond of friendship would develop between them.

Echo found Don to be a decent and caring individual. She sensed a strong gentleness about him, allowing her to relax comfortably in his company. He told her that he once expressed to his friend and fellow retired deputy, Lewis Morell, "This lady says she wants to write about this case and I believe she's going to do it."

Thoughts of Don were a pleasing diversion, but as she entered the prison grounds, Echo felt herself getting nervous again.

She approached the front of the parking area and observed few cars parked at the facility this weekday, assuming most people visit on the weekend.

Echo looked around to acclimate herself to the surroundings. The red brick Administration building stood directly in front of her.

She noticed a man in a corrections uniform going inside.

To her right was a row of red brick buildings, encased by two tall cyclone fences with rolls of razor wire at the top and bottom. Those, she assumed, were the actual blocks where the prisoners were housed.

There were several picnic tables strewn about, each with a wood awning to block the hot summer sun. Echo observed three guard towers strategically placed on the grounds. The Logan Correctional Center has been the home of Russell James for over fourteen years.

Echo shut off the car's engine and began to put her keys in her purse but remembered Geoff telling her that prison rules forbade purses in the visitor's lounge. Taking a few deep breaths in an attempt to steady her nerves, she began to reflect on why she contacted Russell again after all these years.

Echo knew she had the makings of a good human-interest story but after much research to learn about the case, she felt a sort of kinship with the victim's family; for she, too, had experienced the horror of having a loved one taken in a brutal and violent manner.

So, she asked Geoff for his father's address to write him a letter. She wanted the opportunity to share her feelings with Russell concerning Tom's death and her belief that he, like Daniel Sycamore, had been murdered. She wanted to share the moral outrage she felt toward the man who never took moral responsibility for his actions concerning the thousands of deaths he caused.

Echo hoped Russell would feel it too. She believed that if he could, he might see the benefit of his participation in this project; for himself, his victim's survivors and for countless others as well.

"I think he would enjoy hearing from you again," Geoff said. He gave Echo the address, along with his father's prison number. Geoff explained without that number the letter might be returned or could take longer to reach his father.

So, she wrote to Russell. She told him she realized it had been thirty years, but she was wondering if he would allow her the opportunity to pay him a visit. She let him know she wanted to speak with him about something too detailed to put down in a letter. Echo told him that she didn't want to inconvenience him or make him feel uncomfortable in any way.

In his response, Russell admitted that although he didn't

remember her specifically, he remembered the Middleton family with fond affection.

She recalled the last thing he said in that letter: "Please know, Echo, you can talk to me about anything, and you cannot ask too much, inconvenience me or make me uncomfortable in any way. There is nothing that cannot be overcome with love."

Echo understood his response was exactly what she would have expected from him, and she was saddened by the position he caused himself to be in today.

She dashed off another letter to give him her name and birth date for his visitor's list. She added her telephone number and asked him to call collect to discuss a date and time for her visit. And she thanked him for his open invitation to speak freely.

Geoff told her he doesn't visit his father on the weekends as Russell prefers to keep to himself, away from crowds, when the center fills up with visitors. He knows when families and friends come together, passions run high, emotions are stirred and pockets of fights break out.

During Echo's phone call, she told Russell that any weekday would suit her. They chose that Tuesday, so the two of them wouldn't have to shout in order to be heard.

Echo wondered what Russell might look like today and if she would be able to recognize him. She knew he wouldn't have any idea what she looked like as she was only a child the last time that he saw her.

She looked around to find a visitor's entrance. Seeing none, she made her way into the Administration building and walked up to a gentleman sitting at a desk. "Good morning, sir. Where do I go to have a visit with an inmate, please?"

He directed her back out the door to a little cedar and brick building called a Sally Port. Upon entering, Echo noticed a male guard sitting behind a desk.

"Hello, sir. My name is Echo Middleton, and I'd like to visit with Russell James, if I may?" Her voice was friendly but anxious as well.

"Sure, let me check the visitor's list for your name and I'll need to see your driver's license."

As Echo handed her license over, a female guard counted the number of keys on her key chain. "Do you have any money in your possession?"

"Yes, ma'am, I do." Echo reached into her pants pocket and pulled out two one-dollar bills.

"Do I need to run the money back out to my car?"

"No, you're free to use the canteen in the visitor's area to purchase drinks and snacks. Now, follow me, please."

The female guard led Echo into a smaller room where she was instructed to remove her shoes and socks and lift her feet so the guard could see the bottoms of them. She was then instructed to extend both arms out to the side and was frisked from top to bottom.

"Okay, you may put your shoes and socks on now."

Echo complied and was led down a corridor toward the rear of the building and through a back door to the outside. Now, she was on the actual prison grounds. High fences with rolls of razor wire on the top and bottom, surrounded them on all sides.

They walked a few hundred feet to another red brick building and stepped into the foyer. Upon entering, Echo felt a coldness about the place. The walls were concrete and painted an eggshell white. They were bare, containing no happy pictures to assail the dingy drabness.

Echo followed the guard, an attractive lady with long blonde hair tied back in a ponytail. She led her through an entryway, and as they entered the room, Echo saw another guard sitting at a desk that was elevated three feet above the floor level.

The brick walls of this room were pink and a large mural of a carousel was painted on the back wall. The room was filled with tables and chairs. In the corner there were toys to occupy visiting children.

As she scanned the room, Echo noticed a small elderly man standing by one of the tables in the back. She looked to the female guard for direction, and the guard nodded her head toward the man. He had a pleasant smile on his face, so Echo took a deep breath to steady her nerves and made her way over to where he stood.

CHAPTER 4
Sins in the Dark are Brought to the Light
1969

State Police car 329 sat idling in the parking lot of the IGA Food Store in Avery. Inside, Troopers Gary Shelley and Jim Orton received the dispatch from headquarters. The time was 3:09 a.m.

While racing to the scene down Route 114 they noticed Sturnus County Sheriff's Deputy Phillip Jewel, running radar along the highway on his 11 p.m. to 7 a.m. shift. Quickly they drove up to his squad car. Trooper Shelley informed Jewel of the shooting.

An adrenalin rush was evident in Shelley's voice. "We're going to need some backup on this!" he said.

Both cars sped down the highway with lights flashing and sirens blaring. Jewel led the way. The cars zoomed down the two-lane, rising airborne over the railroad tracks at Civic. They reached the U.S. Route 66 junction and headed north for a mile, reaching the station at 3:22 a.m.

Deputy Jewel pulled onto the apron and brought his squad car to a screeching halt. He noticed a young man sitting in an automobile parked on the apron.

As the officer opened the car door, he swung his left leg onto the asphalt, cautiously positioning himself behind the squad car door so that it would provide a shield between him and the man in the automobile.

He reached with his right hand to remove the safety strap, pulled his gun from its holster, positioned it through the open window and pointed it directly at the young man.

With trained eyes peeled on the stranger, Deputy Jewel systematically ordered Brian Redmond out of the car.

"Put your hands on the dash board. Do it now!"

Brian was duly frightened and followed all the orders he was given.

"With your left hand, throw the car keys out the driver's window toward me. Do it now!"

"With your left hand, reach through the window and open the door. Do it now!"

"Step out of the car and stretch your hands up over your head. Do it now!"

Brian followed the officer's instruction as ordered, but inadvertently took a step toward Jewel.

"Stop! Turn around and get down on your knees. Place your hands on the back of your head. Do it now!"

Jewel's voice was commanding and intimidating.

Shaking, Brian complied. The young man now felt his blood run cold. It suddenly began seeping into his brain that he was in a perfect position, through no fault of his own, to become the Sturnus County Sheriff's Department's prime suspect.

With the State Troopers covering him, Deputy Jewel cautiously moved toward Brian. He kept his gun trained on the young man while keying on any sudden movement. When he reached the frightened man, he grabbed Brian's hands that were clasped behind his head. Jewel slipped his gun back into its holster, swiftly brought Brian's hands down behind his back and secured them with handcuffs.

He ordered Brian to his feet and bent the young man over the front of his vehicle to pat him down. He turned all pockets of his clothing inside out. Jewel could feel Brian's body trembling.

He stood behind Brian and gently kicked at the young man's feet, causing him to spread his legs apart. Methodically the officer patted the entire torso and then separately moved down each of Brian's legs. The young man shook in fear; even as he was grateful to God for the officer's presence.

Brian had never experienced anything like this in his entire life. He never imagined being in a position like this, and his fear mounted. Fortunately, his good common sense kicked in and he complied with the officer's demands.

"Take it easy, son, I'm just trying to secure the area here. You'll be alright if you've got nothing to hide. Are you the one that called it in?"

"No, but I reported it to someone off the emergency list inside, and he called it in for me."

Brian couldn't stop trembling. He looked to the left and then to the right. But all he could see were the menacing weapons belonging to the state troopers that were pointed directly at him!

"Okay buddy, you can stand up straight now."

Brian was frightened but he spoke clearly. "I think there's an attendant that's dead inside. I pulled in for gas and found the guy lying in there."

Shelley told Orton to secure Brian in the back of their squad car. And as they crossed the apron the officer noticed a small chocolate milk carton; its spilled contents still wet on the driveway.

"No," Brian told Orton, "I didn't have any milk."

Jewel and Shelley approached the station entrance with guns drawn, eyes shifting left to right and ears perked for human sound. They noticed a V-shaped spring lying just outside the door. Just to the east of the entrance, they saw a large refreshment unit containing milk and orange juice with its door wide open.

Jewel opened the station door from a squat position and was followed close behind by Officer Shelley. Although bitter cold outside, both men now had sweat beading on their foreheads and upper lips. They didn't believe the perpetrator was still on location, but the not-knowing needed resolved.

Their eyes shot back and forth. They searched behind the desk, under the desk, around the counter and glanced at every nook and cranny where a body might lie in wait. The officers noticed money and a candy bar lying on the floor of the main room.

Jewel moved cautiously to the opened storage room door with his gun drawn and nerves on edge. Shelley carefully moved to the bathroom door where he positioned himself to one side as he swiftly turned the handle and pushed the door open.

His eyes scanned the room. With his gun pointed out in front of him, he stepped into the doorway. Seeing no evidence of malfeasance, Shelley reeled and cautiously worked his way over to where Jewel remained in a squat position just outside the open storage room door.

Jewel twisted his neck to peek inside and saw the body lying on the floor. His eyes flashed up, down and all around, scanning far and wide for any possible danger zone.

Seeing none, Jewel cautiously entered the room with Shelley on his heels. Trooper Shelley, younger and with less experience, shot a glance at the carnage sprawled out on the floor. He'd seen several accidents with fatalities along Interstates and highways, but never cold-blooded murder up close and personal. He heard Jewel sigh and saw the wince on the officer's face as his eyes fell upon the young man, lifeless at their feet.

Officer Jewel was a family man with a wife and four children. He guessed his own son, Jeremy, would be about the same age as this young man and he wondered if his son had known him.

Daniel Sycamore was lying directly under a sink flat on his back with his head tilted slightly to the left. Blood covered the right arm and right chest area and collected in the drain by his head. Deputy Jewel bent over the body to check for a pulse. He wasn't expecting to find one. Just one look and he recognized death's presence. But checking was second nature to him. Finding no signs of life, he went to his squad car and called for the coroner and crime scene personnel.

Jewel and Shelley began to preserve the scene, seeing that nothing was touched or moved until additional personnel arrived. Yellow crime scene tape was strung around the perimeter of the station and around Brian's vehicle.

On the counter, the officers saw a half-full Styrofoam cup of coffee that was lukewarm to the touch and a bottle of pop. They saw an Illinois road map and a man's blue jacket lying on the front desk. They noticed the cash register was open and empty except for some small change.

They performed a cursory check in the grass along the highway and all around the outside perimeter of the station. A more thorough canvass would be performed later under the telling light of the sun.

Shelley discovered two $5 bills on the pavement and placed a clod of dirt on each to prohibit them from blowing away in the wind.

In less than twenty-five minutes, the Sheriff of Sturnus County arrived, followed by the coroner and pathologist. The America Ambulance Company pulled in shortly after them with Harlan Vernon arriving close behind.

Soon the station was buzzing with law enforcement personnel from all of the surrounding jurisdictions. A Sturnus County deputy was assigned to document the time and name of all persons entering and exiting the crime scene.

Jewel came out of the station and walked over to the State

Police vehicle. Trooper Orton rolled down the driver's window. The deputy peered into the back seat where Brian sat still visibly shaken by the macabre scene he witnessed.

Jewel was not without compassion for the young traveler. Although the investigation was just beginning, he had a gut feeling that the young man, almost afraid to breathe, was an innocent kid in the wrong place at the wrong time. Still, Brian had become a part of the process.

Deputy Jewel asked Brian in an even-tempered voice, "Would you have any objections to us searching your car?"

"No, you go right ahead. I don't have anything to hide."

* * *

Cecilia Dempsey, Crime Scene Investigator, arrived at the scene just minutes after the coroner. She retrieved Brian's car keys from Jewel and ducked under the yellow police tape that surrounded the vehicle. Along with the car keys, her hands held a small mirror, flashlight and camera.

First, she snapped photos of the exterior of the car; at each side and at different angles from back to front. The license plate was photographed along with the vehicle identification number. Then she opened all four doors and snapped photos of the interior.

She unlocked the trunk, looked inside and found only a suitcase. Opening it, Cecilia discovered clothing, toiletries and a pair of dingy tennis shoes. She looked inside the spare tire well and found nothing but what was expected to be there. The car, registered to Brian and purchased just four months earlier, was clean and free of clutter.

Inside the main body, Dempsey used a flashlight and mirror to search under the driver and passenger seats. She was diligent, deliberate and thorough in her search for evidence that might tie Brian to the crime.

Strangely, she found an open, half-full can of green beans on the floorboard that Brian said he ate while traveling to Missouri. "I don't like stopping to eat once I hit the road," he later explained.

Dempsey dusted for prints but ultimately found no evidence

to link Brian to the crime. No weapons were found, and no blood was discovered in or on Brian's car.

CHAPTER 5
A Time to Remember
1996

"Mr. James, it's good to see you again."

Although both had aged considerably, Echo recognized his face. And now, she remembered the purple birth mark he carried on his bottom lip which she had all but forgotten about. Now, there it was, as prominent as ever.

"It's so good to see you again, too, Echo." Russell stepped forward and wrapped his arms around her in a bear hug. The two sat down at a table and he put her hand into his. He asked how her folks were and she told him both were well.

"Dad is retired and enjoys golfing with his buddies. Mother, having been blessed with a great number of friends, is always on the go."

"And how is Trudy? Do you see much of her anymore?"

"Oh yes, she's very much a part of the family."

Trudy Reardon was Tom Middleton's girlfriend at the time of his death. The couple had talked about getting married someday. Tom even came home while stationed at Camp Lejeune to ask Trudy's father for her hand in marriage. The Reardons were fond of Tom and expected the couple would marry eventually. First, they wanted Trudy to finish her schooling at the Patricia Stevens Business College in St. Louis. They knew that Tom had a little time left to serve, -- about a year, -- and suggested the couple wait until after his discharge to tie the knot. "Then, we'll throw you the biggest wedding you've ever seen," they promised.

The couple had already spoken to Tom's parents and received the same advice the Reardon's gave. In the end, Tom headed back to Camp Lejeune still single but content to wait for now.

But what no one knew, except Trudy, was that she was pregnant. After Tom went back to Vietnam, Trudy never wrote to him about the baby. She chose to keep her pregnancy to herself.

Later she told Mariah, Tom's mother, she didn't want to worry him while he was in Vietnam. She realized he'd have enough concerns to deal with simply by being over there. In February, four months after Tom was killed, Trudy gave birth to Tom's only child, a beautiful baby girl she named Tia Marie.

Echo told Russell about what a good mother Trudy is to Tia, and how Trudy's mother, for all these years, has placed an evergreen basket on Tom's grave at Camp Butler National Cemetery during the Christmas season. "That is until a few years ago when she came down with bone cancer and was forced to stop."

"Yes," Echo continued, "we think the world of Trudy. She is my sister-in-law. If not in the legal sense, than by love and affection. After all, she gave us Tia."

"Oh, I'm so happy to hear that. I'll bet that baby is special to you."

"Yes, she is. I wish I had pictures so you could see just how much she looks like her dad. But you know, she isn't such a baby anymore. Tia is a registered nurse today and, in a few months, she'll be a bride. She's marrying a heart surgeon, and they plan on having children someday. So, maybe Tom will be a grandfather in a few years."

Echo looked at Russell's face and noticed tears forming in his eyes.

"Oh, Mr. James, I didn't mean to upset you. We don't have to talk about this if you don't want to."

"No, no," he said, somewhat embarrassed by the unexpected display of emotion. "It's just that I get a little teary-eyed when I think back on the past."

He pulled a handkerchief from his pocket and wiped his eyes. "You know, I thought the world of Tom. He was a good kid and not wild like Steve was."

Echo only knew Steven James by sight. She couldn't recall a single conversation they ever had. He was seven years older than she and far more advanced.

"I remember the time Steve ran away from home," Russell said. "He put his mother through hell worrying about him. But when he returned, you should have heard how Tom let Steve have it. He told him just how selfish he'd been, putting his mother through that."

Echo was taken aback. *"What? Is he pulling my leg? Doesn't he remember the time when Tom did the very same thing?"*

He was only fourteen years of age when he and his group of friends decided to take off and do some traveling. The boys pooled their money and purchased bologna and bread for the trip, having only that to eat for the seven days they were gone.

As a child Echo shared a bedroom adjacent to her parents' room, with her two younger sisters. Each night while Tom was gone, Echo heard her mother crying.

"What if he needs us and we can't reach him, Marshall? What if he's lying hurt somewhere or worse? What are we going to do?"

Mariah pleaded for answers, looking to her husband for strength and guidance. She knew he would assure her and calm her fears, if only for a while.

"It'll be alright, Mariah," he'd respond. "We've just got to pray and put our trust in God that it will all work out."

"Why can't the police find him?"

"They will, Mariah, they will," he promised her.

Often during that long week, Echo would spot her father, who worked swing shift at the Chicago and Illinois Midland Railroad, on his knees in his bedroom. She knew he was praying for Tom's safe return. She never heard him cry throughout that horrible ordeal but his pain was as great as her mothers.

Echo was furious at Tom for the tears he caused their mother to shed. She hoped when he was found, their dad would remove a pound of flesh from his back side; preferably in the most painful manner possible.

At the same time, however, she wanted him safe and wanted him to come home because Tom was loved and missed terribly.

Echo was in the kitchen when her dad received the telephone call from the St. Louis Police Department. An officer phoned to say the boys had turned themselves in. She remembered the joy and relief that showed on her father's face. Her mother started crying again, but this time they were happy tears.

There was a lot of hugging and kissing when they returned. Echo felt so happy; she didn't want Tom to be punished anymore. Besides, from that time until the day he died; he became sick at the sight of bologna. Maybe that was punishment enough. A constant reminder every time he saw a slice.

Echo smiled at the recall. "Oh, a lot of kids ran away back then and not because they were wild. Some just had a little of the wanderlust in them."

"Yes, that's true," Russell conceded, "but Steven was one who could easily run amok. I had to watch him, sit on him, whereas Tom didn't cause your parent's much trouble at all."

"Oh, he was no angel. But I'd say he was a pretty good kid."

It suddenly struck Echo just how similar Tom and Steve's lives were. They were two very typical American kids growing up in the Midwest. But she also recognized stark contrasts between them as well.

Steve held down jobs all through high school whereas Tom never did. Steve remained in school and received his high school diploma while Tom, to the chagrin of his parents, quit.

After high school, Steve enrolled at Brown's Business College, but not Tom. He was going to be a 'tough guy' so he enlisted in the United States Marine Corp.

Steve seemed to make the better decisions early on. One might think he was much smarter than Tom Middleton. And maybe he was.

But one thing's for sure, Echo knew. Her brother would never have made the decision Steve James made on December 19, 1969. Of that, she had no doubt. Oh, Tom might have enjoyed impressing people with a macho façade, but on the inside, she knew he was as soft as marshmallow crème. Echo couldn't help recall a tragedy he witnessed and the profound effect it had on him.

Tom went to the Taft's Drive-in Dairy on the evening of October 10, 1965, to purchase a cherry Coke. He noticed thirteen-year-old Judy Lazetti crossing 11th Street. Judy was an eighth-grade classmate of Tom's sister, Susan.

Judy reached the curb, but for some reason she stepped back into traffic. Tom later said he thought she must have dropped or spotted something in the street and went to retrieve it.

She was hit by the left bumper of a north-bound truck, and her body was thrown approximately one-hundred feet. The force of the impact knocked both of her shoes from her feet, sending them soaring into the air.

Someone called for an ambulance and the police. Judy was rushed to St. Jonathon's Hospital but died of head and neck injuries at 7:55 p.m.

Tom went to the pay phone on the corner and called home. He was shaken so badly by what he witnessed, that his voice teetered on the verge of hysteria. His mother couldn't understand his breathless discourse but instinctively knew something terrible had happened.

"Calm down and tell me again what's going on," she pleaded in that soothing voice only a mother has. With a trembling stutter, Tom managed to convey the horrible accident he had witnessed. "The police are here now, and they want to talk to me," he said. And then, kind of broken down, like someone with a wounded spirit, he pleaded with her, "Please come and get me. I don't want to walk home all by myself!"

When the two returned, Mariah tried to console Tom, but her efforts were to no avail. That night as he tossed and turned, his mother managed to catnap on a chair at his bedside. She wouldn't be able to sleep in her own bedroom. Tom didn't want to be alone.

No, there was absolutely no way he could have harmed Daniel Sycamore. The fear that must have been on Daniel's face just moments before the first shot was fired would have forced Tom to do all he could to defend Daniel. Echo knew this to be true.

When the Middletons heard the news of the Jameses arrest for the murder of the young man at the station, the whole family was asking, "What if Tom had been with them that night?" To be sure, he could have been in their car, not knowing what they were up to. Even today, Echo cringes thinking about the ramifications of what might have been.

Echo found herself feeling uncomfortable drawing comparisons between Steve and Tom. She knew in all ways that mattered those two boys were completely opposed; in character, in conduct and in empathy for one's fellow man.

In that regard, Tom more readily should be compared to Daniel Sycamore. Both young men had their lives snuffed out needlessly. Both held down jobs at the time of their deaths, Daniel at a service station and Tom in the service to his country. Neither deserved the cards they were dealt.

Echo lowered her head. She didn't like the emotions rustling inside her and knew it was time to change the subject. She decided to direct the conversation to the purpose of her visit. She lifted her head and looked at Russell as she once more prepared to speak.

CHAPTER 6
The Notification
1969

"That's Harlan Vernon pulling in," Trooper Jewel told Coroner Wesley Torrance. He looked at the clock above the door and saw the time was 3:37 a.m. Jewel and Vernon were acquaintances. Jewel's daughter, Betty, and Vernon's daughter, Tessa, were school friends. Phillip Jewel knew Harlan would be devastated.

Torrance looked out the window and saw Harlan walking toward the door. "Alright then. I'm going to need him in here to identify the body."

When he entered the station, Harlan was as white as a ghost. All color drained from his face and he appeared as if he could be sick at any moment.

Simply arriving on the scene and seeing the flashing emergency lights of squad cars and an ambulance unnerved him. Nauseous waves of doom hastened to assail his naturally optimistic self.

Harlan looked to Jewel, still cleaving to the last vestige of hope. "Is he gone?"

Jewel placed his hand on Harlan's shoulder. "Yes, Harlan, I'm afraid he is."

"We're going to need you to make a positive identification so the family can be notified," Torrance said. "He's in the back room. Sir, will you follow me, please?"

Harlan took a deep breath and entered the storage room. "Oh, my God," he exclaimed as his eyes fixed on the lifeless body. He quickly made the Sign of the Cross.

"Our Father," he began praying aloud, his voice trembling on the verge of hyperventilating, "who art in heaven, hallowed be Thy name."

He hung his head. His shoulders violently convulsed as he wept anguished tears of bitter grief and despair. Coroner Torrance stepped out of the room to give the man a few moments to collect himself.

When Harlan emerged, his eyes were red and swollen, but he was composed.

"That's Daniel Sycamore back there."

"Do you have an address for his folks?" Torrance asked.

"Yes, sir. It's in the top drawer of the desk; right there in my address book."

Harlan took a piece of paper from the desktop, grabbed a pen, wrote down the address and handed it to the coroner. His penmanship was erratic, shaky but legible.

"Thank you, Mr. Vernon, I appreciate your cooperation. I better get over to the house. Jack Gallows will be here before too long, and I don't want this family to learn of the demise of their loved one from the news media." Gallows was a veteran newsman with the State Register and the photographer most often used by law enforcement.

Torrance, three times elected to the coroner post, dreaded this portion of his job more than any other. Declaring a lifeless person dead was clinical. But to tell the living of the death of a loved one was emotional, and something in his eleven years of service to the county he had never gotten used to.

He drove in silence to Daniel's parents' house. Positioned six miles southeast of the station, it took just nine minutes to steer his official vehicle onto the driveway. The ringing of the doorbell disturbed the stillness inside the red brick two-story house on Stony Brook in Piedmont.

Daniel's dog, Scamp, a black Lab and German shepherd mix rescued from the dog pound four years prior, made a mad dash to the front door. He began barking with such boisterous ferocity that Torrance feared that some of the neighbors might call the police to report a disturbance.

Suddenly, a light came on and Torrance saw through the lace curtain on the door, a woman and a young man standing stationary at the top of the stairs. An older man hurried down the steps, switched on the porch light and pulled the curtain aside to see the caller standing just outside the door.

The home owner appeared dazed and confused. He wondered who could be ringing his doorbell at this ungodly hour.

He opened the door, but just a little bit. Douglas Sycamore had a quizzical look on his face. "How can I help you?"

"Sir, my name is Wesley Torrance, and I am the coroner for Sturnus County. May I come in to speak with you, please?"

Now Douglas' heart sank to his feet. He opened the door wider for the man to pass into the foyer. He asked himself quizzically, *why is the coroner here? What on earth is going on?*

Janice Sycamore and their son, Dallas, also known as Dally, rushed with trepidation down the steps and joined Douglas in the entranceway. The thought of the coroner coming to her front door in the middle of the night sent shock waves rumbling through every fiber within her.

"Oh my God, what's going on here?" Her anxiety mounted with every passing second. She held her breath waiting to hear the visitor speak.

"Sir, are you the father of Daniel Sycamore?"

"Yes, I am. This is his mother and his brother."

Douglas' eyes searched Torrance's face for any information he might glean from the gravity etched upon it.

"What's happened to Daniel? Is something wrong? Has he been hurt badly? Where is my son? Dear God, what's going on here?" Janice, now panic stricken pleaded to know.

The tall thin woman with light brown hair that fell to her shoulders in a bob was teetering on the verge of hysteria. Douglas put his arms around her. Dallas' bottom lip began to tremble.

"I regret to inform you there has been a robbery at the Harlan Vernon Texaco, and your son has been killed." Torrance spoke as gently as he could when suddenly the air seemed to be sucked out of the room.

Torrance's voice was soft and sincere. "I'm so very sorry."

But Janice's tone was adamant. "No, that's incorrect. There must be some mistake. That just can't be true!" Still, her resolve was fading quickly as the somber face of the coroner remained stiff and unyielding.

Douglas struggled to comprehend the incomprehensible. "What happened?" The family stood in utter shock, unable to grasp the concept.

"It appears he was shot during a robbery."

"He was shot? Who would do such a thing? Do you know

who did it? Did they catch the guy?" Janice asked, stunned.

As the reality of the horrific news oozed into his brain, Douglas Sycamore let go of his final hope that a mistake was made and tears began to form in his eyes.

Janice let out gut-wrenching wails that unnerved her son. Tears began to stream down his handsome face.

Douglas clutched his wife and held her tightly as their world began falling apart. He supported Janice's shaking legs and escorted her to the staircase where he gently sat her down on the lower steps.

Dallas sat down, too, and wrapped his arm around his mother's shoulder as she laid her head on his chest, completely broken and shattered. Her wailing would not cease for hours to come. She sat on that step, folded over. Her arms clutched against her stomach as she rocked back and forth. She cried out in raw pain so deep no words could assuage, "My baby, my poor, poor baby. My Daniel, my good, and loving boy."

Imaginations of the horror of his last moments assailed her senses and tormented her with no respite. Her husband turned to face the coroner. Douglas' voice was painfully weakened. "Where is my son?"

"By now he has been transferred to Hope Memorial Hospital in Starling. There is going to be an autopsy. It has to be done in cases like this. It will be performed later this morning. And when it's over we'll release the body to the funeral home of your choice."

Torrance beseeched the grieving family. "Is there anyone I can call; a friend, a relative, a priest or rabbi?"

Douglas' response was agonizingly calculated. "No, thank you. No reason to spread the pain before it's absolutely necessary to do so. We'll notify family and friends later this morning. Let them sleep and have their peace for now."

"Is there anything I can do for you?" Torrance asked.

"No sir, we'll be okay."

The wailing sobs of Daniel's mother rose to a crescendo and filled the house with sorrow and anguish. Douglas reached for the handle of the front door and opened it for the coroner to make his exit.

Torrance turned to face the grieving father. "Again, please accept my most sincere expression of sympathy for your loss."

Torrance slowly turned and descended the porch steps and

crossed the yard to his vehicle. His heart ached for the family and especially for the young man who was lost to them forever. Daniel's father closed the door and joined his wife and son on the bottom steps of the elegant oak staircase.

Dallas was fearful his mother may never recover from the pain that enveloped her now. He worried for her health. He'd never seen her in raw anguish and wished he could take it from her. Anger and rage began brewing within him like a tempest with every gnashing cry that came forth from the core of his precious mother.

"I swear to God," he said in a voice reeking with singular determination as tears streamed down his cheeks, "they better catch that guy before I do because I'll kill him if I get my hands on him!"

"Hush now," his father commanded as he placed his arm on his son's knee. "That kind of talk doesn't do any good for anybody."

Janice stopped rocking and looked at her husband as tears dropped like rain from her hazel eyes onto her lap. "Why? Why my baby? He was always a good boy and never caused anybody any trouble. How could anyone do this to him? What are we going to do without our Daniel?" Janice began to sob hysterically.

"Come here, dear," Douglas softly said as Dallas moved up a few steps. His father brought his wife closer to himself and wrapped his arms around her. "I don't know, Janice, but we must remain strong for each other and for Dally." He spoke soothingly, although his own pain lay heavy on his heart. Janice put her head on her husband's shoulder, and the two wept bitter sobs of grief while wrapped in each other's arms. Soon dawn would overtake the night sky.

Dally made his way into the kitchen to start a pot of coffee knowing their sleep was over for the remainder of the morning. When he returned to the staircase, he saw his parents sitting broken in a heap of deep guttural crying, holding on to one another for dear life. It was a scene that would stick in Dally's mind forever.

Those strong caregivers who nurtured him throughout his entire lifetime had been reduced to a crumpled pile on a stair step in less time than it took to murder his brother.

He turned and hurried to the kitchen phone. The hour was early, now around 4:20 a.m. He dialed the phone number to the home of Adaline (Addie) Bushera, his fiancé.

Addie and Janice had become close since the young couple's

engagement ten months previous. The wedding date was set for Saturday, July 26, 1970, at Saint Mary's Catholic Church.
Daniel was to be his brother's best man.

I've got to call Addie. She's a nurse. She'll know what to do. She will help soothe my parents' grief. Otherwise, I'm afraid I'll lose my whole family before this day is over. Especially mother. I don't know how much her heart can withstand.

Janice was recently diagnosed with pulmonary heart disease and was being treated with medication and diet.

"Mrs. Bushera, may I speak to Addie? It's very important, ma'am," he said when his fiancé's mother drowsily answered the phone.

The weak and quivering voice of her future son-in-law rattled her. "Dally, of course. Is everything okay?"

"No. Nothing's okay. I just really need to speak to her, please." Dally fought back tears as he struggled to maintain his composure.

"Hold on a minute, Dally, I'll go upstairs and get her out of bed."

Amelia set the telephone receiver down and climbed the steps to her daughter's bedroom. Something about the tone of Dally's voice frightened her. He just wasn't himself.

"Hi Dally, what's going on," Adeline asked sleepily.

"Can you come over to the house, Addie?"

"Right now? You want me to come over right now? Dallas, what's going on? Is something wrong?"

"It's Daniel. The coroner just left the house. He came to tell my parents that my brother was murdered at the Texaco station. He's dead, Addie!"

And after speaking the inevitable, Dallas Sycamore broke into a heap of his own. He dropped the phone and fell to the kitchen floor, the reality of the situation finally taking hold. He cried grievous mournful tears for the only brother he would ever have.

"Oh, my God. No. No." Adeline shrieked. "What happened? Are you sure?" She hoped against hope that a mistake had been made. But Dallas wasn't responding any longer. The telephone receiver dangled from the cord to the floor next to where he laid.

"Hello. Hello. Dallas, are you there? Hello?" Getting no response, Addie raised her voice, "Dally, I'm on my way. Just hold on. I'll be there as fast as I can." She hung up the phone and screamed for her mother. But her mother couldn't understand the blubbering words her daughter was trying to convey.

"Calm down, Adeline. Take a deep breath and tell me what's going on!" Amelia was duly frightened by her daughter's hysteria.

"Oh, mother," she cried, "it's Daniel, Dally's younger brother. He's been murdered at the Texaco Station where he's been working during Christmas break!"

"What? Oh, dear God, please don't let it be so!" Amelia raised both hands to cover her mouth as tears welled in her eyes. She threw her arms around her daughter. "How did it happen?"

"Dallas didn't say any more than that. I guess he couldn't talk. So, that's all I know right now. I've got to go over there to be with him. He needs me and he wants me there." Addie couldn't stop her hysterical sobbing and struggled to catch her breath.

"You go on upstairs, honey, and get yourself dressed," her mother said soothingly. "I'll wake your father so he can take you over to the house. You are in no condition to drive yourself."

"Oh mom, I'm so scared for Dally and his family. Through all the pain and suffering that lies ahead, nothing will ever be the same again."

Al Bushera was already out of bed and dressing when Amelia entered the bedroom. He had been wrenched from sleep by his daughter's cries. "I heard," he said, dazed and confused by it all. "How dreadfully awful it is for Dallas and his family. What is this world coming to? I can't believe it and I can't imagine what that good family is going through right now. It's mind-boggling; the inhumanity of it all!"

"Al, when you drive her over, accompany her to the door, then come right home. Dallas said the coroner just left the residence. So, you can imagine how fresh and raw this must be. They need time alone to grieve with just the family. I'll get a ham at the store, and we'll go over to the house later this afternoon. Oh Al, it's such a terrible thing that's happened." Amelia began to cry with abandon. In all her charmed life, she never imagined this could happen to family or friends. She threw her arms around her husband and wept bitterly.

***

Echo never saw her father cry until the night two Marines came knocking on the Middleton's' front door. She was at home that Sunday evening watching the weekly television show, "Laugh-in," starring Goldie Hawn.

Two soldiers in full dress Marine uniform climbed the steps and knocked on the door. Echo's brother, Ted, invited the men into the house.

Marshall Middleton was reading in the kitchen. He came into the living room and stood beside an upright chair that separated him from the two soldiers.

Echo listened to the words spoken by the taller visitor. "Mr. Middleton, we regret to inform you that your son, PFC Thomas Middleton was killed in action in Quang Tri Province, Vietnam."

Echo turned to see the soldiers and had a look of disbelief on her face. She knew how embarrassed these men were going to be when they learn of the terrible mistake they made. Not for the slightest moment did she believe otherwise.

These men didn't know her brother or they would have known that Tom could take care of himself. *Maybe he lost his dog tags in a rice field, and they were discovered lying by the body of an unfortunate soldier. Yes, something like that must have happened,* she thought.

In simple truth, Echo was a sheltered kid. She didn't know bad things happened to good people. She returned her attention to the television.

It was only after the soldiers told her father they would return the next day to speak with her parents again did she look back. She couldn't see her dad's face as he walked around the chair to shake the soldiers' hands. But when he shut the door after their exit and made his way to his bedroom Echo saw the side of his face. One lone tear trickled from his eye onto his flushed clean-shaven cheek.

When he emerged from his bedroom, Marshall was composed. He sent his eldest child, Patsy, in her red Corvair to the A & P Grocery Store to retrieve her mother and youngest sister, Annalisa, who walked there about an hour earlier.

Marshall put his arm around Patsy and escorted her to the

back door. "Don't say anything to Mom about this, dear. I'll tell her when she gets home. It's going to hit her hard, and she deserves a few minutes of peace before she must know."

Patsy told her father she was glad it was dark outside. "Maybe Mom won't notice my puffy red eyes." She grabbed her purse containing her car keys and headed out the door.

When they returned, Marshall lifted the groceries from the car and placed them on the kitchen table. Mariah was her usual jovial self. As she scurried around putting groceries away, she talked a mile-a-minute about the price of hamburger.

Mariah didn't notice the silence in the room; an oddity with six active children living at home. And she didn't seem to notice that the family was all gathered in the kitchen with faces drawn.

On a normal October Sunday evening, there would be baths drawn for school the next day, television watching, last minute homework, and a sundry of other activities.

But there wasn't anything normal about that Sunday night. Eventually, Mariah would sense the peculiarity for herself.

She placed the last of the canned goods into the pantry and turned to see the faces of her husband and children. All eyes were glued to her. Now, she looked confused. "What's the matter with everybody?"

Marshall, leaning against the kitchen counter, asked his wife to come over to where he stood.

"Why? What in the world is going on here?" Mariah's eyes pleaded to know.

Marshall asked once again in a soft cracking voice as he extended his arms compassionately toward her, "Please come here, Mariah. I've got bad news to tell you."

The look on her husband's face must have convinced her that her worst nightmare had come true.

"Oh, dear God, Marshall, what's the matter? Is it one of the boys?"

With three of her four sons in the service, Mariah had good reason to fear that something might have happened to one of the boys.

Neal was in the Navy and was stationed on a ship off the shores of Vietnam. He went on land to collect body bags for transportation back home. Tom and Shawn, the eldest son, were

Infantrymen entrenched in the thick of things. All three would serve at least one twelve-month stint in Vietnam.

As circumstance had it, Tom and Shawn ran into one another just two months before Tom was killed. It was at Da Nang that Shawn found himself walking by a Marine post and looked inside its open door. One can only imagine the excitement he felt seeing his brother shooting the breeze with his comrades.

The two were able to spend that entire day together. The memory of it is one of Shawn's personal treasures. The next day Tom's unit moved out of Da Nang. There would be heavier fighting for him as his squad moved closer to the Demilitarized Zone, (DMZ). When the news came of Tom's untimely death, Shawn was back home on "Rest and Recuperation," commonly referred to as R and R.

Shawn served the majority of his tour in Vietnam as a meat inspector for the Army stationed at a hotel in Saigon that was used for Army headquarters. That hotel would be bombed by Viet Cong forces, and many soldiers would lose their lives. Shawn was one of the fortunate ones. In the end, two of the three Middleton sons were awarded the Purple Heart medal with Tom receiving his posthumously.

With trembling and fear, Mariah walked over to where Marshall stood. She had already begun to cry. He put his arms around his wife's waist and held her tightly to brace her for what she was about to hear.

"Yes, dear, it's Thomas."

"Oh no, Marsh, has he been hurt really bad?"

"He's gone, Mariah."

Marshall's heart was breaking upon seeing his wife's grievous look.

Echo's own tears drenched her face, a reaction to the sound of her mother's agonizing painful wails. The image of Mariah's legs going limp so that her father was virtually holding up dead weight was seared in Echo's mind forever.

With his left arm secured around her waist to keep her from falling, his right arm stroked the hair on her head as it rested on his shoulder. Tears streamed down their faces. They stayed in that position for what seemed to be an eternity.

Time would eventually soothe the Middleton's pain but it

would never erase Echo's memory of her father's loving words, spoken to his wife as he held her close to him.

"You hold on to me, Mariah, and I'll hold onto you and together we'll get through this."

Echo learned from watching her dad on that terrible evening so many years ago that tears were not a sign of weakness. But those who are capable of feeling might shed them from time to time.

Her father was a well-spring of strength from which the entire family drew. He held it all together even as his own pain and grief came crashing in from all around. He was a pillar of sanity in a world that seemed to have gone insane.

As for Echo, she never blamed God for what happened to Tom in the late morning of October 26, 1969. But she could still recall her sister, Susan, returning home from a date on that fateful evening. Her family was gathered in the kitchen with faces drawn and no one speaking. Sue came through the front door and entered the kitchen on her way to the bathroom. She stopped but only for a second as she laid her purse on the table.

"What's the matter? Did somebody die or something?" she flippantly asked, seeing the dreadful looks on her family's faces.

Marshall and Mariah glanced at one another and followed Sue into the little half-bathroom just off the kitchen. Echo couldn't hear her parents convey the dreadful news, but she heard her sister's horrific gut-wrenching screams.

"There is no God. There's absolutely no God," she bitterly bellowed, "because if He existed, He would never have allowed this to happen. Where was He, Dad, when Tommy needed Him? How come He didn't help my brother when he desperately needed Him to do so?"

Susan spewed the words in agonizing heartbreak. After a good cry, all three exited the bathroom with morose faces, irritated eyes, yet together and whole.

Echo heard the gently soothing tone of her father's voice coming from the bathroom that night, but she couldn't make out the impassioned words of wisdom he imparted to Sue. And she would never know for they are Susan's alone to treasure.

CHAPTER 7
A Chance to Give Back
1996

"Geoff told me about the clemency hearing to be convened later this year," Echo said to Russell, sitting in the prison's stark visitor's lounge.

"Yeah, but now I wish I'd never gotten involved with it in the first place!"

"Well, why not?"

"Oh, I don't think there's any chance of me getting out of here and it just builds false hope for the children. I told them not to get excited and put the cart before the horse. But you know how that goes. With all the publicity that could be generated over it, it's just going to bring it all back up again."

"It doesn't bother me anymore, but my grandchildren weren't born back in 1969. Yet, because some have my last name they're going to be gawked at, stared at and have fingers pointed at them for something they never had a part in. They'll have to suffer, and that's what really bothers me."

"I don't care about myself; they can't do any more to me. I've been incarcerated for almost 28 years, and I'm numb to it. All the pain, the shame, and humiliation; I've dealt with all that years ago.

"I have a brother who has children. I have to think about them, too. They are all innocent people."

"Sure, I'd like to receive clemency in order to spend my remaining years at home. But I'd just as soon die in here then to cause the family any more pain and suffering. Still, they wanted me to go for it and that's the only reason why I agreed."

"Well, I'm sure they love you very much and want you home with them," Echo responded.

"Yes, they've been good to me, and one day I'd especially like for my grandchildren to know that I used to be a decent man."

Echo could see the pain etched all over Russell's face. "Oh, I'm certain they realize that, Mr. James."

Surely a measure of decency remained that allowed him to feel empathy for his grandchildren. But the paradox wasn't lost on Echo. She wondered if he felt compassion for the Sycamores who would never have grandchildren through Daniel. And she wondered if he considered the re-victimization that they would have to endure through all the media attention the clemency hearing would thrust upon them. She noted that he hadn't even mentioned them.

"Well, I sure don't feel like a decent man and haven't for quite some time now."

Echo hoped the right words would come to her in order to convey her intentions. "That's sort of what I wanted to talk to you about, Russell. Did you know when we moved from the old neighborhood, we moved just three miles down the county road that ran in front of the Texaco station?" Echo looked directly into Russell's light blue and teary eyes.

"No, I didn't." An expression of surprise overtook his face. Echo could see his astonishment.

"And I met Daniel Sycamore there a few times."

"So, you knew him?"

"Not well. But I spoke with him there on a few occasions. We talked about kids we knew in common from our high schools. It was just your typical conversation when you're first getting to know someone."

"And there's something else. Daniel and I have aunts that are sisters. Now, I didn't know that before Daniel told me. So, later I asked mom and she said it was true."

"Wow, I had no idea," he responded.

Silence permeated the room for a few moments. Only the fan perched on top of the guard's desk, humming on high speed, interrupted the stillness until Russell finally spoke.

He looked at her quizzically as if he were contemplating where all of this was leading. "I had no idea where your family moved to, Echo."

She told him about her parents selling their house to the proprietor of the station about two months after the murder. She could tell these little coincidences were not lost on him.

"Wow, that's strange," he said.

"Yes, it is and that brings me to the main reason why I'm here." She swallowed hard and took a deep breath.

"I would like to write about your particular circumstances, Mr. James, and afford you the opportunity to apologize to those you hurt the most. We all have walked different paths. Some, either through their own dealings or due to elements out of their control, have suffered great pain along the way. It is my belief that through that pain some of the world's greatest lessons can be learned."

Echo grew fearful he might jump up and walk away from the table. But he didn't move. She turned her face toward him trying to grasp what he might be thinking.

"Additionally, you might shed some insight into what you feel led to your downfall. There's nothing new under the sun. Yet human beings seem to repeat bad behavior. Society must learn what devastated, deadened or influenced some folks to take the road they did. If we learn these things, that knowledge will allow us the opportunity to eliminate the causes and cease the repetition."

"People perish from a lack of knowledge and if you would share your insights, folks prone to similar stimuli might learn to deal with their inadequacies before wreaking mayhem on others."

With elbows on the table, Echo cradled her head in her hands and looked at Russell. He appeared thoughtful, pondering.

She felt uncomfortable asking him to relay the details of his worst mistake. Yet, she couldn't help believe that a remorseful man would want to give back.

"Let me ask you something, Echo. Why should this old adjudicated case spark an interest in you? Why dredge up the past?"

"My interest peaked when memories were exhumed by Geoff's phone call concerning the clemency. That's when I went to the circuit clerk's office and studied the details of Daniel's murder. I hadn't known anything about it up until then."

"But as I learned, I couldn't help recalling my own brother's death and the numbing sense of loss that was so devastating to my family. I see many similarities between Tom and Daniel's lives and deaths."

A look of confusion overtook Russell's countenance. "Forgive me, Echo, but war is different than murder. Your brother was killed in a military action; not murdered. Surely you can't see similarities between Tom's death and the death of that boy. I guess I just don't understand." Russell looked at Echo skeptically.

"Yes, the correlation makes perfect sense to me. After all, to mar by incompetence is a definition of murder. So, when the President of the United States goes before congress and lies about a Gulf of Tonkin incident that never happened and he is given carte blanche to do as he pleases over there because of that lie, it's like a drunk driving behind the wheel of a car.

I am outraged still at Johnson's incompetent execution of a war that caused so many deaths. I can only hope the sobering weight of our military casualties hung like an albatross around the neck of Lyndon Johnson until the day he died!"

"To my way of looking at it, Tom had his organs pierced and shredded by shrapnel and automatic rifle fire as a direct result of lies from the top office holder in the land. So, it sure feels like murder to me. If not by intention, than by gross incompetence. Senseless and wasteful, the injustice is undeniable!"

"Wow, I never thought about it that way. You've got an interesting take on it, though," Russell bent forward in his chair and placed his elbows on the table. "So, you want to write a book about this case?"

"Yes, I do."

"Well, Steven is the one you need to talk to. There are a few years back there I have no remembrance of." Russell looked at Echo straight faced and sober while she hoped her disbelief was not etched all over her face.

During her research, she learned the James men spent the previous afternoon into the wee hours of December 19th bar-hopping in the St. Louis area. She wondered if Russell had pushed the murder into the recesses of his mind, having his senses dulled by alcohol. Yet, was it even possible that an abhorrent act could be forgotten in a drunken stupor? Echo knew she wouldn't be so fortunate to forget; no matter how much alcohol was consumed?

She felt saddened at what she perceived to be an excuse to avoid the matter. Still, she couldn't be sure. This was their first visit in 30 years. What Echo was certain of was her single-minded vision to write this story. So, she kept her disbelief to herself. She understood the imperative of keeping the lines of communication open. She was concerned that Russell would close the door and remove her name from his visitor's list.

Echo began to realize that her brother might well be her ace in the hole. She had talked so much with Russell about Tom, sharing memories with one another. And as they sat together, she witnessed a grown man cry at the mention of his name.

"You mentioned Steve. I would like to speak with him. Do you think he would respond if I wrote him a letter?"

A sense of relief seemed to sweep over Russell's countenance. "Oh, sure he would, Echo."

"Then, I'll do that."

Just then the guard sitting at the elevated desk walked over to their table.

"They're serving lunch now. Will you both be eating today?"

"Would you like to go over, Echo?" Russell asked.

"Oh no, I really should be heading back to Starling."

Russell looked up at the corrections officer "Alright, then, I'll be going over in just a few minutes."

"Very well." The guard turned and made his way back to his station."

"Will you come to see me again, or write and stay in touch?"

"You can count on it. You and I have a lot to talk about yet."

Russell hugged Echo, but as she started to leave the pretty female guard with the ponytail instructed her to wait because the male guard would take Russell into another room first. He would remove his socks and shoes and be searched before making his way over to the prison cafeteria.

They want to make sure I didn't give him anything illegal, she thought to herself.

After a few moments, Echo was escorted out the same door she entered just two and one-half hours earlier. The guard led her to the sally port, and she went alone to the parking lot and climbed into her car.

She took a deep breath and exhaled, placed the key into the ignition and started the car, preparing to leave the prison grounds. She wondered if anything she said came out right.

Russell was 40 years of age the last time she saw him. He was a handsome man with dark hair and impeccable dress. Now his hair was white, and his face bore telltale signs of a hard life that aged him far beyond his 70 years. He appeared small and frail.

Echo looked forward to the time they would speak again. As she mentally rehashed the morning's events, she was grateful Russell had asked her to stay in touch. It was a start. She had her memories of the decent man she had known him to be and she banked on the belief that some degree of decency remained within him.

Although not a gambler, she bet he would stand up and do the right thing, knowing full well the memories of her childhood were really all she had to go on."

Echo drove off the parking lot onto the road, placing the prison in her rearview mirror. But she stopped the car and looked back at the complex. The rain had ceased and the sun was shining.

He was inside having lunch. He wasn't able to go to McDonalds Restaurant like she was planning to do. He would eat what was served to him. He didn't have any other choice.

It suddenly struck her as ironic how the decision he made on December 19, 1969, took all ability to make further decisions from him once he was arrested. His own conduct caused him to be stripped of the power to decide anything for himself. She shook her head back and forth in disgust as she pondered the wastefulness of it all. She took a deep breath and exhaled audibly, turned back around, put the car into drive and headed for the highway.

CHAPTER 8
Person or Persons Responsible
1969

Sturnus County Sheriff Teddy Roland broke with protocol by making the call to his top Investigator himself. "Don, we've got a murder at the Vernon Texaco on Route 66 at Glenrose. Get over here ASAP!" Don Delario had been sleeping soundly until the ring of the telephone disturbed the silence in his bedroom. Yet, he managed to answer on the first ring.

"I'm on my way, Sheriff."

As Chief Investigator, Don would be in charge of the case.

The DeLarios lived just a short distance from the station and were quite familiar with it. Don quietly rose and started dressing in the dark not wanting to disturb his wife. Still, she turned over to speak to him.

"What's going on?"

The three-quarter moon hanging in the sky did little to shed light through the curtained bedroom windows. Don moved toward the bed where she was lying. He bent down and kissed her on the cheek. "There's been a murder. Now, go back to sleep and I'll call you later."

He drew the bedroom door closed and navigated through the house and out to his unmarked Sheriff's car.

Carla was accustomed to the telephone ringing at all hours of the night. She'd been married to the Chief of Detectives for twenty years. Quickly, she said a prayer for the lost soul, whoever that might be, and drifted back to sleep. Don arrived at the station at 4:10 a.m. The first person he spoke to was Sheriff Roland.

"What have we got?"

"The young attendant, a kid named Dan Sycamore, was robbed, shot and killed."

Don let out a gut-wrenching groan. "Oh, no. Not Danny! Is he from Piedmont?" A look of horror erupted on the sergeant's face.

"Do you know him?"

"Oh, Lord. Yes, he's the son of a dear friend!" Don raised his hand to the forehead of his stunned face and rubbed it fitfully. He felt like he'd just been sucker-punched!

Sheriff Roland wasn't surprised as people in this area of small cloistered towns usually know one another all their lives. Generations of those that are born in the area usually tend to stay in the area.

The department was short on manpower and although the sheriff had the utmost confidence in Don's competence, he was equally concerned about any perception of impropriety.

"Are you going to be alright handling this? Perhaps I should turn the investigation over to the State Police."

"Please don't do that, Sheriff. I can handle it. I will put my personal feelings aside. I'll do my job. You presented me with the "Most Professional" certificate at the Awards Banquet last year, remember? So, you can't take that back now."

Roland considered the sergeant's words for a moment. "Alright, Don, the investigation is yours for now. But you keep your emotions intact. Just clean, honest investigative work is what we need here."

"And that's just what you'll get, Sheriff," Don responded sincerely. "Has the family been notified?"

"Yes, the coroner headed to the house about twenty minutes ago."

Don winced. The thought of what his friend was going through right now was almost too much for him to bear. He shook his head to clear his mind and began his investigation in the storage room. The body was removed but a chalk outline of the corpse was visible. Yellow crime scene marker cones stood at sites of blood splatter, dropped money, a V-shaped spring and a chocolate milk carton's spilled content. Walls, doors, handles and other surfaces were darkened with finger print powder from which prints were collected.

Don saw the partially dried crimson on the concrete and pulled a handkerchief from his pants pocket to dab his eyes. He said a silent prayer for Danny and for the family that loved him.

He squatted down surveying the area and noticed four BBs near the sewer under the wash basin where blood stained the floor. Dominic Kenney, Investigator with the State Police, photographed them before Don carefully placed them into a plastic bag. He and Kenney thoroughly went over the entire station, inspecting it with a proverbial fine-tooth comb. Each room was searched for any articles of evidence that might pertain to the case.

While checking the restroom, Don spotted splintered wall tile protruding outwardly. Some plaster in powder form and small pieces had fallen to the floor.

Don went into the storage room; to the opposite side of the splintered wall and found a hole created by what he thought might be a slug. He carefully measured the center of the opening twelve inches up on the wall from the concrete floor.

When he was finished with the measurements, Cecilia Dempsey brought a saw from her tool kit and cut out the area around the hole. The slug was found lying in the inner space between the walls of the bathroom and the storage room and had dropped down to the plating. Sergeant DeLario picked it up and handed it to Cecilia who placed the slug in a brown manila bag.

The time was now 6:10 a.m. Cecilia, a thirty-year veteran with the Crime Lab, had just twelve more days to work before retiring. Her plan was to return to Oceanside, California, where she was born and reared and where her mother, two brothers and sister lived.

Cecilia dusted various items for prints collecting fifteen exemplars to be used for the purpose of comparison. With a little good luck, a successful identification match could lead to the killer or killers.

She would remain at the station until approximately 7:30 a.m. Later that morning, she would make her way to Hope Memorial Hospital to attend the autopsy on the body of Daniel Sycamore.

Don went back into the storage room one last time that early morning as he wanted to make sure nothing was overlooked. The light was on and he drew the door closed. His eyes canvassed the area from ceiling to floor.

Now they fell upon the inside of the storage room door two to three feet from the bottom, and he moved closer for a better view. What he saw appeared to be the print of a right heel and sole of a shoe. It looked to have been made by a shoe that contained moisture when the print was placed on the door but it dried and was now visible. The heel bore an impression of a cat's paw. The sole print was smudged and appeared to have slid down and over to one side along the door.

Don stuck his head out into the main room. "Hey Dominic, can you come in here and take a picture of this door for me?"

"It's a good thing you stopped me when you did. My car's warming up outside. I was just preparing to head back into Starling. I only have four shots left in my camera. Is that going to be enough?"

"Oh sure. If I need more, I'll get Gallows. Is he still around?"

"No, he left about fifteen minutes ago. What did you find in there anyway?"

Don stepped back allowing Kenney to enter.

"Wow, that's a clean, legible heel print."

"Yes, it is. I've got a feeling that shoe print was placed there when someone kicked that door shut. I don't know if it's going to amount to anything right now, but I'd hate to leave it behind. I'll talk to Cecilia Dempsey before she leaves for the morgue and have her check the bottom of Daniel's shoes. But I'm betting that print was made by a wicked evil-doer."

"I think you're right. And if you can find the person that planted that print there, you'll find the murderer of the station attendant. I'll grab my camera. Be right back." Dominic headed out to his car.

Sergeant DeLario collected the BBs found in the storage room and placed them in his pocket. The autopsy would soon begin. He made his way out to his unmarked squad car and started the engine.

He sat back in his seat, closing his eyes. He'd seen blood many times before. But the sight of the spilled blood belonging to Danny gripped like a vice around his lungs and he struggled for air. Thoughts of his friend's fresh, raw grief sent waves of sorrow to flood his senses.

Soon, he would make the fifteen-mile trip to Starling and to the morgue at Hope Memorial, but not before making the six-mile jaunt into Piedmont to the home of Douglas and Janice Sycamore. There he'd make a promise to his buddy. "Neither hell nor high water will stop me from finding the person or persons responsible for Danny's death."

CHAPTER 9
A Marring Incompetence
1996

Echo was happy to depart the prison free to go as she pleased. She drove her vehicle onto Interstate 55 South and cruised along at sixty miles per hour.

At Williamsville, she took the exit and navigated onto Ann Rutledge Road toward the McDonald's Restaurant at the Love's Travel Stop. She walked up to the counter and ordered a cheeseburger with no catsup, French fries and a diet soda. She chose a seat in a booth where the sun permeated the window with warm, golden rays that hit the floor like a spotlight. As she unwrapped her sandwich, her mind traveled back to just minutes before when she sat with Russell James.

It was Russell's "war, not murder" and "killed in action" comments that seemed to have unsettled Echo. Both were factual of course but simplistic as well. They showed Russell never considered that Vietnam casualties mounted due to the bungling execution of the conflict by an incompetent Commander in Chief. It was, after all, lies from the top that embedded American combat troops in trenches and foxholes with no competent strategy to win.

Echo knew that most historical experts agree Lyndon Johnson fabricated the August 4, 1964, Gulf of Tonkin incident. And his fiction directly led to U. S. combat troops becoming wholly involved in Vietnam. Johnson's deceit exacted an enormous toll on the nation.

Just seven short months after the Gulf of Tonkin tale, on March 8, 1965, the first United States Marines combat troops arrived in Vietnam.

As she sat enjoying her cheeseburger, Echo thought of the many injustices the Vietnam soldier suffered; from the irresponsible lies of the president, to name-calling and violence from fellow Americans when they returned home.

Echo picked up another French fry and dabbed it in catsup

before plopping it in her mouth. She knew she need not look any further than Johnson's "I will not seek" speech to discover his lack of credibility. In that March 31, 1968 oration, Johnson talked about de-escalating the war but additional combat troops were being sent to Vietnam.

He said that America's strength was in its people's unity. But in that same speech he stated there was division in the American house. The inconsistency of his words is indisputable and quite puzzling. I will never be able to comprehend how a man could look straight-faced into a camera feed going out to the nation, and speak such striking contradictions, she thought to herself.

As she sat consuming her lunch, she pondered why Johnson didn't rethink his Vietnam policy, if the president knew the American people weren't unified. But he didn't and Americans died. Instead, Johnson went on to say if peace doesn't come through negotiations, Hanoi needs to understand our common resolve is unbeatable.

Once again, Echo snickered at his ludicrous forked-tongue statement. *What common resolve was he referring to when just moments before he spoke of the division existing among the American people? He seemed to speak out of both sides of his mouth. How could anybody believe a single word he said,* she wondered.

Echo took another bite of her cheeseburger and a drink of her diet soda. She began to recall the turbulent times of the 1960s and the volatility on the home front.

Protests against the Vietnam debacle were taking place on the grounds and steps of town squares in most major cities across the nation. Starling, Illinois was no exception.

A rather large protest rally was held on the town square in the summer of 1968. Echo could almost feel the searing heat of the protesters' anger; simply by recalling it. None of the Middletons were at the protest that day, but the family sat riveted; watching the report of it on the 6 p.m. and 10 p.m. news.

The boiling sun did little to subdue the incessant mantras that rose from the crowd to a crescendo and dispersed into the stifling air. Chants of rebuke were repeated over and over again, in unison, "LBJ, please go away," and "hey, hey LBJ, how many kids did you kill today?"

The protesters' voices were loud, purposeful and nearly

frenzied! The activists at this protest seemed to place the onus where it belonged, squarely on the shoulders of the Commander in Chief and not on those who bore the burden of carrying out his dirty work. But that wasn't always the case.

To many Americans, the Vietnam soldier represented the war itself. There were no ticker-tape parades welcoming the Vietnam veterans' home; just protests on town squares where a uniformed soldier might find himself engulfed in peril as deadly as dodging bombs and grenades in the Asian rice fields. The Vietnam debacle pitted brother against brother and Lyndon Johnson will forever own that shame.

In early March, 1965, perhaps Johnson didn't realize what the full impact of his lies would be on the nation as he sent combat troops into Vietnam. But on March 31, 1968, surely, he knew the costly weight of his actions. Still, he chose not to stop the madness. Instead, like a coward, he announced he would not seek or accept the nomination as the democratic candidate for the presidency in the next election. He would pick up his 'bat and ball glove' and hightail it out of the White House.

Surely his Vietnam mistakes had come full cycle, and he knew full well he had abdicated his responsibility to the American people. What a wonderful opportunity Johnson let slide by not taking responsibility for his actions, admitting his failure and setting into motion the steps necessary to bring our men home.

Echo grimaced in bitter recall.

An immediate withdrawal would not have been possible after involving U. S. troops so deeply over there but he should have attempted to make a start. Countless casualties died the next day, the next month, the next year because he didn't. It needn't have happened.

It was as incompetent to continue in Vietnam as it is to drive drunk and plow like a torpedo into another vehicle that causes death.

To Echo, Johnson's actions were gross negligence at minimum. But when he turned his back and walked away from the White House, abandoning the soldiers he sent to Vietnam in the first place, his incompetent culpability rose to murder!

U. S. troop numbers were at their highest point in 1969. Johnson's approved maximum number in Vietnam was 549,500.

Echo closed her eyes, as contempt for Lyndon Johnson rose

within her from that dark hole where she pushed her anguish and disdain for him in order to cope with the damage he caused. She could think of him in no other way than as a thug. His reign of terror, she believed, cost a lot more than the shattered lives of its soldiers. The country's morale hit the skids.

Justice for my brother will have to come as history records the truth about the Vietnam fiasco with Johnson's incompetent escalation void a plan to win. A complete explanation of his bad decisions was owed; just as it was with Russell James. Johnson not only owed it to those like my family that lost a loved one, but to each citizen, for the demoralizing consequence of his incompetence.

Possibly, Johnson thought his position as president placed him above doing that. Maybe he just didn't have the character required to do so. And maybe, too, he didn't feel the need for the nation's compassion or want its people's forgiveness.

They said it was by way of shrapnel from a grenade that took Tom's life, but I know that was simply the method. The man behind that grenade, responsible for it, I believe, is the thirty-sixth president of the United States. I can see it no other way.

Time had done nothing to alleviate the contempt Echo held toward the man who walked away from the mess he created in Vietnam and the division he caused on the home front as well. The nation, after all, was left to wonder what on earth we were doing there. After his 'will not seek' speech, protesters held up signs that simply read, "Thank you."

Echo slurped the last remnants of soda from her paper cup. She picked up the tray and plopped it on top of the garbage bin. She slung her purse over her shoulder and exited through the side door onto the parking lot.

The humidity after the rain was thick and stifling. She hurried to her car, turned the air-conditioning unit on full speed and drove off the parking lot toward the Interstate for the trek back into Starling. As she drove, her mind reverted to a more pleasant time before life dealt a dose of cruel reality.

It was only a couple of years before Tom's death that Echo carried her Barbie doll across the street to meet her friends. Her destination was the Martin Luther Grade School, the gathering spot for all the neighborhood children to enjoy an array of activities.

She headed toward the front of the school where her friends

were already waiting for her. But just as she began her passage across Matheny Avenue, she heard a voice holler out, "Hi, little girl!"

Echo looked over her right shoulder and saw a soldier in uniform about half of a block away. He raised his right arm and waved when he saw her look at him.

Somehow, she couldn't place who he was, so she continued to cross the street. Echo heard the soldier holler again, but this time she ignored him.

It's hard to imagine now, how it never registered, having three brothers in the service at that time, that the friendly soldier might just be one of them.

When she arrived at the school, she put her things down and turned to look at the soldier again. Just as she did, she saw him walking up the sidewalk that led to her family's front porch.

"Tommy!" Echo hollered in eventual recognition, running back across the street as fast as her little legs would take her. Her heart raced from the excitement.

Mariah must have seen Tom coming as she met him on the front porch and had both of her arms wrapped tightly around him. Her eyes filled with tears. She was so happy to have him home again!

When she finally let go, Tom scooped Echo up into his arms. She put her arms around his neck and hugged him.

"How come you didn't wave to me?" he asked.

"I didn't know who you were."

"Oh, come on. You haven't forgotten your big brother already have you?"

Feeling somewhat embarrassed Echo told him that she hadn't. He put her down and rubbed the top of her head.

"And you won't ever forget me, will you?" Tom spoke in a tone that was more commanding than inquisitive. "Promise me now that you won't ever forget me."

"No, I won't. Ever," Echo assured him. "I promise never-ever will I forget you!"

Mariah opened the front door, and they crossed the threshold into the house. Cassie and Annalisa came scurrying in behind them.

Marshall was at work that Saturday afternoon but would have a pleasant surprise when he arrived home that evening.

Surprise indeed, for Tom hadn't told anyone the specific date he'd be home on military leave.

The Grand Avenue exit that would lead Echo into Starling was fast approaching. She slowed her Prelude to safely execute the turn. She pulled into the Stop-N-Shop Grocery Store parking lot and turned off the engine. Before going into work, she needed to pick up a few things for her meeting with Don on Saturday.

***

That same evening Echo wrote a letter to Steven James asking if she could pay him a visit but he never responded. It was later while talking with Geoff she learned Steve received her correspondence but wasn't interested in meeting with her.

Geoff told Echo once that Steven has been institutionalized and is a bitter person. That letter was the last contact Echo would have with Steven. She didn't want to push the issue.

Just let sleeping dogs lie, she thought to herself.

CHAPTER 10
Like the Back of my Hand
1969

Don arrived back at his office; a man on a mission. He needed the afternoon shift to come in early. As he entered the command center, he handed the call-out list to the deputy dispatcher, Ethan Rigsby.

"Call the second shift. Let them know they're needed in here right away. Then call the third shift and see if any of them want to work a double. I need all the men I can get!" He thanked the dispatcher before he reeled and headed back to his office. He sat down at his desk and picked up the telephone to call District Nine of the State Police. Trooper Michael Henry took the call.

"I'd like you to check on any traffic stops made overnight, prior to and after the murder at around 3 a.m., along U. S. Route 66 between Bloomington and St. Louis."

"Yes sir, I'll contact the other districts along the route, and we'll get the information for you," Henry said.

About a half-hour later, the men from the 3 p.m. to 11 p.m. shift had arrived at the station along with others from the graveyard shift. Sergeant DeLario laid out the first plan of action.

"We'll meet at Vernon's Texaco Station and split into three groups. The first group will canvass the area in the fields and along the highway on both the north and southbound lanes going in a southerly direction to the Route 114 junction."

"The second will cover the same area but in a northerly direction to the Glenrose overpass."

"And the last group will take the county road in front of the station and canvas both sides and in the fields for about two miles, in a westerly direction."

"Remember gentlemen, we're looking for weapons or anything that might shed some light on the person or persons responsible for this crime. There's nothing out there you might find that isn't important to us right now; so, collect it all. Now, are there any questions before we get started?"

The officers remained silent.

"Sheriff, do you have anything you'd like to say, sir?"

"Just do a thorough job, folks. We want the person or persons responsible for this murder, and we want that badly!"

"Alright then gentlemen, I'll see you in the field." Don headed back into his office to retrieve his winter jacket. The deputies filed out of the room and made their way to their squad cars for the short trip to the Vernon Texaco station.

***

At two o'clock on the afternoon of December 18, 1969, Steven James called his wife, Bonnie, at her office at the Tippy-Toes Day Care Center where she worked as a secretary, to ask for their check book. He told her he was leaving town with his father and wanted to take some money with him.

"I have it with me. You'll have to come up here to pick it up. But just so you know, we don't have any money in the account."

"Well, that's alright then. I'll ask dad if I can borrow from him."

Bonnie waited to hear back, but he never called. She wouldn't see or speak with him again until late the next evening on December 19, at approximately 8 p.m., when they arrived home with their hands full of bagged items.

Both father and son, from all appearances, seemed to have had a very successful shopping trip. Russell purchased four new shirts, and his son purchased a knit shirt, a few records and one other item as well. Steven took a seat at the kitchen table and raised his right leg. "How do you like my new shoes?"

His wife seethed at the sight of him showing off the black imitation alligator loafers he was wearing.

"Well, for God's sake, where did you get the money? I thought you didn't have any. Don't you remember calling me looking for some? How in the world can you justify buying a new pair of shoes? You know we don't have money to throw away like that, Steve!"

Bonnie looked at him, waiting for a response but he made no reply which angered her even more. The couple lived in his parents' house, and she didn't like to argue in front of them. But this time she couldn't contain herself.

"You act like money grows on trees and now I won't be able to finish the Christmas shopping for having to pay your father back. I suppose that's where you got the money?" Still, Steven sat silent at the table feeling somewhat embarrassed.

Bonnie fumed at her husband's apparent irresponsibility. "Where are your old shoes? I'd like to see just what was so bad that you needed another pair."

"Oh, C'mon, Bonnie, I had to buy a new pair, honey. I twisted my ankle and the heel on my right shoe came off."

Bonnie folded her arms in front of her in a defensive stance. "Oh, that's not a likely story. If that's the case then why didn't you find a repair shop and try to have it fixed?"

"I didn't know where to locate a shoe repair shop in St. Louis. Besides, if it couldn't be fixed immediately, was I supposed to walk around in my stocking feet?"

Bonnie was angry but made a special effort to restrain her indignation. His parents were at the kitchen table listening to the diatribe. "Well, we just don't have the money," she said in defiant resignation.

Steven hung his head. "You're right, honey. I'm sorry."

"Okay, but the next time you want to go on a shopping spree you and I will need to go over the finances first."

Steven was relieved to put the spat behind him. "Yes, I promise. But for now, I need to take these damn shoes off. My right foot is killing me!"

Bonnie gasped as her husband removed his shoes and socks. "Oh, my gosh, look how swollen your ankle is!"

Steven held up his right leg so his mother and father could see. "It's hurting like a son-of-a-gun too!"

He looked over at his father and made eye contact. "I must have done it when I twisted my ankle and the heel on the old shoe fell off."

"Yeah that's probably when it happened," his father replied.

"No way," Bonnie said in jest. She was one who loved to tease and insert her jabs whenever she could. "You know how your

73

temper gets the best of you. You probably were pissed off and started kicking at something again. We all know that's what you do when you are angry. Isn't that right, Mom?"

"Oh, he's got a temper alright," Margaret said with a smile.

Steven's face flushed although he smiled appropriately. He shot a sheepish look at his father, then looked at his wife. "You think you know me don't you, smarty pants?"

"No, I don't think I know you. I know that I know you; like the back of my hand."

CHAPTER 11
The Best Intentions
1996

Don arrived a little earlier than expected that Saturday, and Echo raced to the door to greet him. "I hope you're hungry. I fixed lunch; spaghetti with meat sauce."

"Oh, you shouldn't have bothered."

"It wasn't any bother at all. Besides, you're always picking up the tab. So, this one is on me. Come into the kitchen, Don. The sauce is simmering on the stove."

Echo opened the top portal of the double oven and peered inside. The garlic bread was beginning to brown. "Just about five more minutes is all."

She walked over to the kitchen table and sat down across from Don. "So, tell me how your visit with Russell James went?"

Echo looked up at him and smirked as she shrugged her shoulders. "Well, I found myself struggling to separate my childhood memories of him from the reality of his situation today. I felt awkward, clumsy with my words, and completely out of place. Still, he didn't banish me forever, so I believe it went as well as it could, considering the 30-year absence."

Don smiled compassionately. "I can understand your anxiety, but I wouldn't concern myself too much. The more you visit the easier it will become to see him in his present circumstance. You're not that little girl today and neither is he that kindly neighbor. I predict lucidity will prevail in the weeks and months to follow."

Echo removed the pre-cut garlic bread from the oven and drained the noodles in the sink. She grabbed tongs and silverware from the drawer and retrieved dinnerware from the cabinet. The two filled their plates and sat back down at the table.

"This is good, Echo. Thank you."

"She smiled broadly from ear to ear. "You're so welcome."

Don took on a more serious tone. He looked directly at Echo as he spoke. "You know that Russell and Steven James are only half of the story, don't you?"

Echo had a perplexed look on her face. "I'm not sure what you mean, Don."

"Well, there's another family that was deeply affected by the murder the Jameses committed.

"Yes, I understand now. You're referring to the Sycamores."

Don nodded. "That's correct. They're good people who never sought the nightmare they lived through. They have a completely different perspective. And I believe it's equally important that you hear from them as well."

"Don't you think they'd resent my drudging up the painful past?"

"I think they'd resent the exclusion. If you give the murderers a voice without affording equal opportunity to the victim's family, your book won't be worth the paper it's written on."

Echo sat back in her chair with a dejected look on her face. "But at this point, I'm unsure what route the book will take. And what right do I have infringing on people's misery when I have nothing to offer in return? Wouldn't that be unfair? Maybe this isn't the time to reach out."

"Would you rather they learn of your contact with Russell James and draw inaccurate conclusions concerning your intentions? Why not tell them of your plans and say you're unsure of the outcome?"

"Allow yourself to be vulnerable. Permit them to decide if they want to contribute. I'm just afraid your hesitation might be construed as a snub or worse. They may conclude you're trying to free a murderer. And that would be most unfortunate."

"I never thought about it that way. I just didn't want to add to their pain before I had something to offer them. However, I see now. Certainly, they should learn my intentions from me, firsthand, rather than from anyone else. Do you think they'd agree to see me?"

"I believe they would. Douglas Sycamore was a close and dear friend. We were high school buddies. People say we were like brothers, and I suppose that's true enough. I was best man at his wedding. In fact, his firstborn son's middle name is Donald after me. I watched those two boys grow up. My wife and I loved them as if they were our own."

Echo was surprised by the revelation. "Oh, I didn't know

that!"

"Douglas and Janice are gone now, but I will speak to Dallas. I feel it's important and best to be out front with your plans for the sake of everyone involved."

"I wish I had thought of that. Please let Dallas and the rest of the family know that I'd like to meet with them."

"I'll certainly do that for you. When will you visit Russell James again?"

"I'm going up early on Thursday. I plan to be there at 8:30 a.m., the start of visiting hours. Russell prefers early visits to accommodate his work schedule."

"Don, about the Sycamores. I hope my dreadful thoughtlessness doesn't strain our friendship. I'd hate that more than anything!"

"Not a chance, young lady. I know you have the best intentions."

CHAPTER 12
No Longer on the Premises
1969

Harlan Vernon and his employee, Jeremy Summer, took inventory and discovered $524.84 was missing from the register; but that wasn't the only thing. Jeremy discovered it while counting oil cans in the back.

"Hey Harlan, where's the shotgun?"

Harlan came out from behind the desk and hustled to the door of the storage room. "I don't know. It's supposed to be standing up against the wall right here in the corner!"

He stuck his head around the door for a look but the 12-gauge double-barrel New Elgin shotgun was not in its usual place.

"Jeremy, search around in there. See if it might be in the restroom. I'll check the front. Who knows, maybe one of the officers hauled it off as evidence."

The men set about scouring the entire station, but the shotgun was nowhere to be found.

"I'll call the employees. Maybe one of them used it for hunting," Jeremy said.

"Yeah, that's a good idea." Harlan reached for the address book containing the employee phone numbers and handed it to Jeremy, who began to re-think his last statement. He turned to face Harlan.

"Then again, why would they do that? They know that shotgun doesn't work half the time and is beyond repair."

Harland nodded his head in agreement. "Still, we have to check."

He followed Jeremy over to the phone. About two years prior, Vernon purchased the shotgun at Washburn Sports Store and took it to the station where it was kept stashed behind the storeroom door.

The workers used it for target practice on field mice that infiltrated the station from the surrounding cornfields. But now the right firing pin was defective, and the left firing pin didn't work and had been removed.

By early afternoon, all employees had been questioned. According to all of the workers, the shotgun was behind the storage room door the last time they saw it.

Vernon then picked up the telephone and placed a call to the Sturnus County Sheriff's office and asked to speak with Sergeant DeLario. He wanted to let the chief investigator know the shotgun was not on the premises.

"I appreciate you calling to inform me of that," Don said. "Also, will you please look at your receipts for any credit card purchases. If you have any local charge accounts, I'd like the names and addresses of those people, please."

"I'll start on that right now, gather the information and let you know just as soon as I can," Harlan said.

CHAPTER 13
Not by a Longshot
1996

Echo's eyes scanned the visitor's lounge as she waited for Russell on that Thursday morning. Her mind couldn't help but think how dreadfully mundane prison life must be day after day, month after month and year after year. She observed the same guard sitting at the same desk. The same fan was spinning at the same speed.

It felt as if she were witnessing life without living and human warehousing without interest. There was no feel for past or future, but for sanity's sake, a presence in the moment repeated over and over again. The realization sent chills down her spine.

Echo saw the same dulled smile on Russell's colorless face when he came into the room. He wore the same Department of Corrections navy-blue pants and light blue shirt issued to all inmates. They sat down at the same table to reminisce the past before discussing the present.

"Do you remember, Echo, I told you I wanted my grandchildren to know I used to be a decent man?"

"Yes, I do remember that."

"Well, before my incarceration things were pretty good for me and my wife. We didn't have all we wanted, but we had all we needed. We had a roof over our heads and heat in the winter in a home we owned outright. I had a good job, and we paid our bills on time. We were in good health, and we had healthy children."

"We were happy, and I had my volunteer work with the Khoury Baseball League where I was named the Circuit Director. I still coached a team -- Tom's team -- until 1965."

"We built three baseball diamonds inside the big race track on the fairgrounds. Tom and his buddies helped us with that. I talked Mr. Quinn, a local landowner, into allowing us to build three diamonds on his property. That's how Quinn Park was born."

"But things started to change. I began to get sick. First, I developed a bronchial condition that turned into pneumonia. Over the next few years, I entered the hospital several times with depression. I wasn't able to work. And in November 1969, I made application and was scheduled to enter a veteran's hospital on January 3, 1970. Unfortunately, as you certainly know, I never made it."

"Yes, and what a tragic shame that was for everyone concerned. I'm sure you've had a mountain of regret."

"Indeed, I have. More regret than I could ever articulate. It haunts me still, all the 'what ifs.' What if I was admitted to that hospital sooner? My life would have turned out a whole lot differently."

He shook his head in disappointment.

"Anyway, through all the sickness I believe something must have happened to me because I can't remember incidents that occurred back then. I wish I could. But the truth is I don't remember harming that boy. I don't remember anything about it. Don't get me wrong. I'm not saying I didn't do the crime. I simply don't recall ever being present at that gas station."

Echo's shoulders drooped, and she exhaled audibly. She felt that heart-dropping sensation when she finally got it; finally realized he wasn't going to account for his actions or offer a genuine apology to the people he harmed. He wasn't going to and she didn't possess the ability to make him do otherwise.

She certainly wasn't the one that he would confess his sins to. After all, she was just a child when they were acquainted. What could she say to him that would change his heart now to make him want to do the right thing?

Still, Echo's inner voice whispered he was lying. His words just didn't ring true. His face and body language told her that even he didn't believe a single word spewing from his mouth, although he wanted her to believe his fantasy. So, she decided to keep her doubt to herself for now, to sit back and just listen to him speak. She resigned herself to hearing whatever he wanted to tell her. The floor was his.

"Back then I had medical procedures, and I wonder if that would account for my memory loss. Between May and June of 1967, I spent five weeks in the hospital undergoing a series of electroshock treatments. Then in March 1969, I received additional electroshock therapy."

Echo didn't know anything about that medical procedure and didn't want to participate in a discussion without having some knowledge of it. Still, she couldn't dispel the question that gnawed at her. Was it possible a man receiving a series of electroshock in 1967 and again in March 1969 could suffer memory loss of an incident that hadn't even occurred yet? Afterall, the murder happened a full nine months after his last treatment?

Russell seemed to recall quite well incidents leading up to and directly following the murder of Daniel Sycamore. Remarkably, the memory loss encompassed only the time frame of the crime itself.

Later, Echo learned that few electroshock patients do experience memory loss but experts agree it's centered on the time of treatment or before and certainly not as long as nine months afterward. Although not a psychiatrist, it seemed to Echo that Russell James suffered from a voluntary memory loss.

It troubled her that he wasn't truthful even after all this time and at his age with facing his own mortality. She wanted to change the subject and leave the table so that he wouldn't see the disappointment she felt. She rose from her chair and scurried to the vending machine. "How about some popcorn and a soda?"

"Sure, that sounds good."

After purchasing the popcorn, she placed the bag into the microwave, and the scent of heated kernels filled the room. When finished, she opened the bag, allowing the steamy heat to escape into the air. She handed Russell a can of diet Pepsi and placed one in front of her chair as well.

Echo sat back down at the table. She reached out and placed her hand on top of Russell's. She refused to give up just yet. "You know what, Mr. James, I still believe good can come out of the carnage, even if you don't recall the murder itself."

"Could you concentrate on the things that led up to it and the ramifications thereafter? Could you discuss those things that influenced you toward that end and the misery you created for yourself and others? Because if you can, and you're willing to share it, then Daniel wouldn't have died in vain and all needn't be a total waste."

"Oh, boy, I can't believe you said that. It's like Deja vu!"

Echo looked at him curiously. "What do you mean?" She

was interested in knowing where he was going with this. She had been around him long enough to surmise he was diverting the subject; something he did quite often.

"That's exactly what my mother said when Steve and I were convicted. "What an absolute waste you've made of your life." Mom shook her head and cried, mortified by it all."

"That poor, good woman. My heart breaks when I think of all she endured." He looked down at his folded hands resting on the table. "When my mind conjures up the image of her learning from her sister, Luella, of our arrest in Durham, I feel so ashamed."

Russell reached into his pants' pocket and pulled out a cotton handkerchief and brought it to his face. "I'm sorry, Echo. I get emotional talking about this." He wiped his eyes and placed the handkerchief back in his pocket. Echo shifted her gaze from his face. Her heart pumped compassionately for the tired, old man sitting across from her.

His regret for the pain he caused his loved ones was real. Echo wondered though, if after all this time, he felt that same compassion for the Sycamore family. If he did, she knew the suffering both families endured could count for something, if only he would speak to it. And what a good thing that would be.

She let go of the hope of hearing Russell James account for his crime. She knew there was nothing she could say to entice his efforts at recall. But what about some kid out there that has absolutely no idea what prison life is all about but is heading in that direction anyway? Could Russell muster the courage to share the lessons he learned through his incarceration and the warning signs he missed along the way? Echo wanted to find the answer to those questions. She wasn't ready to give up. No, not by a longshot.

CHAPTER 14
A Clinical Death
1969

Dr. Jackson C. Grant, Director of Laboratories and Pathologists at Hope Memorial Hospital since 1963, began the autopsy on the body of Daniel Sycamore at 8:05 a.m. Cecilia Dempsey signed the log book as required for all persons in attendance at autopsies.

The victim's body heat was reduced upon the doctor's initial examination at the station. However, at that time, no signs of rigidity were present in the jaw or limbs, and the muscle tissue retained reactivity. The doctor determined death occurred not more than an hour prior to Daniel being found.

Now, in the morgue, the doctor observed large amounts of partially dried blood on the right side of Daniel's attire. The clothing was removed and turned over to Dempsey who arrived on the scene just moments before. She looked at the bottom of Daniel's shoes before placing the items into plastic bags. Then, she took patent prints of Daniel's ten fingers. When completed Dr. Grant began to examine the various wounds to the body.

Two wounds, one an entrance and the other an exit, were situated on the right forehead. The bullet traveled under the skin and exited without fracturing the skull.

The next wound went clear through Daniel's right arm. The hole on the inside of the arm was large with a tearing appearance and the hole to the outside of the arm was much smaller and less jagged. Wadding and shot were removed and handed over to Cecilia. She placed the shot and wadding into separate plastic containers, sealed them and placed her initials on the containers.

Doctor Grant noticed bruising on the right side of Daniel's chest. He determined this was caused by the force of the shotgun pellets pushing the arm into the right chest area.

The fatal wound was positioned behind the victim's right ear. A good amount of brain matter was caked over this wound.

The bullet entered the skull and Dr. Grant, using a probe, traced its course through the brain to the opposite side of the head. The Doctor removed the .38 caliber bullet and turned it over to the crime scene investigator. Cecilia took placed it in a plastic bag, sealed and initialed it.

The autopsy took about two hours to complete. The cause of death was massive destruction to Daniel's brain.

As he finished, Dr. Grant looked down at the lifeless form lying on the cold steel table and found himself lost in thought. *This was somebody's son, brother, nephew, friend. It was just hours ago that he had a life, until some vicious murderer took it from him.*

He thought about Daniel's folks, people he did not know. Dr. Grant's heart went out to them. He was a trained professional accustomed to seeing death having performed hundreds of autopsies throughout his career. But whenever he had to examine young people, it always bothered him. At no time did it bother him more than at times like this, when a hideous murder was involved!

Grant stood over the body with his chin in his hand, slowly shaking his head from left to right. His consternation rose as he looked down at the remains. He hoped whoever did this would get just what they had coming to them.

What a waste, he thought. *A young man out doing his job, only to be snuffed out. Who knows what potential follows him to the grave?*

The doctor looked at Cecilia. "We're all finished in here."

As the two professionals turned to walk away Dr. Grant put his hand on Cecilia's shoulder. "I think I've had just about all I can stand of this room for one morning."

"I understand completely," Cecilia responded.

Grant reached for the handle on the door leading into the hallway and stepped aside to allow Cecilia to pass through. DeLario met up with them in the hall outside the autopsy room just moments after it was completed. The Doctor gave the sergeant a summation of the wounds inflicted upon Daniel's body.

When hearing of the single-bullet entrance and exit wounds on the victim's forehead, DeLario's mind flashed back to the station.

He recalled finding the bullet that caused the hole in the drywall just twelve inches from the floor. He now realized only one conclusion could be drawn from that evidence. Daniel Sycamore had been methodically executed. He had to be down on the cold concrete floor, maybe wounded, but defenseless, as his killer or killers took aim and opened fire.

Don was incensed. He shuttered at the cruel callousness of this brutal murder, and his resolve was reaffirmed. He would do whatever it took; work day and night, to bring justice to Daniel and his family and friends. He handed the BBs over to the crime scene technician.

"Oh, by the way," Cecilia said to Sergeant Delario, "that cat's paw heel imprinted on the store room door, was not made by Daniel's shoe."

The threesome shook hands and Don walked down the hallway to the elevator that would take him up and out to the parking lot. He hopped in his car and headed back to his office in downtown Starling.

On the following Thursday, Susan M. Kutchar, Crime Technician in the Joliet office received a box from the State Crime Laboratory in Starling. The contents of the box contained Cecilia Dempsey's individually packaged items of evidence that were collected at the autopsy and at the station.

The wadding removed from the massive wound to Daniel's right arm was measured and determined to be of twelve-gauge. All pellets retrieved from the body and the station floor were weighed and determined to be number six shot.

Two bullets, one removed from Daniel Sycamore's head and one from the wall of the storage room were received. The more pristine bullet was determined to be of .38 caliber with five lands and grooves with a right-hand twist.

* * *

A letter arrived at the Middleton home on Matheny Avenue around the middle of November, 1969. In it, Captain W. B. Clary, U.S. Marine Corp, detailed the circumstances and forensics surrounding the demise of Thomas Middleton.

The letter stated: "Thomas was assigned as a Grenadier of the 2nd Platoon. On 26 October, 1969, the entire Battalion was engaged in a large-scale operation against the Viet Cong in Quang Tri Province just south of the Demilitarized Zone."

"At 10 a.m., your son's squad was moving along a trail and came under attack by Viet Cong using grenades and automatic weapons. Penetrating shrapnel wounds with multiple entrances of the lower left abdomen, right upper abdomen and right palm assailed the body causing massive internal hemorrhage. Additionally, penetrating shrapnel wounds with multiple entrances of the lower right back, lower left back and upper left posterior forearm assailed the body with apparent gunshot wounds and caused massive internal hemorrhage."

"Thomas fell victim to a Viet Cong grenade. His passing was instant. The last rites of his faith were administered by Commander J. A. Lowell, a U. S. Navy Chaplain."

CHAPTER 15
The Beginning of Disillusion
1996

A month passed since Echo's last visit with Russell. Apparently wishing to withdraw from face to face visits he now seemed to prefer telephone calls on Saturday mornings.

Echo's requests to see him were falling on deaf ears. There were excuses like, 'I'm busy at my job.' That is until his annual parole hearing rolled around, and he wanted her to attend.

The whole thing was leaving a bad taste in Echo's mouth. She felt as if she were being conned by a con. Slowly, she began to see the kindly neighbor in a different light.

After asking Echo to attend, he told her to think about it. He knew someone outside his family speaking up for him might weigh favorably with the Parole Board. He desperately wanted her voice.

Yet, she really didn't want to go. Echo felt uncomfortable as she had strong misgivings about any contribution she might make. She didn't want to appear as one who supported the notion that his punishment had been satisfied. How could a sound determination be made when he dodged accountability?

Mostly, she had no desire to be perceived as choosing sides as if this were some baseball game at Martin Luther Grade School on Matheny Avenue. Echo just never wanted to be put in that position!

Had there been an issue of judicial error, she would have jumped in with both feet, but that wasn't the case. She had a different agenda. She found no quandary in separating moral issues of accountability and repentance from the issue of legal debt. Assisting in freeing Russell from his lawful obligation never entered the picture.

Still, Echo was afraid to refuse to attend for fear he would cut off all ties with her. She had given up hope he'd ever account for the crime he claimed not to remember. She just couldn't imagine he wouldn't want to talk about the precursors to the murder and the lessons he'd learned after. So, she agreed to attend the annual affair at his request.

Only one Prison Review Board member, Mr. Stanley Post, was present. He would create an audiotape recording of the hearing for the rest of the board's perusal. If the board recommended or refused to recommend parole for Russell James it was of no consequence to Echo. She had no dog in the fight.

Still, she wasn't without a modicum of sympathy. He'd been in prison a long time, and his age weighed advantageous for parole since, statistically, older prisoners don't repeat their destructive behavior.

Post asked Echo her name and connection to Russell. She told him that her family used to be neighbors to the Jameses and the kindness Russell showed her brother. She said her presence there was at Russell's request. She made no other statement but sat listening as Geoff spoke next impressing her with his passion.

His love for his father was evident in Geoff's pleas for his release. He and his wife would bring Russell to live with them and Geoff would introduce his father to his larger Christian family at his church to support and uplift his dad as they had so richly done for him.

"Thank you, sir," Post responded. He, too, seemed moved by Geoff's passionate plea.

"Mr. James, this is your hearing and your chance to speak to the board. Is there anything you'd like to say, a statement you'd like to make? You know from previous hearings I will be sharing this audio recording with my peers. This is your chance to be heard."

"Well, I'd just like to say that I am sorry. I don't really want to talk about it as it's very emotional for me to do so, but I'd like for the board to know that I am truly sorry!"

Stanley Post appeared genuinely surprised. "In all of your parole hearings, you never apologized for your crime." He looked at Russell hoping he might elaborate, but he would not speak further on the matter.

"Mr. James, you know the rules. We won't talk about or discuss anything you don't wish to. This is your parole hearing, not mine."

"Well, thank you very much," Russell responded. "I just can't bring myself to talk about it right now."

"Mr. James, would you be willing to submit to a mental evaluation?"

The question had never before been asked of him. Echo thought she saw hope stir within him that reflected in his eyes as he shot a quick glance at Geoff. He seemed happy to oblige as if it might benefit him to do so. "Yes, I would."

"Very well then. A date and time for the evaluation will be scheduled, and the test will be administered here at the center. Now unless you have anything further to add, that will conclude this parole hearing."

"No, that's about all I can think of, sir." Russell smiled politely, rising from his chair. He reached across the desk to shake Post's hand before turning and exiting through the door where a correctional officer stood guard throughout the entire hearing.

Geoff and Echo followed directly behind him, and the three were escorted into the visitor's lounge.

Echo was pleased to have heard the remorseful words that had eluded Russell James throughout all the long years of his incarceration. But she was leery as well.

She found it curious that he didn't want to elaborate on it with Mr. Post. She thought if he were truly sorry for what he did, that it would behoove him to share the entire gamut of that information with someone who had the power to recommend parole. Still, how could he be sorry for something he claims he don't remember doing?

Echo began to suspect his words weren't sincere but were an attempt to manipulate the board. Surely those highly educated men and women were not easily swayed or deceived.

Echo and Russell took seats at their usual table while Geoff meandered over to the vending machines.

Echo smiled warmly, trying to elicit more information. "I think you surprised Mr. Post with your apology today." But Russell wasn't buying into her attempt to push him to engage in an in-depth discussion concerning it.

"Echo, I've got regrets for a lot of things in my life, as I think most people do. We've all made wrong choices and bad decisions at one time or another."

"Is that what you meant when you said you were sorry? Your everyday wrong choices and bad decisions? Is that really all the 'sorry' you were referring to?"

However, he didn't respond. Instead, Geoff inadvertently interrupted the conversation while standing at the vending machine. Echo sat silently stunned.

"I'm sorry I can't stay any longer, Dad. There's a special project at work occupying my time, and I need to get back to it."

"Oh sure, son, you go ahead. I certainly don't want you in trouble at work."

"Do either of you want a soda from the canteen before I go; chips, candy bar or anything like that?"

"Oh no, thank you, Geoff, I really can't be staying either. I have to return to work by 1 p.m. and grab some lunch before I do. So, if you don't mind, I'll leave with you so the guard will only have to make one trip over to take us out."

Truth was, Echo just had to get away from Russell James. She was so disgusted with him trivializing the worst 'wrong choice' or 'bad decision' he ever made. Other people's feelings didn't matter. His narcissism shone in the light of his callous disregard for the Sycamore family. There was no sympathy for their suffering at all.

Echo's involvement with Russell had turned her stomach. She needed a breath of fresh air to clear her head and remove the stench from her nostrils. She suddenly craved a large glass of water to wash away the foul taste the whole thing was leaving in her mouth.

"Well, thank you for coming, Echo. It means so much to me."

"You're welcome, Mr. James. I'm glad I came. It has been an eye-opening, very enlightening experience." The sarcasm that spewed from Echo's mouth was surely complimented by the look on her face.

Russell never reacted to it. A warm cordial smile smoothed out his appearance. Geoff walked around the table and wrapped his arms securely around his father. "I love you so much, Dad. I'll be back to see you on Wednesday."

"I love you too, son. Drive home safely."

As Echo watched the interaction between Russell and Geoff, she was impressed by the caring forgiving spirit within the son that had such love for the man who shattered his world many years ago.

It was striking to witness the good son's arms wrapped around the weaker shell of his father who could have been much more than Inmate C-25017.

As she watched the scene unfold before her, Echo was struck with the knowledge of how fortunate Russell was, despite his present circumstances. His son loved him unconditionally in spite of every flaw and character deficit he had.

"If you're ready to go I can take you over now," the guard said. As Echo stood to leave Russell reached out and gave her a hug.

"You drive home safely, too, young lady."

"I sure will," she responded, repressing her ire. Never could she recall a moment she was ever more grateful to leave a person's company than at that time.

CHAPTER 16
Crimson on Purple Hearts
1969

Unlike Tom Middleton, Daniel didn't have a military escort standing at the foot of his casket on Tuesday, December 23. But he did have a colossal police presence from the Sturnus County Sheriff's Department.

Plain-clothed detectives sat inconspicuously mingled amongst the large group of mourners, eavesdropping on conversations before the service began at 2 p.m. They hoped to pick up clues that might lead to the arrest of the person or persons responsible for the execution style death of Daniel.

Outside the church, deputies worked diligently to write down every license plate number on the cars that were parked in the church lot, and the streets that surrounded it. Plate numbers were inputted into the computer in order to establish the name on the car's registration so that criminal background checks could be processed.

When the church emptied and the funeral cortege headed to the cemetery, the visitation log was brought to the Sheriff's department. Every page was copied. Then every name listed thereon would be processed through a criminal background check.

In the choir loft, a plain clothed deputy stood in the shadows with a camcorder recording the presence of every individual that entered the church.

***

At 11 a.m., on the day of the funeral, the Sycamores and 40 relatives and close friends traveled to the Curry Funeral Home in Piedmont, for a private viewing.

Cars lined up behind the hearse that would carry the body to the church at noon for a two-hour public viewing before funeral services began. Both of Daniel's grandmothers and his Grandfather Sycamore were present along with several aunts, uncles, cousins and close friends like Carla DeLario.

Don regretted his absence at the funeral home where Carla would represent the family. He chose instead, to be at the church with his detectives as they set about observing the interactions of the mourners making up the large crowd. Janice and Douglas understood completely. Shari Bellows, Daniel's girlfriend, rode to the funeral home with Danny's mother, father, Addie and Dallas.

The clothing Daniel wore to his final resting place at the Holy Cross Cemetery in his mother's family plot had been delivered to the funeral home on Friday afternoon, and arrangements were made at that time.

Daniel wore a crisply starched white business shirt under a navy-blue vest and a matching double-breasted jacket, navy blue dress pants, socks and black patent leather shoes. His tie was red with dark blue pin stripes.

The family gathered in an alcove to wait for the funeral director, Benjamin Banister, to escort them to the visitation room where Daniel's body lay.

As they waited, Douglas' mind drifted back to the last time he saw his son alive. Bittersweet emotions tugged at his heartstrings. It was on that final Thursday night as his son scurried down the steps and shouted out, "See you later, Pop." Daniel headed out the front door on his way to work, happy and carefree, with a bright future looming ahead of him.

"Be careful out there, Danny boy," his father shouted from the kitchen.

In all the remaining years of his life, Douglas Sycamore could never erase the sound of that front door slamming closed or Daniel's footsteps on the porch before he descended the steps to the sidewalk.

"Mr. and Mrs. Sycamore, if you're ready will you follow me, please?" Benjamin smiled compassionately.

Janice and Douglas looked at one another, frozen like a deer caught in the beam of headlights, locked both of their hands tightly together and walked apprehensively behind the funeral director. The rest of the entourage followed closely behind. No one spoke.

Benjamin led the mourners down a short corridor to a room

that was closed off by lace-curtained French double doors. He opened them, exposing an area filled with rows of padded folding chairs. Many floral arrangements and plants lined the walls and surrounded an open casket at the front of the room.

"Come in, please." Benjamin coaxed the mourners to follow him to the casket as he gently held the arm of Janice Sycamore.

As she approached, her eyes fell upon her child. No signs of the trauma that assailed the body just days before were visible.

The handsome face, with heavily applied makeup to the forehead, appeared no more than to be sleeping soundly.

Shakily, Janice laid her hand on her fallen son's chest. Tears trickled down her cheeks. She cried out in a quivering brokenhearted voice, "Oh Daniel, oh my precious baby. I'm so sorry. Forgive me, son, for not being there to protect you. I love you, Daniel, and I always will."

Douglas wrapped his arms around his wife as she collapsed broken in his arms, sobbing inconsolably. It was a sight no one witnessing would ever be able to erase from their mind.

The raw pain of the spoken words of Janice Sycamore rose above the mourners and filled the room with such sadness. There wasn't a dry eye in the group.

Benjamin walked over to Douglas as he held his wife and placed his hand gently on his shoulder.

"Is there anything I can do or get for you?"

"No," Douglas responded. "We're okay now."

"Then I'll give the family some privacy but if you need me, I'll be just down the hallway." He exited the room and closed the double doors behind him leaving family and friends alone in their grief.

Shari walked up to the casket. The direction her life was supposed to go had been altered forever, and nothing would ever change that. She was devastated. In disbelief and grief, she hung her head and wept bitter anguished tears.

Shari turned and walked over to where Janice and Adeline now sat, taking a seat next to Daniel's mother. Douglas was standing to the side of the casket sharing wonderful memories of his son with family and friends.

Daniel's grandmothers were engaged in conversation although tears had reddened and swollen their eyes.

"I just don't understand it," Delphine Sycamore said, weeping and dabbing her eyes with her Kleenex. "I would have taken that bullet for him. I've done everything I've ever wanted to do. There's nothing else I have to live for."

Bridgette Denney, Daniel's maternal grandmother wrapped her arm around Delphine. "Hush now. You mustn't talk such foolishness. The good Lord has it under control. He's on His throne, and all will yet be well."

"Now, how is that so," Delphine asked, sarcastically, "when Daniel is lying there in his casket? How come He didn't show up to protect Danny that night?"

"Oh, He was there, rest assured. He'll never leave us or forsake us. He saw Daniel into heaven. I know He did!" Bridgette's words were filled with confidence. She hugged Delphine in a loving gesture of comfort and support.

Douglas walked over to Janice who had stopped crying and was enjoying stories her family members were telling about Daniel. Some of the stories she'd never heard before. Like the time at Aunt Sally's house when Danny climbed the neighbor's cherry tree and ate the unwashed fruit until his belly ached.

"I fixed fried chicken, Daniel's favorite, but he couldn't eat another bite. He was too filled up with all those cherries!" Aunt Sally laughed until she cried at the memory.

Cousin Barry shared the time when Uncle Buck took him, Daniel and Dallas to the Sturnus River to do some fishing. But all Daniel caught was an old nasty, high-top tennis shoe.

Now, the French doors swung open, and Benjamin Bannister quietly entered the room. He walked over to where Douglas and Janice now sat.

"Folks, it's time we should be going now. We'll start in the back, form a single-file procession past the casket and exit the opened side door for the trip to the church."

"Yes, sir, we understand." Douglas looked over to his wife as she once again began to cry with abandon. Addie handed Janice a Kleenex.

When it was their time to leave, Janice walked up to the casket. She bent down and kissed her son's cheek for the last time. In her hand, she held a piece of paper. On it was a poem that she composed; staying up all night to complete it. She wanted the right words to go with Danny; to be with him throughout eternity. She wrote them from the very soul of her being, through bitter tears and grievous heartbreak.

> Someday, my precious child, we will meet again,
> where death cannot divide us, where new life will begin.
> It must be so, Dear God, it has to be,
> for I would surely cease to live without that hope in me.
> Sleep well my sweet boy, Daniel, in fear and pain no more.
> In due time I will come to you. Keep watch along the shore.

"Come on, dear," Douglas said soothingly as he gently took his wife's arm and turned her toward the door.

Swiftly, she recoiled and turned back to the casket. "No! Not yet." Her voice was tearful and shaky. She opened the paper in her hand and, silently read the words she penned on it.

Benjamin Bannister walked up to her. She looked at him beseechingly. "Will you please place this in Danny's hand. I want it to go with him, so he'll know to look for me."

"Certainly, ma'am. I'll do that right now, before we leave for the church."

Douglas and Janice watched the kindly mortician. Janice thanked him, then turned toward the door to make their exit. Douglas placed her hand in his, and she laid her head on his shoulder. The two walked out of the room with tears of sorrow on their faces and their hearts broken; yet, they were strengthened and emboldened by their love for each other, for Dallas and for the son they were taking to his final resting place today.

Douglas turned to face his wife after they entered the limousine. He was curious about something. "What was written on that piece of paper, dear?"

"It's a secret I wrote to Danny and it's his alone to keep."

* * *

When they entered the church 30-minutes before the scheduled public viewing many mourners had already arrived. They rose to attention as the casket entered the room and was wheeled to the front.

Benjamin Bannister and his assistant, Joseph Horst, raised the lid of the casket, straightened the lining and allowed the mourners to come forward and pay their respects to the family of the slain young man. Benjamin made sure the paper was still in place in Daniel's hand.

In ten-minutes' time, the church was packed to the gills with family, friends, neighbors, ex-classmates, co-workers, Harlan Vernon, Don DeLario and his detectives. It was the largest group of mourners ever to attend a funeral service at the Piedmont First Presbyterian Church or any other church in the area up to that time.

Forty-seven cars and trucks would accompany Daniel to his final resting place. Don arranged for traffic to be cordoned off with barricades on the busiest streets along the procession route to the cemetery. Officers in plain-clothes were on scene there, scanning the crowd for anything or anyone seeming to be out of place.

The Christian Women's Presbyterian Auxiliary prepared food for the mourners to be served in the church basement recreation room after the trip to the cemetery. The food had to be reheated as the extremely large caravan caused a 45-minute delay in their return.

* * *

Unlike some of the less fortunate soldiers, Tom's body was shipped home arriving at 4:24 a.m., on November 5, on GM&O train number five, taking ten days to reach its final destination. The Storrie Funeral Home was notified and waited at the station to transport the body to the funeral parlor.

Tom arrived in full Marine dress uniform and had already been embalmed by American personnel at the Tan Son Nhut Mortuary outside Saigon. Paul Storrie called Marshall Middleton later that morning. He wanted to know if there was a preference for clothing for their son.

"No," Marshall responded, "we'll bury him in his military dress."

"He looks good, Mr. Middleton. His body is well preserved.

The mortuary in Vietnam did a good job under difficult conditions." Paul spoke as compassionately as he could, assuring the parents that Tom was whole and his face was unscarred.

"Would you like to view the body before making plans for the wake?" But neither parent could bear to do it.

The wake was held from 5 p.m. to 8 p.m., on November 6, 1969. The immediate family arrived an hour earlier for a private viewing of the body.

The casket was already open, exposing the upper half of the body when Paul Storrie escorted the family into the large room where Tom's body lay. A United States Marine Corp Escort, Lance Corporal Matthew C. Edwards, stood at attention at the foot of the casket.

Echo looked up at the soldier, but he never returned a glance her way. Instead, he stood erect and perfectly still throughout the entire wake, never batting an eye. Her brother, Shawn, now stationed at Granite City, wore his Army dress uniform.

Mariah Middleton had prepared herself for this moment. Although tears ran down her face, she moved closer to the casket and placed her hand on Tom's chest. Echo saw her mother look up and give a half-hearted smile to Paul who had been a classmate of hers at the Sacred Heart Grade School.

"Well, it sure is him, Paul. There's just no denying that handsome face."

"Do you want to have an open casket, Mariah?"

She turned around to get her husband's approval, but he had walked away from the casket and stood to face the wall. Both hands were in his pants pockets. His head hung down and his eyes were staring at the floor.

Viewing Tom's body had delivered a hard blow to his father. The old saying, "seeing is believing," now rang so true.

Simply hearing the awful news might leave a small flicker of hope that some mistake could have been made. But seeing casts a whole different light on the matter. Now they knew, their eyes having seen; that their son and brother was gone and would not be coming back again.

Mariah Middleton looked over at her husband once more. His back was still toward her, so she made the decision for the both of them.

"Yes, I believe we will show him, Paul."

"Then I'll give the family some privacy now."

Paul placed his hand on Mariah's shoulder. "If you need anything at all, I'll be in the next room on the right, just down the hallway."

"Thank you, Paul." Mariah watched as the funeral director made his exit from the room.

Echo moved closer to the casket. Dreaded disappointment shook her being at seeing with her own eyes the body that was so indisputably her brother, Tom. So, in those times after it was over when doubt crept in, she forced her mind to refer back to Storrie Funeral Home and those first painful moments of viewing his body.

Except for the discoloration of his light brown hair which now was reddish, most likely due to the chemicals used by the mortuary, he could have been mistaken for someone sleeping soundly. He appeared to rest peacefully now.

The same wasn't true for Echo's brother, Shawn. When she looked at him, he was looking into his brother's casket. A stone-cold frozen stare ravaged his face. For a moment, she thought he had stopped breathing and it startled her.

What's with him? Echo thought, noticing no tears in his eyes. His color drained, and he looked as if he had just seen a ghost.

Finally, he moved to the right side of the casket and sat down in a chair where he remained for the entire evening. He didn't have a single conversation with anyone that night. He spoke only when he was spoken to. He seemed locked away in some painful place of his own. Echo had no understanding at that time of the turmoil that was raging inside her oldest brother.

Shawn had been to Vietnam and knew firsthand the hell Tom went through. He witnessed the bombs going off in every direction. He saw the Viet Cong give candies to the Vietnamese children. He heard their instruction to go over to the American soldiers and pull the pin on the grenade they'd been given.

And he knew also there were people in his own country, fellow Americans, who protested the war and hated the sight of a soldier in uniform. 'Baby killers' they were called.

People came from all over to pay their respects. Many folks the Middleton family didn't know but had a son, husband, brother or nephew in Vietnam and just wanted to extend their sympathy to the family. Paul Storrie opened an adjoining room to accommodate the massive group of mourners.

It was well after 10 p.m., before the family left the funeral home. Shawn, who sat so stiffly in that chair rose from his seat and walked up to the casket once again before turning to walk out.

Echo was standing several feet behind him and saw his shoulders shaking uncontrollably. Her mother noticed too, and went to put her arms around him. They turned to leave, and Echo walked ahead of them out the door.

She crossed the parking lot and reached for the handle on the car. As she did, she turned around to see her mother's hand resting on Shawn's back. He was bent over losing his stomach in the bushes.

As a kid, Echo assumed her brother had contracted the flu but today she had a better understanding of the bedlam assailing his psyche at that time.

Family and friends were all emotionally sick at the loss of son, brother, father-to-be, friend and fellow countryman. Shawn felt that pain also, but so much more. He knew first-hand the waste of so many lives in a war that was never intended to be won and only he and those like him would ever understand what it was like to return home to violence perpetrated against them simply because of the uniform they wore. Echo came to understand it had all came crashing in on Shawn that night. So much so that it sickened him physically as well.

Shawn never talked about his Vietnam experiences with Echo or anyone else in the family for that matter. He was the oldest son and the Middleton's second born child. The age difference between him and Echo was nine years. His silence, Echo believed, was to protect the innocence of his younger brothers and sisters.

They were growing up in a country that hadn't seen a war on its mainland since the 1860's and had no idea what it was like to dodge bombs or move cautiously around land mines planted beneath them.

They were fortunate; so much more so than the little Vietnamese children. Exploding bombs and detonated grenades were commonplace for them. To be sure, Shawn didn't want the knowledge of such things to plague the minds of his brothers and sisters.

Echo asked him one time after he returned from Vietnam

what it was like to be in a war.

"You shouldn't be thinking about things like that. You ought to be outside playing and having fun with the rest of the kids your age!" Seeing the look on his face, Echo knew their conversation was over.

At the time, she thought he just didn't want to talk to his kid sister; after all, Echo was just a child. In retaliation, she stuck her tongue out at Shawn and ran out the front door heading over to the Martin Luther Grade School where a neighborhood ball game was being played. Ted was up to bat, so she grabbed his ball glove and hit the outfield.

Echo couldn't recall ever speaking to Shawn again on the matter. Although many years later she wanted to, she knew any attempt to broach the subject would be futile. He was never going to engage in a conversation of that nature. He had already grieved the loss of over 58,000 American soldiers and the maiming of countless others.

He shared their pain and understood it, for Shawn was one of them. In a letter sent home from Vietnam, he wrote, "I don't honestly know what we're doing here. God, help us. This is insanity!"

That was past him now. He had successfully placed it behind him. He refused to dredge up the awful past. He had faced the ghosts of Vietnam, so that they no longer haunted him.

Echo wouldn't be so fortunate. When Tom was killed, she was just a child. At the age of thirteen and in the turbulent 1960's, what affected her most concerning Tom's death were the tears and heartache endured by the adults in her life. She had no real comprehension of death's finality.

Her parents, those to whom she ran to when she was hurting, were now hurting themselves. They had sheltered and protected her and her brothers and sisters all their lives, and there was nothing she could do to alleviate their sorrow. That hurt Echo most of all.

To this day, Echo can still recall her grandma crying uncontrollably at Storrie Funeral Home asking over and over again, "why, why." It was painful to witness and caused her to cry right along with her grandmother.

The sight of her dad and Uncle Martin escorting 86-year-old Grandpa Middleton up to Tom's casket seared in Echo's youthful mind. She witnessed the tears streaming down that wonderful old man's face. She heard him tell her father while standing at the casket, "I'm an old man, Marsh, and he was so young. I just don't understand why it couldn't have been me instead of Thomas. I've lived my life and his hadn't yet begun." Her grandfather shook his head and cried, and Echo shook her head and cried.

All the old folks in her family, the people that she admired and loved so much, were grief stricken and suffering inconsolably. They hurt and cried so she hurt and cried.

Their tears caused her tears. They were working out their grief, and it was painful to witness those strong supportive caregivers unable to make the situation all better again. The entire episode left scars on Echo's soul that she hadn't yet begun to comprehend.

And even to this day, her mind finds no relief from her most bitter re-occurring nightmare. On a rice field in Quang Tri Province, Vietnam, her tears for what was lost, -- numbered like clover and pouring like a monsoon -- fall heavy on silenced Purple Hearts.

CHAPTER 17
Good Trumping Bad
1996

Echo walked with Geoff out to the parking lot. By coincidence their cars were parked side by side.

"You're a good son, Geoff," she couldn't resist saying. "It's evident in the way you care for your father."

"Well, don't let me fool you. It hasn't always been like that. There was a time when I detested my dad. I abhorred my grandmother for having him, my mother for marrying him, and I loathed my last name. I had no idea I possessed the capacity to hate that much. When I think about it today, it scares the daylights out of me!"

The two reached their vehicles and stopped to chat.

"You wouldn't believe how low I sank after the death of Daniel Sycamore. And if it weren't for the Lord's mercy, my father-in-law's guidance and a judge's pity, I don't know where I'd be today. Most likely inside those walls we just came from."

"It must have been quite a journey." Echo spoke compassionately.

"It felt like a trip into hell, but I wouldn't change one iota because it brought me to the place where I am now."

"I have peace inside me, the love of a good woman and family, and I am surrounded and uplifted by good friends. What more could I ask for? Life is good."

Geoff leaned back against the passenger door of his car.

"I remember my friend, Blake Lufton, was at the house that morning in January 1970, when my dad and brother were first arrested."

"We were fourteen, out of school on Christmas break, and guided by our entrepreneurial spirits we decided to grab some shovels and head outdoors. It had snowed the night before, so we knew there was good money to be made."

"We canvassed the area going door to door in my

neighborhood looking for jobs. I remember feeling rather accomplished that day with all the money we were collecting for shoveling snow off driveways and sidewalks. Some folks even paid us to scrape it off their cars. We then went over to Blake's neighborhood and canvassed there."

But when we finished, all I wanted to do was head home and strip off my wet clothes. My toes and fingers were stinging, and my nose felt frostbitten."

"You know, Echo, it doesn't get that cold anymore like it did when we were kids. Back then the snow reached the windowsills and stayed until the onset of spring."

"You're right about that," Echo said confidently. "I remember walking to school and the cold air caused tears that formed tiny icicles that hung from my eyelashes!"

"Yes indeed," Geoff said, chuckling. He shook animatedly, as if he could feel the cold down to the bone by simply recalling it. The two laughingly recoiled at the frigid memory.

"Anyway, I was looking forward to getting warm and dry. But when I returned home at about 4 p.m., thoughts of my freezing toes, fingers and nose rushed right out of my head the moment I saw my mother's face."

"She was sitting all alone at the kitchen table looking as if someone in the family just died. It startled me and almost took my breath away! My Grandma James was at the house and had Bryce and Melissa upstairs cleaning their bedrooms."

"I looked over at mom. "What's wrong?"

"The look on her face; I'd never seen it before or since. It was one of abject terror. I braced myself, afraid to death of her reply."

"Your father and brother have been arrested for armed robbery in Durham!"

"Mom found out from Samantha Org when she went to the neighborhood grocery store to purchase something for supper."

"Have you heard the news?" Samantha asked. "They've arrested your husband and son."

Mom snickered, waiting for the deliverance of the punch line to a joke. "Oh Sammy, what are you talking about?"

Sammy always had a funny anecdote to share with her customers. She was short, gray-haired and portly with a huge personality. Her laughter rose from her toes, so boisterous and hearty that her ample belly bounced up and down with every gregarious giggle. Sammy was friendly and folks enjoyed a warm welcome whenever they entered her family's store but, on this day, she wasn't in a joking mood and she wasn't kidding around.

"Margaret, seriously. It's all over the radio. They've been arrested in Durham for robbing a jewelry store. I'm so sorry to be the one to tell you. I just thought you ought to know." Samantha sensed she had exceeded her boundary and shamefully hung her head. "I'm so sorry Margaret," she kept repeating over and over again.

"It's alright Sammy. There's obviously been a terrible mistake." Margaret's face conveyed shock and unbelief all rolled into one frozen daze. Her appearance drained of all color. "I must go home now. Will you please add these groceries to my bill?"

"Yes, of course," Sammy began. But mom was already out the door crossing the street in a panic. That's how we began our wretched decline into the pit of hell itself."

Compassion for Geoff swept over Echo. "It must have been difficult for your mother being left alone to care for you and the little ones."

"No doubt she had it rough. Her only source of income came from working in the kitchen at St. Jonathon's Hospital where she barely made enough money to support herself, let alone all of us. But thank God for my Grandma James. She moved in and used her minuscule Social Security check to supplement mom's wages. She was a good woman who blamed herself for the mayhem her son and grandson created."

"She used to cry such pitiful tears telling my mother how sorry she was that she failed as a parent, but the failing was never hers to bear. Nevertheless, she felt deeply responsible somehow and was determined to see to it that the three remaining James children didn't have an opportunity to go astray. I know she had the best intentions but she ruled like a drill sergeant over the little ones and was unrelentingly brutal on me."

"That woman didn't give me a moment's rest. I think it must have been my age that pressed her to straighten me up before it was too late but I wasn't the one that was out running around doing things I shouldn't have been doing and I'm certain she could sense the resentment growing leaps and bounds within me for my father and brother."

"Well, I saw how Mom and Grandma were struggling to make ends meet, so I dropped out of high school in my junior year and took on two jobs to help supplement the household income."

"I thought it was the right thing to do, but I soon realized without a high school diploma I'd work at minimum wage for the rest of my life. So, I went back to school and tried to manage my studies in-between two jobs. It was an impossible feat, yet I felt a sense of duty to the family."

"With Dad and Steve absent, I felt the weight of the world on my shoulders. I didn't have much of a life. I was, by this time, an eighteen-year-old boy carrying my father's obligations. I hated him for that and hated the people that looked down their noses at us because of him."

"We lived with the shame, with no reprieve for years. We couldn't afford to move for anonymity sake. We were forced to stay in that old neighborhood where everyone knew about the crime, and some whose torment was relentless, refused to let us forget. They'd shout taunts of "killer's kids," and "daddy deadly! Certainly, that stung in more ways than one. After all, 'daddy' took his eldest son down a road no loving father ever would. And I asked myself, "How does a father do such a thing?"

"Steve was responsible for his actions, surely. He was grown and his choices were his own. Still, visualizing a father and his son walking side by side down that destructive path; I just couldn't conceive it. Yet, I knew the truth, and I had to face it."

"My whole belief system eroded. Every good thing he ever tried to teach me became bile in my belly. It was all a bunch of lies. Our family life was nothing more than a smokescreen."

"He was the head of our household, yet he brought disgrace upon the entire family and here's the kicker – he did the crime and the whole family had to do the time. I couldn't help think how selfish he was to never consider the whispering and naysaying he would bring upon all of us."

"Needless to say, I was hanging by a thread and I remember when it finally broke. That's when I totally gave up and resigned myself to the probability that I wouldn't amount to any more than Dad or Steve and probably end up incarcerated just like them."

Echo shook her head "Oh no, Geoff. Seeing the man that you've become today, I can't imagine anyone envisioning that scenario for you."

"Well, it was rough back then and I had no hope, Echo. It was on a Saturday. I worked in the morning and had a few hours before I had to be at my evening job. Feeling exhausted, I went home and crawled into bed but failed to set the alarm to wake me in time for work."

"Well, I was sound asleep when my grandmother plowed into my bedroom."

"Get up right now. You're late for work!"

"I said to her, "What," as I tried shaking myself awake."

"Get out of that bed right now," she said. "I'm telling you boy if you don't watch your step you're going to end up in the same place as your father and brother!" I can still feel her anger raining down upon me to this day."

"I don't know why, but something just snapped in me. Oh, I know my grandmother meant well, and she loved me very much. She wanted the best for me, but I just didn't need to hear her say those words. I was doing all I could to stay in school and maintain passing grades while working two jobs. A little bit of appreciation, I believed, might have been in order."

"Well, I'm ashamed to say I didn't hold back. I yelled and cursed at that good, old woman like a sailor. And I can still see the horror etched on her face as she stood frozen. I remember having the impression that no one had ever spoken to her in that manner before."

"I told her I was tired of her dictatorship, and I was moving out. God, forgive me, I told her to stay out of my face or I'd smash hers with my fist. That's when I decided to drop out."

"My girlfriend and I applied for a marriage license, and were married at the court house. We moved to Peoria where I began to take every kind of drug imaginable. To make matters worse, I began to deal in it. I had a buddy that would bring it in from Florida, and my job was to distribute it. Boy, did I ever make the dough. You just can't imagine!"

"Anyway, we were married about three years, and my wife couldn't take it anymore. She moved back to Starling, and we were separated for 22 months."

"Interestingly throughout this time, her dad would call to see how I was doing. He'd say he loved me and if I ever wanted out of the mess I was making of my life, all I had to do was ask for help."

"He always ended our conversations with, "I'm here if you need me; even if you just want to talk.""

"By this time the Drug Enforcement Administration was hot on my tail and was wire-tapping my phone. I was scared they were going to put it all together and arrest me. I could feel it in my bones that it was just a matter of time. I resigned myself to believing a long prison term loomed in my not-too-distant future."

"Still, it wasn't just the threat of prison gnawing at me. My life was in shambles. I was a broken man who was crying myself to sleep at night."

"I lost everything important to me. My wife and daughter were living with her parents and I missed them terribly. I hadn't seen my mom or grandmother since the day I left for Peoria and took the cowardly way out. I never said I was sorry for leaving the way I did. I was too busy wallowing in the miserable morass of self-pity."

"So, feeling empty, shattered and desperate, I picked up the telephone and called my father-in-law. I told him I was as broken as a man could get. "I want to come home. I want to straighten out my life. I want my wife and daughter back. Will you help me? I feel so hollow and alone."

"Yes, son," he responded through tears of his own. "You come on home now. We'll be waiting for you with open arms. Don't waste any more time. We're waiting, son."

"I remember the depth of gratitude I felt at that moment. The unconditional love and forgiveness that flowed from that man took my hardened heart and melted it like butter. I didn't know what it was about him that tendered such mercy for me, but I knew I wanted it for myself."

"I loaded up my Jeep Cherokee with my personal belongings, turned the keys over to the landlord, walked away from a whole lot of money and headed back home."

"My father-in-law took me in. I told him kind of broken down-like that I couldn't continue the way I was going any longer. My father-in-law took my hand and prayed with me, and I never looked back from that moment. I actually felt a physical release, like shackles being lifted from all the hatred I carried in my heart. I felt like Ebenezer Scrooge on Christmas morning!"

"My father-in-law helped me set up a meeting with the State's Attorney's Office to plead guilty to drug trafficking and to take my punishment. I told them every illegal thing I ever did and spared nothing. By the time I was finished they knew it all. And that's when I went before Judge Wilbur Chambers, the exact man who presided over my father's trial and had sentenced him to death."

"He asked me all kinds of questions about growing up without a father, the shame of Dad's conviction and how it affected me. And miraculously, the judge sentenced me to five years' probation. I couldn't believe it. I just knew it had to be divine intervention!"

"Now, go and do well," the judge said, "and make your community proud of you."

"I thanked the judge repeatedly and I cried like a baby. I told him I truly appreciated the second chance he was giving me, and that I would never make him sorry for the leniency he showed toward me."

"In the following months, I visited my dad for the first time in seven years. I wanted him to know I forgave him and Steve. I hugged him and held him close and for the first time in my life, I knew how it felt to give that perfect unconditional love as it was given to me by my father-in-law."

"Dad thanked me. We sat crying for the longest time. We held hands and let out all the angst. He asked what brought me around to see him again. I sat back and thought for a few moments."

"I explained we're all sojourners through this life and I finally came to understand that I was carrying the heavy weights of anger, strife, bitterness and hatred. And once I let them in my travel bag, my heart, I owned them and all the adversity they created."

"I finally understood the power those burdens have to inflict anguish. Their torment is worse than any devastation ever inflicted upon me by anyone other than me. Indeed, the hold they had on me was a vice grip worse than all the shame, humiliation and degradation my father and brother ever put upon the family."

"I learned through hard work and prayer how to put these things down. Today, if it's not everlasting, I rid myself of it before it takes hold, like the stinging albatross I once wore around my neck. I've been there and done that, and I'm never going back."

"Additionally, I came to understand as I had been forgiven, I should forgive. So, I'm just simply beyond judging anyone."

"We're all human beings capable of making horrific mistakes. The good Lord knows I made my share. And I'm just grateful to have His mercy in my life."

Echo and Geoff stood silent for a moment listening to the birds chirping in the tall oak trees on the prison grounds.

"Well, I better head back to work," Geoff said, rounding the back of his car to the driver's door. "It's been good to see you again, Echo."

"Good to see you again, too, Geoff. Thanks for talking with me."

"Well, thank you for coming. Drive safely back home."

"Of course, and you do the same."

Echo contemplated the words Geoff spoke as she climbed inside her vehicle. She was happy for him. He had successfully laid down the manacles of bitterness, anger and hatred from days past.

Geoff had been to hell and back. What didn't kill him seemed to make him stronger. He possessed an inner strength that amplified Echo's admiration for him. His life was filled with peace, joy and unconditional love that equipped him with the ability to forgive the father and brother that hurt him so cruelly.

However, it wasn't like that for Echo. She loathed Lyndon Johnson for what he did to her family. And with the same degree of intensity Geoff had before his epiphany. Echo couldn't understand how he could forgive so easily. The whole idea was repugnant to her. Yet, oddly, she believed it was the most magnetic and appealing attribute Geoff James possessed.

Something was gently stirring inside Echo although she returned to it an indifferent and defiant ear until all that she could hear from deep within her were the screeching rants of hatred, anger and bitterness.

Echo placed the key into the ignition and started her vehicle. She turned the air-conditioning unit on low and adjusted the radio before pulling off the parking lot.

CHAPTER 18
Sweet Justice Indeed
1969

The Red Ruby Lounge was located on the eastern edge of Starling's downtown business district. The building consisted of two rooms. The larger front room contained the bar along with several tables and chairs. A shuffleboard stood along the west wall. The smaller room had a dance floor and a slightly elevated stage where musical groups performed. The lounge played host to blues and jazz musicians from as far away as New Orleans.

The two rooms were connected by a small hallway where the restrooms were located. The lounge had red and white lighting and was dim upon entering. Its clientele was primarily African-American.

Russell and Steven James stuck out like sore thumbs. They were two of only a few Caucasians who came into the place. By now, the black clientele was accustomed to seeing them. Some of the regulars even considered them friends and welcomed them as a part of the established group.

* * *

Don DeLario and Lewis Morell entered the Red Ruby Lounge at 2 p.m., on a Friday afternoon on a tip Don received from an informant. Cody Collins, twenty-four, was a petty burglar and small-time marijuana dealer.

Cody called Don at his office. "I have an item in my possession you might be looking for. I'd like to get it off my property."

The two agreed to a clandestine meeting in the parking lot of the St. Theresa Grade School off Parchment Drive. Cody was waiting when Don pulled up alongside his car. Both exited their vehicles and walked to the back of Cody's Chevrolet Impala. He unlocked the trunk and retrieved a twelve- gauge, New Elgin sawed-off shotgun and turned it over to Don. Collins also handed over the name of the man who gave him the weapon.

Don's tone of voice was as serious as a heart attack. "Do you know where we can find him?"

"He works at the Red Ruby Lounge downtown," Cody responded.

Don placed the shotgun in the trunk of his unmarked squad car. He handed Cody a twenty-dollar bill, climbed into the driver's seat and made the journey to the Harlan Vernon Texaco Station for a positive identification of the weapon. When he arrived, he saw Harlan sitting behind the desk, and Jeremy was outside pumping gas. Don retrieved the gun and walked inside.

"I need you to take a look at this, Harlan. Can you identify it as your missing shotgun?"

Harlan didn't hesitate. "Yes, that's it. There's just no mistaking it. See the letters here on this handle, HVT. Daniel carved those letters himself. They stand for Harlan Vernon's Texaco. It's been altered, -- the barrels have been sawed off, -- but this weapon has a missing firing pin that you will find in the cabinet right over there."

Jeremy Summer came into the station and identified the weapon also. "That's definitely it. I was here when Danny carved those initials on the handle. Will finding this shotgun help catch the murderer?"

"If I can trace it back to the person or persons that removed it from the station, you bet it will and that's exactly what I intend to do!"

Jeremy beamed wide-eyed, revealing his excitement at the possibility. "Wouldn't it be so cool if the identification of this gun, through the letters Danny carved on it, led to the capture of his murderer? Wouldn't that be the ultimate perfect justice? I can almost envision it, -- Danny reaching back from the grave to tie the noose around the neck of his killer!"

Harlan Vernon couldn't hide the fact that he, too, was thrilled by the prospect. "I can't imagine a more appropriate scenario, with one exception; to allow Danny's parents to carve his initials into the noose around the neck of the killer when he's caught.

It's like an eye for an eye."

"Yes," Don responded. "That would be sweet justice indeed!"

CHAPTER 19
Wires that Linked Them
1996

Echo was loading the breakfast dishes into the dishwasher that Saturday morning when the telephone rang. She dried her hands and scurried to answer the incessant ring.

"Hello."

"This is a collect call from an inmate at a correctional facility. Will you accept the charges?"

The computerized recording was, by now, familiar. Echo heard it every time Russell James telephoned.

Echo spoke clearly into the receiver. "Yes, I will."

A few seconds of silence followed before Russell's voice traversed the wires. He sounded upbeat in spite of his most recent disappointment. "Well, good morning."

"Hi, Russell. Geoff called me with the news last night. I'm sorry to hear the Prisoner Review Board recommended that your parole be denied."

"Yes, that's why I was calling. I wanted to let you know. But don't you fret about that. I never expected to be granted parole anyway."

"Well, fortunately, you still have the clemency hearing."

"Yes, whenever the Governor finally decides to schedule it. Still, it doesn't matter as it's just going to be more of the same thing. There's no way I'm ever getting out of here. You can trust me on that. I simply try not to dwell on it. It's too tormenting to do so."

"I understand completely," Echo responded. "I wouldn't want to set myself up for a letdown, either."

"Yeah, so when daydreams of being released enter my mind, I pick myself up and I get busy. It's a lesson my mother tried to teach me, and one I should have heeded. Had I, maybe I wouldn't be sitting here today. I can recall her saying so many times, "Idleness is the devil's workshop."

"She must have been a wise woman," Echo interjected.

"She was. She knew the benefits of hard work; whether it's the fruits of a plentiful garden or the sound of a purring engine. No matter what I chose to do, I would have experienced the satisfaction of accomplishment."

"I should have kept busy until the only thing left to do was crawl into bed from sheer exhaustion. I think a sound mind may have been my reward and just maybe that's all it would have taken to lift the awful depression I suffered. Certainly, all the electroshock treatments did nothing for me that a little hard work wouldn't have accomplished."

"My mother wondered for the rest of her days if there was anything that she could have done differently to alter the destructive course her son had taken. Truth is, the lesson had always been there through Mom's good example. I just didn't have the good sense to follow it. The bottom line is I have no one to blame but myself. I made bad choices; the consequence is a great pain to many people. My mother wore that pain on her face and you could see it in her eyes. So, today I choose to live my life the way she lived hers. And when bad thoughts enter my mind, I pick myself up and get busy. My mother's lesson is finally learned."

"Mom stood steadfast. She never once questioned our participation in the murder of that boy on that early morning back in 1969. She believed in our innocence until the day she died."

"I'm sorry for your loss, Russell."

"Yes, thank you, Echo. I still miss my mother terribly sometimes."

The dreaded automatic recording came over the line. "This telephone call will disconnect in one minute."

Echo looked at the clock on the wall. "Boy, the time flew by!"

"It always does," he responded.

"I sure would love to pay you a visit." Echo was anxious to sit with him again to look in his eyes and evaluate for herself the veracity of his words. But there was no response immediately.

"May I come to the center next Thursday at around 8:30 a.m.? I promise not to overstay my welcome." She could sense his hesitancy.

"Well, I'm not sure what my work schedule looks like for that day. I'm afraid you might have to wait if I'm stuck in the middle of something." It was the best pretext he could muster on the spur of the moment.

Still, she pushed forward anyway in spite of his excuse. "Oh, I don't mind. Besides, if I have to wait too long, I will simply tell the guard I'll come back another day. The weather is supposed to be pleasant. It could be a great day for a car ride."

"Well, alright then," he said in resignation. "You come along and I will see you on Thursday."

"Wonderful. I'm looking forward to seeing you again. It's been six weeks since the last time I was there."

"Same here," he started to say. But his voice was cut off. Echo couldn't hear his last words as the connection was broken and dial tone flooded the wires that linked them.

CHAPTER 20
Just a Matter of Time
1969

When Don and Lewis Morell entered the Red Ruby, they were looking for Herschel Johnson, identified by Cody Collins as the person who gave him the sawed-off shotgun. The officers found the African-American, twenty-six-year-old male busy at work mopping the bathroom floors.

"How are you doing, Mr. Johnson. I'm Sergeant DeLario and this is Detective Morell with the Sheriff's office. We'd like to talk to you about a twelve-gauge shotgun recently in your possession and identified as one used in a murder."

Herschel's eyes grew wide. "Woah now. Hold up. I don't know nuthun' about no murder!" He looked at the officers; boldly defensive.

"No, sir, we're not accusing you. We're just trying to sort this thing out. We'd like you to come down to the station to help us tie up some loose ends."

"Oh, I'll come down there alright because I ain't got nuthun' to hide. All I did was try to get that shotgun fixed. I didn't kill nobody, and you're not going to pin no murder on me. I got two hours to work. When I'm done, I'll clock out and come down there."

"Here's my card," Don said. "Just tell the desk sergeant you want to see me. We'll see if we can get this thing ironed out."

The officers shook hands with the young man and piled into the unmarked sheriff's vehicle, driving four blocks back to the Sturnus County Complex. Neither knew if Herschel would follow through on his promise.

Still, Don grabbed a recorder, loaded it with a new tape and placed it on the table in a conference room. It was 4:15 p.m. when Herschel entered the Sheriff's Department and asked to speak with Sergeant DeLario.

Herschel was escorted into the detective bureau conference room where Morell sat waiting. The chief investigator pressed the start button on the recorder.

"Okay sir, go ahead and just tell us what you know about this shotgun, how you came to have it and your actions with it afterward. Please start at the beginning and take us through step by step."

"Well, it started at about 10:30 p.m., on Sunday, December 21. I was at the Red Ruby Lounge when I ran into Russell and Steven James. I've known them since the time I was a kid. Russell's mother lived a few doors down, and Steve and I would play when he came to visit his grandmother."

"The Jameses always came to the Ruby to see Leroy Drake whenever he returned home from Chicago. Roy's real close to his mama and comes back to Starling regularly to visit her. The Jameses get along pretty well with him and the Ruby has always been Roy's favorite watering hole."

"I've known the guy myself for about five years. But I never really cared for him all that much. He comes off as arrogant to me."

"Now, I hear tell that Drake and the Jameses have a fencing operation going on. Items are copped in Chicago and transported to Starling. The loot is stowed in the James' garage until they can sell the items. Then the money is divided between the parties. I've heard the operation is pretty sweet, financially speaking. But, like I say, this is just what I heard. I don't know if it's true or not."

"Anyway, at about 10:30 p.m., Leroy, his girlfriend, Rose, and I arrived at the Ruby at the same time outside the entrance. I saw Steven pull up, let his dad out at the front door and park the car."

"Russell and Leroy shook hands while Steven locked the car doors and ran across the street to join us. He reached for the door handle and said, "I'm going inside. It's freezing out here!"

"We all sat together at a table in the main room. None of us knew Rose but she was friendly and sexy as hell in her short tight little red dress." Herschel rolled his eyes in recollection. A broad grin crossed his face.

"Anyway, Rose was talkun' about a stripper joint in Chicago Heights. I never figured out if she owned the place or just worked there. Anyway, when a fight broke out in the back, it got all of our attention."

"Joe Wright, another regular at the bar, was feuding with Leroy over a wristwatch he purchased from Roy that didn't operate. Before we knew it, Roy was in Joe's face in a flash and that's when

I heard Joe say, "You better get the hell out of my face before I jack you up!"

"Leroy pulled back his right arm and flung it smack-dab in the center of Joe's left cheek. Joe put a wrestling move on Leroy and took him to the ground! The next thing I knew a chair comes sliding across the room, and Joe has Leroy Drake flat on his back, penned to the floor. Rose stood at the table screaming like a banshee. "Stop it. Stop it!"

"That's when Russell pulled a chrome-plated, shiny, black handled revolver from his pocket, sitting right there at the table."

Don shot a look of unexpected surprise at Detective Morell. Neither officer had mentioned anything about a revolver. "Do you know the make or caliber of this revolver you're talking about?"

"I know it's a .38, that's for sure. I've seen him with it many times and could tell just by looking at the bore size"

Herschel Johnson continued without missing a beat, not realizing the interest he had peaked in the two detectives. "Me and Steve remained at the table standing up next to Rose so we could see the action."

"Joe was on top of Leroy, fixun' to throw a punch, when the pistol was pressed to the side of his head. Then, I heard Russell holler out, "Looks like you better let him up if you don't want your brains blown out!"

"Well, Joe jumped off Leroy, and Leroy stood back on his feet. Joe was really pissed. He said, "You son of a bitch, you wouldn't mess with me if you didn't have that gun in your hand!"

"And that's the truth, cos Joe could make hamburger out of Russell James. You know, Joe is a three-time state wrestling champion. Yet, with the gun pointed at his brain, what else could he do?"

"Pete, the bartender, grabbed a twenty-two pistol he kept behind the bar and hurried over to the fight. "That's it," he said angrily. "You boys gonna come in here and act like that, you can leave and never come back. You take your trouble someplace else. I mean it. I ain't gonna put up with your crap!"

The two men stood glaring at one another with Pete right dab in the middle of them. "I have a bar to run. I can't be standing here all night long!"

Finally, Joe turned and walked away. He took a seat at the

bar and looked over to where the crowd was still gathered.

Pete stared, stink-eyed at the gun in Russell's hand until he placed it back in the pocket of his jacket. Then, Russell and Leroy turned and walked back to the table. Both Joe and Roy avoided one another the rest of the night with no further trouble between them.

Don's curiosity peaked. "Now, we asked you down to the station to tell us what you know about a 12-gauge shotgun, but that's not the weapon you're talking about, right?"

"Naw, man. I told you it was a .38 caliber revolver. I'm gonna get to that shotgun in a minute."

"Alright, Mr. Johnson, let me ask you something. Was this the first time you saw this revolver?"

"Naw, man, I seen that gun lots of times. Russell be carryun' it around with him for a while now."

"Can you be more specific with the dates and times that you saw the weapon in his possession?"

"Well, there was the time I went over to their house to get money that Steven owed me. Mrs. James was at work and the kids were at school. I sat at the kitchen table and watched Russ clean that gun. I asked him if I could look at it, and he handed it to me. Believe me, I gave it a thorough going over. It was definitely a .38 caliber."

"When did this take place, Herschel?"

"On December 6, my mother's birthday. I'm sure of the date because I wanted the money to buy my mom her birthday present, and Steven was late paying me back."

Don looked at Morell and instinctively knew the two police officers were thinking the same thing. A .38 caliber revolver, coupled with the stolen shotgun in the hands of the James boys, creates probable murder suspects.

"Okay sir, please continue. You left off on December 21."

"Okay, so, Pete announced, "last call", and Leroy bought everyone at the table a final drink. We finished and headed for the front door and said our goodbyes on the sidewalk. Leroy and Rose went to their car and I was on foot. Steven offered me a ride home so I walked with them to the parking lot and hopped into the back seat."

"Okay now, sir, just so I have this straight – you are stating that on December 6, 1969, you saw a .38 caliber revolver in Russell James' possession; some fifteen days prior to the incident at the bar on the 21st?"

"Yea man, straight up, that's what I'm tellun' you. Only I saw it many more times than that. It's just that the 6th is the pinpoint time I'm sure of, cos that's momma's birthday."

"Can you identify it if you saw it again?"

"C'mon, man, I know that weapon. Of course, I can identify it."

"Thank you. Go ahead sir. I just wanted to confirm that. Please continue."

"They asked me to have another drink at their house before they took me home. So, we go there and the kitchen light above the sink was on, but the family was asleep. Russell grabbed three glasses and the wine bottle from the refrigerator. We sat down at the table and he pulled that revolver out of his pocket and put it on the table. It was the same gun I saw on December 6th"

"Where on the table had he placed it, Herschel?" Lewis asked.

"Right smack dab in the middle; like some damn centerpiece."

"He took his coat off and hung it on a coat rack in the foyer there. When he returned to the table, he opened the cylinder."

"How many bullets did you observe, if you remember?" Don asked.

"I saw three bullets in the cylinder and two open positions." Herschel was positive about that. "The gun was definitely a five-round revolver."

This revelation was not lost on either law enforcement officer.

We have three bullets in the chamber and two empty positions, with two bullets expended at the station. It's a possible murder weapon, Don thought to himself.

"Thank you, please continue, sir."

"Now, this is where the shotgun comes in. I asked Russell if he had one I could use cos my momma makes the best rabbit stew and I wanted to go hunting. Well, Russell said they did, and Steven went outside to get it. I didn't see where he went, but I think it was in their garage with all the stolen goods. When he returned, he had the shotgun and a hacksaw in his hand. He put the shotgun on the table and starting sawing off the barrels."

"I told him, "Whatcha think you're doin', man, it ain't gonna be no good now. But Russell said, "No sweat, cos this wasn't the best shotgun in the world anyway. But if you want it, it's yours to keep."

"I knew once Steven sawed the barrels off, it would be no good to go hunting. But if they were going to give it to me, then I was going to take it."

"I took it home and I took it apart and saw one of the firing pins was missun.' So, I went to Washburn Sports to buy some 12-gauge shells. I took an old piece of plywood to the backyard to see if the other firing pin still worked, but it wouldn't fire."

"You were still planning to use this weapon for hunting?" Lewis couldn't hide his astonishment.

"Naw, man. Ain't you heard nothun I said? I know a sawed-off shotgun won't hold a pattern. But they gave it to me, and I was sure nuf' gonna take it. Maybe I would sell it – I didn't know what I'd do with it."

"I got in touch with Cody Collins to see if he could fix the pin. He's good at fixun' things you know. I figured maybe I'd see what he could do with it. I talked to him on the phone and told him I'd bring it to his house where he placed it under the back porch for safe keeping. They had lattice work there but a piece had fallen down. The opening was big enough to crawl under the porch. He said no one would bother it and he'd look at it in the next few days. And that's all I know 'bout that shotgun."

* * *

After Herschel left the sheriff's department that late afternoon, Don and Morell lingered in the conference room. They could hardly contain their delight. "What a bombshell he just dropped on us!"

Morell smiled excitedly. "That's just what I was thinking. Talk about good fortune just falling into our laps."

"It's like manna from heaven, him mentioning that revolver when all we were aware of was the recovered shotgun. I'd sure love to get my hands on it. I'll bet you that it's the very gun that fired the bullet into Danny's brain!"

"Now, that's a bet I'm not going to go against," responded Morell.

Don was feeling hopeful. "Maybe we've turned the corner in this case." He picked up the telephone sitting on the conference table and placed a call to Lieutenant Matthew Sebring, head of the robbery division at the Starling Police Department. He wanted to inform him of a fencing operation within his jurisdiction and to ask him to do nothing until Don had an opportunity to question the suspects in a murder investigation. Sebring agreed.

The two detectives stood from the conference table; their job finished for now. Don reached for the switch to turn off the light. "We're going to nail them, Lew. I really believe we're on the right trail now."

"Yes, sir, it's just a matter of time."

CHAPTER 21
Time Spent with Dallas
1996

Echo crawled out of bed at the crack of dawn. Throughout the night-time hours, her mind raced with anticipation at finally meeting Dallas. She was nervous and edgy. Insecurity was gnawing at her confidence.

After a breakfast of coffee, toast and banana she began trying on several items of clothing to choose just the right outfit to look her best. She sought a professional yet approachable appearance. She settled on a casual brown boot-cut cotton pant suit with a sleeveless button-down crème-color silk blouse and matching jacket. Her makeup had been applied with great care. Still, it did nothing to settle her anxiety.

She looked at the clock mounted on the living room wall. The time was now 9 a.m., and the meeting was set for an hour later. All groomed, dressed and ready to go, she peered out the window expecting Don's arrival at any moment. Not seeing him, she nervously paced back and forth across the living room floor. She didn't know what she would say, or what she was going to do.

She looked out the window once more to see Don navigating his 1995 Ford Bronco onto the driveway. Quickly she grabbed her jacket and purse and hurried outside locking the front door behind her. She scurried over to the driveway and climbed into the passenger's seat.

"Good morning," Don said pleasantly.

Echo's voice was shaky as she shut the door and fastened her seat belt around her. "I sure hope it is."

"Well, now why wouldn't it be a good morning?"

"Because to tell you the truth, I'm really scared. I feel like an interloper into the Sycamore's most personal pain."

"You said you wanted to write a book, remember?"

"Yes, but even that's in question considering Russell's claims of amnesia. I'm afraid the Sycamores will have to re-live their worst nightmare when Russell may never give an account of his actions or their consequences."

"You know, I've never done anything like this before and now that the rubber is meeting the road, I feel like a fish out of water, clumsy and awkward, not knowing what to say or do. The whole idea of writing a book, along with my 'jump in and get your feet wet' attitude, short of counting the cost, has left me feeling completely out of my league. I feel as if I'm encroaching on some hallowed ground where no decent person dares to tread. God knows I'm all too familiar with that. It's where Tom abides with me, and where Daniel abides with them, safe and protected until we see them again."

Don looked at Echo with compassion. "Hey, C'mon now. You're getting yourself all worked up. There's nothing to fear. These are nice people. They know you want to write a book, and they're looking forward to speaking with you. Their minds are open with no pre-conceived notions."

"Even so, we don't have to do this if you don't want to. You can back out, change your mind and not meet the Sycamores today. I can turn this car around and take you back home and make your apologies to the family. Maybe you need a little more time to collect your thoughts."

"Oh no, I don't want that at all," Echo declared. "I started this and I want to see it through. I know I can relate to their pain. It's just that I'm afraid my inadequacies will emphasize my inexperience."

"Well, there's one thing I know for sure. You can't let fear guide your steps, young lady. If you're afraid to reach beyond your comfort zone you'll never know what you could have achieved."

Don looked over at Echo compassionately. "You've got to go with your gut. What does it tell you to do?"

"My gut tells me to rise above the fear. That's why I'm here at this exact moment. I'm not a quitter, Don. What I know is that my heart possesses a great passion for this endeavor. And I don't know anyone other than me, whose life crossed paths the way it has with both victim and felons. Now, for what purpose I don't know."

"I'm compelled to go forward to discover where it might lead. My heart is sure, but my mind is certain to interfere, causing mistakes along the way. And that's the whole crux of the matter."

"Oh, you're bound to make mistakes, Echo. But you can't let those mistakes beat you up. You learn from them and get going again. Let me tell you something. From the time you contacted me, I wanted to help. I, too, felt compelled somehow. So, I believe you should do this but I'm not going to tell you it will be easy. Nothing worth fighting for ever comes without a struggle."

"You know, fear does funny things to people. It has the power to convince you that you're inadequate, unable, and that you can't do the things that are placed on your heart to do. It can overtake your desires and stop you dead in your tracks, so that nothing good can come from your efforts."

"Don't be robbed of the opportunity you've been given to do something good. Do what your heart tells you and rise above the fear. And know that it's okay to stumble. It wouldn't be the end of the world and certainly nothing that couldn't be fixed."

"Oh Don, you always know exactly what to say. I can hear my own father talking just listening to you!"

He looked at Echo and smiled.

She felt less tense now, emboldened by the words of the gentle man who was navigating southward on Interstate 55, rising up a slight incline about a quarter of a mile from the Glenrose exit.

"There's the site, Echo. I can barely imagine now the way it used to be."

Echo peered through the window as if she were seeing the location for the first time. "Don, can we stop for just a moment?"

Don took the exit ramp to the county road that ran in front of the now defunct site of the Vernon Texaco Station. He pulled over to the side by where the station used to stand, just west of the south bound lanes of U. S. Route 66. He put the car in park and turned off the engine. Both exited the vehicle in silence.

The landscape had changed drastically and nothing appeared as it did on that fateful day in December. The station had been razed long before to make room for the bigger Interstate 55.

A little south of where Vernon's Texaco used to stand and east of the north bound lanes of the old Route 66 stood the remnants of Cruther's Marathon station. It remained trapped in the shadow of that fateful day. A thick plush blend of fescue and Kentucky blue grass covered the space where the asphalt and concrete apron used to lie.

The spot was peaceful and quiet now with no human habitation. Life had ceased here and voices stilled. A silent reverence remained that was disturbed only by the sound of rubber tires rolling along on the hot asphalt pavement of the Interstate.

After a few minutes, Don and Echo slowly turned and walked back to the Bronco. Neither spoke. Both felt powerless to understand the brutal events that occurred here so many years ago.

They climbed inside the vehicle and fastened their seat belts around them. Don pulled off the shoulder and drove back onto I-55. He drove four more miles before exiting onto Paradise Way.

"Here we are. This is their house." Don looked at Echo who appeared calmer now. He pulled onto the purple and amber stamped concrete driveway. The brown brick ranch-style house was spacious with an attached three-car garage. A large pole barn sat in back at the edge of the property. The corner of a sun-sparkling vinyl-lined in-ground swimming pool could be seen from the driveway.

Echo walked around the car to where Don stood waiting for her. An attractive auburn haired, thin but shapely middle-aged woman opened the front door and stepped out onto the porch that ran along the entire front of the house.

The woman had a pleasant and welcoming face. There was kindness in her eyes. And Echo began to wonder why she had ever been so nervous.

"How are you, Adeline," Don asked, wrapping his arms around the woman in a bear hug.

"I'm good, Don. It's so good to see you again. And you must be Echo," she said, extending her hand with a disarming smile.

"Yes, ma'am, my name is Echo Middleton, and it's my pleasure to meet you."

"Likewise, Echo. Please come in and I'll introduce you to my husband."

The three stepped over the threshold into the comfortable but stylishly decorated living room. Dallas Sycamore came out of the kitchen to greet them.

"Hi Don, good to see you again." Dallas scampered over to where the retired chief investigator stood and the two men embraced.

Echo looked closely at Dallas's face. Although her memory was vague, she had seen many newspaper clippings of Daniel and had the uncanny feeling she could be looking at his double. The physical similarity was remarkable.

"Dally, I'd like you to meet Echo Middleton," Adaline said.

"Ms. Middleton, I'm happy to make your acquaintance. I've heard from your Aunt Maybelle a lot of good things about you. She is my aunt's sister, you know?"

"Yes, actually I did know that." Echo smiled pleasantly but kept to herself the fact that Daniel was the one who first told her.

The room grew awkwardly silent. Fortunately, Adaline came to the rescue. "Won't you have a seat? May I offer you something to drink, coffee, tea, soda or water?"

"No, thank you," Echo responded. Don, however, agreed to a cup of piping hot coffee.

The foursome sat down in the family room. Echo looked out upon the calming sun-soaked water that sparkled like diamonds in the swimming pool. She breathed deep and exhaled quietly.

"Help me, Lord," she silently prayed.

CHAPTER 22
Finding the Perfect Patsy
1969

One week passed since the brutal murder of Daniel Sycamore, and the conniving shenanigans of the Jameses were raring to have a go again. The night of December 26 was cold and blustery. The temperature had dropped to a bitter 9 degrees. Russell and Steven went to the Red Ruby Lounge to listen to a blues band that was booked to play the club that night.

The place was packed. All the chairs were occupied. They found a couple of empty bar stools and sat down. Pete sat two glasses of Lancer's rose wine in front of them. He didn't need to ask what they wanted to drink. He made it a point to know what his regular customers liked and to have it ready for them the moment they entered the establishment.

"How you boys doing tonight?"

Russell smiled, as Steven took out a five-dollar bill from his wallet and placed it on the bar. "Pretty good, Pete."

"You boys are gonna love this band tonight. Look at the crowd they've packed in this place!" Neither father nor son could recall the Ruby ever being crowded like this before.

"They're taking a break right now, but they'll be starting up again real soon."

The Jameses downed their first drinks and ordered another round. It was close to 10:30 p.m. when they heard the most beautiful sound coming from the back room.

The Smooth Notes, a four-piece band, featured Andre Tinsley on saxophone, Willie Lawrence on drums, Weston Ronny on the keyboard and Lil Turn as the main attraction. The Smooth Notes had been performing together for nearly ten years, and their sound attracted people from miles around.

The band generally played the clubs in Durham but by word of mouth, the talented group was making a name for themselves and branching out beyond the confines of that city.

Another black club, Big Daddies, was the first to invite them over to Starling. Some of its regular clientele were at the Red Ruby this night to enjoy the smooth, sultry music.

"Do you hear that sax back there? Come on. I want to see who that is!" Russell rose from his seat and motioned for his son to follow him. He bent down and picked up the bar stool knowing none of them were bolted to the floor. Steven grabbed his stool and began to follow his father into the next room. At first, Pete objected, but then waved them on. "Go ahead, take the barstools with you. Just don't leave them in there. Bring them back up to the bar before you leave." There were no other seats available in the entire place.

The Jameses found a little free space just inside the doorway and put the bar stools down there. The two men sat silently soaking in the soulful sound of the Smooth Notes. They didn't seem to have a care in the world. Their mood was relaxed and sociable. Their demeanor revealed no signs of the violence and brutality they engaged in just one-week prior. They sat focused on the music, absorbed in the mellow rich sound, tapping their feet to the gentle beat.

The Smooth Notes finished playing the last song before taking their final break. Andre Tinsley carefully laid his sax down on the stage floor and walked toward the bar to get a drink.

Russell stood as Andre approached. "Man, that's the sweetest sound I think I've ever heard!"

"Thank you. I appreciate it."

"You care to join us?"

"Well, I was just on my way up to the bar."

"What are you drinking? I'd like to buy you one."

Andre smiled warmly. "Oh, whatever's on tap would be fine."

"I'm Russ James and this is my son, Steve."

Andre shook hands with the only two white men in the bar, and Steven offered the man his chair.

"My name is Andre Tinsley. It's good to meet you both." He smiled cordially as Steven headed up to the bar.

Andre was a small man himself, standing about 5' 7". He was of thin build and appeared the hippy type. He wore a two-inch heel boot, a flowered shirt that was not tucked into his beltless bleached-out and faded blue jeans. He wore a gold bracelet around his right wrist and a gold chain around his neck. His long hair hung to the middle of his back, tied into a braided ponytail.

He was an independent soul that walked to the beat of his own drum. He was soft-spoken, almost to a whisper, with his warm smile revealing his gentle trusting spirit.

The bartender was working feverishly to keep the customers hydrated. "Hey Pete, I need a beer."

"Hang on, Steve. I'll be right there as soon as I take care of the folks before you." *That boy needs a good dose of patience,"* Pete thought to himself.

"Where in the world did you learn to play like that?" Russell asked Andre.

"I got my training in New Orleans at the same place and time Fats Domino got his." Steven returned from the bar and handed the draft beer to Andre.

Andre raised his glass and took a hearty drink. "Thank you, sir." Steven remained standing, seeing no other vacant chair. "Do you give lessons? I have always wanted to learn how to play the sax."

"I have before but only to students that are serious about learning. I love it too much, and I have no patience for anyone who isn't dedicated to the music or is afraid of a little hard work."

"Oh man, I'm not afraid of a little hard work, and there is nothing I would love to do more than to learn how to play the sax!"

Andre grabbed a napkin from the nearest table and asked for a pen. A lady sitting beside him opened her purse and handed him one. He jotted down a number and handed the napkin to Steven.

"This is my telephone number. When you want to start on them lessons, you give me a call, and we can talk about the price."

Steven folded the napkin and placed it in his wallet for safe keeping. "Great. I'll be calling you for sure!" He looked at his father through conniving eyes that Andre did not notice.

Russell chimed in, "Where will you be playing next? I would love to bring my wife to hear the group. I know she'd enjoy it."

"We're going to be at Mr. Gee's in Durham tomorrow night. Love to have you bring your wife and come out to see us."

"Where's Mr. Gee's?"

"It's right on El Rio Street as you come into Durham. You can't miss it."

The other band members began making their way back to the stage for their last set. Andre stood from the barstool and Steven sat back down. "Thanks again for the beer."

Russell nodded. "You're welcome."

The father and son team continued drinking as they listened to the last performance by the band that evening. The crowd roared for more when they finished, and Lil Turn bid the audience a good night.

Russell drank down the remaining contents of his glass. The father and son waved goodbye to Pete and exited the bar, heading for the car that was parked in the lot across the street.

CHAPTER 23
Kindred Spirits
1996

"So, he's going to get a clemency hearing," Dallas said sarcastically. "Well isn't that real special. Tell me, Ms. Middleton, do you think the Governor will be so kind as to give my brother a clemency from the grave?"

"No, sir, he doesn't have that kind of power. Only God can do that."

Adeline patted Dally's knee as she sat next to him on the sofa, trying to subdue the beast within him. "Calm down, honey, this isn't her fault."

"It's okay. I'm alright. I'm calm." Dallas fixed his eyes upon Echo who was sitting across from the couple on an over-stuffed La-Z-Boy recliner. Don sat on the love seat listening to the repartee beneath the open-curtained picture window that looked out onto the swimming pool.

Echo lowered her head. "I'm sorry, Dallas."

"No, no, I'm not angry at you. I suppose I'm just frustrated at a system that would consider clemency for a murderer when the same can't be afforded the victim. My brother is gone, and he's never coming back. So, why should his killers be able to re-enter society?"

"It's a matter of fairness, and I hope the Parole Board takes that into consideration. I mean, if someone can bring Danny back, then, by all means, let's get it done, and we can discuss returning the killers to their family. That's the only way to handle it."

"Remember, they were sentenced to death. So, they've already been given a sort of clemency from the electric chair. Yet, there will never be clemency for Danny. What's done is done and there's no reversing it."

"The article in the newspaper about the clemency hearing said the murderer was plagued with arthritis. I understand the difficulties of aging. I can remember my dad before he passed with all the aches that he had due to his old age. I understand and I can even sympathize with the elder James; but only to a point."

"I'm more interested in knowing if he and his son can understand the pain we've had to endure. It's much worse than anything he may be suffering from now. I wouldn't wish this on my worst enemy. Not even them!"

Dallas sat back in his chair, and the room grew silent.

"I know it's a different set of circumstances," Echo said nervously, "but I believe I can relate to the pain you've had to endure, Dallas."

Not sure just what Echo meant, a quizzical look affixed his face. "Oh, really, is that so?" He leaned forward in his chair; intent on listening to her explain.

"Yes, sir, I've experienced it through the death of my own brother. You see, his demise feels like murder to me."

Dallas was more confused than ever. Adeline was just as surprised. *What murder? What on earth is she talking about,* they wondered? Quizzical looks affixed their faces.

The room grew silent for a few awkward moments when finally, Don began to attempt an explanation.

"Actually, what she's trying to convey is," he began, but Echo interrupted him.

"Don, please, may I explain?"

Dallas and Adeline looked at Echo. Don acquiesced and silently sat back on the loveseat clasping his hands together in his lap while all eyes fixed upon the petite lady, who appeared dwarfed by the size of the over-stuffed recliner she sat in.

"We have the common everyday criminal element that walks our streets and fills our newspapers with tragedy on a daily basis. He'll rob a gas station, for example, and for reasons no rational person can appreciate, will murder the attendant. He is the thug that does the deed. His victim's blood is on his hands. When discovered, Lady Justice will mete out punishment. The Jameses belong to this group."

"But there is another type. The Elitist, I believe, is the one who rarely serves time for his crime. This type will lie, bold-faced to the American people, and never bat an eye as his lying connivance takes a death toll on the people he was sworn to serve. This criminal seems to stand above due process of law, never having to face responsibility for his actions."

"He never does the dirty work himself. Yet, his victim's blood is on his hands and it is my opinion that Lyndon Johnson belongs to this group."

"One of the definitions of the word 'murder' in the "New Webster's Dictionary and Thesaurus," is to mar by incompetence. Lyndon Johnson marred so many through his incompetent Vietnam policy. And thus, it was with my brother, Tom, and over 58,000 of his comrades. As survivors of this criminal, our only hope is that historical truth will mete out scathing justice for our loved ones."

"It's true, Tom wasn't a casualty of the violence plaguing the streets of this nation, but his death was brought about by a power zealot who lacked the character to put my brother's life before his own political agenda."

"My conscience is clear, and I have no problem comparing the two. From my perspective, it seems that both have character flaws that render them all too human."

Echo addressed her comments directly at Dallas. "I suppose you might find it harder to visualize a Commander in Chief as a murderer. I think that's because we perceive them as something better than the average citizen, smarter, more capable, etc. However, the truth is Lyndon Johnson put his pants on in the same manner as Russell and Steven James; one leg at a time. I cannot morally, and shall not ethically, hold Lyndon Johnson in any higher regard than I do them. Johnson was in a position of power, trust and authority and he sorely abused it."

Dallas and Adeline sat listening intently, immersed in the emotional conviction coming from the lips of the young lady speaking. No one interrupted. No one wanted to.

"It should not matter to us whether it happens because of the false sense of power that a .38-caliber revolver gives to the perpetrator or whether it happens because of the complete abuse of power. Lord Acton's words ring true, 'Power tends to corrupt; absolute power corrupts absolutely.'"

"We all know that good can come from evil. I learned some valuable lessons at an early age. I learned there are chameleons in this world that are wolves in sheep's clothing. They will change suits at every turn to satisfy their own lusts. Most especially, I learned that moral standards are absolutely essential requirements for anyone who has power and authority to make decisions that affect my life. My vote must be well thought out and calculated, and I must be politically engaged."

"It has been twenty-seven years since my brother's passing. When I think of him now, I smile and I don't cry as I did when the wound was fresh. The same is not true when it comes to Lyndon Johnson. I loathe him still. My hatred remains raw and open!" Echo lowered her head and sat silent now.

The tone of Dally's voice was gentle and soft. "Your passion is intense. I never thought about the Vietnam casualties in quite that way but I think I'd be remiss if I failed to admit that I should have. Your points are well taken. I never had to do a tour there. I spent the majority of my time in Germany but my respect is huge for those that did. I'm sorry for your family's loss."

Echo smiled warmly, appreciative of his understanding.

"Certainly, knowing how you feel about Lyndon Johnson, though, you can understand why we will fight tirelessly to keep Russell James in prison where he belongs, with no clemency whatsoever."

"Oh, I do understand. If I were in your shoes, I'd feel exactly the way you do. I think we are all accountable for our actions. If a person does the crime then they must be prepared to do the time."

"Oh, speaking of the time." Don rose from the love seat and Echo instinctively followed suit.

"I promised Dallas and Adeline we wouldn't overstay our welcome. They have a prior commitment; a church function they must attend."

Echo reached for her purse sitting on the floor next to her chair. She grabbed Don's coffee cup and saucer and followed Adeline to the kitchen sink. When they returned, Echo stood next to Don.

Dallas reached down and hugged Echo, unable to resist. "It's my pleasure to have met you. I enjoyed hearing your insights concerning your brother. Thank you for sharing them with us. My pain, like yours, is less intense with time. I, too, enjoy reminiscing all the good times my brother and I shared. It's the outrage at the injustice that lingers."

Echo couldn't have agreed more. "Yes, that's certainly the angst, isn't it?"

"I hope we will meet again real soon, Echo."

"I'm looking forward to it," she responded.

"Shari Reilly, Danny's girlfriend at the time he was murdered, told me she's looking forward to meeting you also. She believes something good will come from speaking with you. Now, frankly, I'm not sure resurrecting the pain and sorrow is such a good thing but I'm willing to give it a try."

Echo smiled warmly. "I can't ask for more than that."

Dallas shook Don's hand as the visitors prepared to leave. "Let's have dinner one-day next week." Dallas looked to his wife for approval.

"Oh yes, that would be great. I'll invite Shari and Patrick. They're very anxious to meet you, Echo."

Dallas reached out to shake Echo's hand. "I wish we had more time today. You're as passionate about your brother as I am about mine. We can relate to one another's pain. We've become members of a club that neither of us ever wanted to join. It's sort of like we're kindred spirits now."

CHAPTER 24
With Criminal Intent
1969

Russell was growing impatient with Margaret. He went to the bathroom door and rapped on it gently. "Are you about ready in there?"

Margaret hated being rushed. "Give me a minute, will you? I'm hurrying as fast as I can!"

When she exited the bathroom, she walked over to Geoff and kissed him on the cheek. Bryce and Michelle had already taken their baths and by now were sleeping soundly in their beds.

"We won't be late, honey."

"Oh Mom, don't worry. Seems like you never get out. Go and have a good time. Everything will be alright here."

Geoff waved goodbye as his parents walked out to the car parked in the driveway. Their first stop was the Mill Restaurant where they had reservations. Russell ordered two prime rib dinners with baked potatoes and garden salads drenched with the Mill's ever-popular house dressing. He ordered a carafe of wine.

After dinner, the couple loaded into the car and made the drive over to Mr. Gee's Lounge. Russell hoped Andre Tinsley would remember him.

The black-clientele bar was crowded, but the first-time visitors managed to find a table for two toward the back of the room. Andre spotted the conspicuous couple almost immediately and approached them. He extended his hand. "Russell, isn't it?"

"Yes, and this is my wife, Margaret. Margaret, this is the man I was telling you about that Steven wants to take saxophone lessons from."

Margaret flashed her warm friendly smile. She was a full-figured woman with black hair that glistened as a strobe light rotated on and off her head. She had a trusting face, and folks were always comfortable around her. Margaret could disarm a junkyard dog with her charming personality. "How do you do, Mr. Tinsley?"

"I'm pleased to meet you, Margaret."

"Won't you join us for a drink, sir?"

"Oh, I wish I could, ma'am, but the band is just about to start playing. I appreciate the both of you coming over tonight, though, and I'll come around again when we take a break."

***

Margaret was enjoying the music every bit as much as her husband was, and she told Andre when he was able to join them. "I think Steven could learn a lot from you. You're very talented with that saxophone."

Andre would recall being impressed with Russell's persistence that night concerning the sax lessons for his son. "He seemed to want them badly," he later told the police.

"If you're not in a hurry to get back home, you're welcome to come over to the house where we can talk about setting up those lessons. It's located just two blocks down the street."

Russell's eyes lit with excitement. "We'd be happy to come over."

Margaret nodded in agreement and smiled although she would have preferred to get back home to the children.

***

The trio arrived at the Tinsley residence at 2 a.m. Aretha was awake and awaiting her husband's return. She heard his car crunch the gravel driveway and heard the sound of the garage door lifting at the back of the house. She heard another car pull onto the driveway as well.

She peeled back the shade and peered out the window. She wasn't expecting company and hastily set about tidying the living room.

The three entered through the back door into an enclosed porch area. A street lamp located in the alley behind the garage afforded a little light to the darkened rear entryway. Russell's eyes scanned the area. Andre unlocked the door that led into the kitchen and introduced the couple to his wife.

Aretha cordially greeted the guests and then began to prepare coffee for everyone.

The foursome sat down in the small but cozy living room. Their conversation centered on the sheet metal industry with Russell describing the pitfalls while Andre listened politely.

"I was foolish to trust him," he later admitted. "The only reason I invited them to the house was to tie down the lessons but he didn't ask me one thing about them. I should have known there was more to the story."

It was now 2:45 a.m. and Margaret was ready to go. She stood up from the sofa, not waiting for her husband's approval. She knew if he had his way, they would still be sitting in that living room well after the sun came up.

"Well, we don't want to overstretch our welcome," she said politely. "Thank you so much for your kind hospitality."

Russell didn't want to make a fuss. He stood with a mollifying smile on his face.

Andre was the one who broached the subject of the lessons as he walked the husband and wife to the door. "What do you want to do about them?"

"If it's alright with you, Steven and I will stop by next week to discuss the arrangements and a payment plan."

Trusting and amiable, Andre Tinsley nodded his head. "That's perfectly fine with me."

***

On Thursday of the following week, January 1, 1970, Russell and Steven returned to the Tinsley home. Since it was a holiday, the Jameses knew Andre wouldn't be at work. They found him lounging comfortably on the sofa.

When he invited them into the house, the conversation centered entirely around saxophone lessons. Steven appeared as eager as ever. The three agreed the instructions would begin on the following Monday, at 6 p.m., at Andre's house and every Monday after that for nine more weeks, followed by an assessment on the progress. An agreeable price to all was reached.

Still, the price of the lessons was irrelevant. The Jameses would have agreed to any amount Andre required. They had no intention of paying because the lessons were never going to occur. They were, after all, a ruse for their criminal activity.

The Jameses said their good-byes, shook hands with Andre and headed for their car. Andre returned to the warm and cozy spot on the sofa, completely oblivious to activities outside his home.

***

The devious duo climbed back into the car, and Steven started the engine. "I noticed Andre was napping on the sofa," Russell said. "His eyes looked heavy and tired. So, I'm not concerned about him. It's Aretha that worries me now because she was in the kitchen cooking, and that kitchen window looks out onto the driveway."

"That's okay, Dad. I can get into the back porch from the other side of the house if I use the neighbor's driveway."

Russell looked over at his son. "When your mother and I visited, I noticed there was no lock on that rear door leading to the back porch. You should have no problem getting in. I saw a chair back there that has a skirt at the bottom. The duffel bag should fit underneath it. If you place it back far enough no one will see it there."

"Let's pull out of here and drive over to Hardee's Restaurant. I'll swing back on foot." Steven was as cool as a cucumber.

"If they spot you, son, tell them we're tracing our steps trying to locate my wallet. Just act natural and be yourself."

Fortunately for them, Steven wasn't seen, and he made the drop-off without a hitch. Within fifteen minutes he was back at the fast food restaurant, just three blocks from the Tinsley residence. He hopped in the driver's seat and pulled off the concrete parking area onto El Rio and the scheming duo headed toward Starling.

* * *

    Andre would later speak with the Durham police detectives. "I was always a trusting individual, almost to a fault. I just didn't realize they were up to no good, with criminal intent, or else I would have never had anything to do with them!"

    "I would've never agreed to give Steven lessons, and they would never have been invited into my home where my children and my wife were. There is just no way I would have allowed that to happen. Not in this lifetime. It makes me feel like such a fool not to have seen it!"

CHAPTER 25
A Harsh Reality
1996

"I want to show you something," Russell said as Echo entered the visitor's lounge that Thursday. He handed her an envelope. "Go ahead, open it."

She looked at the postmark on the front and saw it bore the name of the town of Denton, Texas. Removing the contents, she observed a sort of home-made greeting card. On the cover was a picture of the image of Jesus. Underneath the picture was the handwritten caption that said, 'Jesus loves you.'

She opened the card and saw a picture taped to the inside of a thirtyish-year-old man and woman surrounded by four little children. The hand-written caption below the picture read, 'And so do we!'

Echo studied the face of the woman. She looked across the table at Russell and then glanced back down at the picture again; smiling at the recognition.

"Oh, my goodness, it's precious little Melissa; except she's not so little anymore! I haven't seen her in 30 years, yet I still see that little five-year-old child staring back at me from inside those big brown eyes. She was the cutest little girl and I can see that she has turned into a beautiful woman. Is this her family?"

"Yes, that's Sam, her husband, and the children's names are Sammy, Jacob, Nathan, and Heather."

"Well, they're a good-looking bunch and I'm sure you're very proud of them."

"Yes, I am. My daughter and her husband are fantastic parents with the best-behaved children I've ever seen."

"They have a prison ministry in Texas where they speak to the convicts about the Lord and His love for them. Melissa tells them about me and Steve. She speaks of her love for us in spite of the shame we brought upon her. She has adjusted and matured without my support, but I can't say the same for Bryce. He is so angry with me, even today."

Bryce James was Russell's youngest son. He was six years old when his father was arrested. Melissa was just five.

"He feels I abandoned him, and there's no way I can argue against that. He needed me to be there for him and I wasn't. He doesn't come around to see me."

"He was married once but he and his wife split up. I hear his drug habit and hers was the cause of their downfall. They had a child, a little girl. Bryce's wife didn't want the baby so he took custody of her."

"Geoff knew the child wouldn't be properly cared for. So, he asked Bryce if the baby could live with his family. Bryce responded with an absolute no, that he would never walk away from his children like I did. Believe me, that stung. Sometimes, the truth is the most painful reality."

"Eventually he realized he couldn't take care of her and agreed to turn custody over to Geoff. Still, Bryce was allowed to see her whenever he wanted to. Yet, I'm told he doesn't visit her at all."

Echo lowered her head in sadness. She could just imagine the far-reaching ramifications of Russell's lethal conduct. When he killed, it was as if he threw a stone into a calm and peaceful lake, where the ripples spanned out beyond the rock, creating a cataclysm for his victim first and then for so many others.

She sympathized with Russell's plight. But she couldn't help think how fortunate he was to be afforded the hope that Bryce might someday change his mind and want to see him; when the Sycamores are denied the hope of ever seeing Daniel again in this life.

Russell is allowed hugs, kisses and human touches with his family while the Sycamores are relegated to the touch of a cold, marble headstone that stands above where their beloved son and brother lay. Their hope now lies in a heavenly reunion where visits with hugs, kisses and touches can never again be severed by the cowardly acts of those seeking to do harm.

Echo desperately wanted to see Russell's compassion for the Sycamores, but it just didn't seem to be within him. She realized that now. She visited with him too many times not to have observed a scintilla of empathy. It was beginning to make her feel dirty, just sitting in the same room with him. He was not the man she thought he was.

Who is this man? She wondered.

Echo suddenly realized that she never really knew him. She was beginning to see that her memories of him were juvenile and skewed, based solely on the teachings of her childhood that demanded respect for her elders, coupled with the kindness he extended to Tom. And when that truth finally settled in Echo's head, she became emboldened by it. No more would she hold back for fear of offending him. She was ready to confront him.

"I was thinking about the Sycamores. Do you have the same empathy for them that you possess for your loved ones?"

He didn't respond and his jowls clenched. Still, she refused to let that faze her. Instead, her indignation increased with his. She had reached the point where it really didn't matter if he were to banish her without further ado. She just couldn't tolerate the discrepancy any longer. The abundance of remorse and compassion he carried for his own family, was grossly lacking when it came to the Sycamores.

There were other stories she could write without having to deal with a narcissist's stinking thinking. Echo didn't need it or want it any longer. She wasn't going to beg like a dog for a bone or subvert her principles.

The look on Russell's face said it all. Echo hit a nerve and she could see anger rising within him. She felt anxious and uneasy, but determined. She would not back down. Considering all the visits and phone calls, it was time for a 'come to Jesus' moment. She paused for a few seconds to collect her thoughts.

"When you speak of the suffering your children have endured, I can see your pain is as raw as a festering wound that just won't heal. Yet, you have never shown any empathy what-so-ever for the Sycamores. Why is that? I just don't understand."

"Well, it's pretty hard to feel compassion for them when they're the ones that keep me and Steve in here. We've already spent more time behind bars than most who are convicted of the same crime, committed in the same era and sentenced under the same laws. When we first entered the system, I figured we'd spend about ten years of incarceration; no more than that."

Echo was staggered to realize what little value he placed on Daniel's life, trivializing the seriousness of his crime. "Ten years -- ten years for murder!" She wondered what on earth she had been thinking to visit with a man who didn't seem to have the moral compass of a hoot owl? She felt like shaking the dirt off her feet and running to her dad just to breathe in a little goodness for a while. Instead, she couldn't help speaking her mind.

"I bet the Sycamores would have opened the bars for you themselves if Daniel was allowed to leave his grave after just ten years!"

Echo couldn't believe the speed with which the sardonic words flowed from her mouth without a single thought for their consequence.

Russell sat silent but the look on his face was one of contempt. He was not pleased with the way this conversation was going. Still, Echo forged ahead.

"How can you blame them for wanting you to stay in prison? Can't you understand you took their child away from them and eradicated every hope and dream they ever had for him?"

"Look, I can understand; but only to a point. After so many years have gone by, -- literally decades, -- haven't we run the gamut of punishment and retribution?"

"Well, what about the gamut of the Sycamore's punishment? They'll never be free. Death is their only reprieve!"

"I can't change that though, and after thirty years what more can they do to a person? Aren't we simply warehousing prisoners to satisfy a cruel and sadistic compulsion to watch human flesh rot into mere shells of themselves?"

"I realize there are prisoners who can never be freed for they will repeat their crime. Still, the vast majority of convicts who made bad choices with dire consequences are people that are better than the sum of their worst mistake."

"I could be let out of here today, and they'd never hear another peep from me again. I know it and they know it. Yet, the Sycamores are not about to let that happen. They write letters to the Parole Board and we don't stand a chance."

"For several years back then I had a hard time figuring out why I couldn't catch a break with the Board; considering my good prison record. I never dreamed that boy had parents that were running the show. The thought just never crossed my mind."

Echo's lower jaw dropped wide open in disbelief. "Listen to you," she said in disgust. "The Sycamores lost their son, were robbed of him for no good reason, and all you want to talk about are the injustices you think you've suffered."

"Well, I'm not going to listen anymore. Daniel was a person, with parents and a brother, and they suffered a great loss at your hands. Rest assured your problems are not their fault."

"Daniel was a young college man," she continued. "He was taking care of business. He was working that night. He was doing what he was supposed to and he was where he should have been."

"The same can't be said for you and Steven. The two of you put yourselves in the wrong place at the wrong time and with evil intentions. I find it bizarre how angry you are at the Sycamores for desiring retribution. Can you honestly tell me you wouldn't want the same thing if the roles were reversed? How can anyone contemplate parole for you when you can't take your eyes off yourself long enough to consider the devastation you caused?"

But he never answered. Instead, Russell James sat clenching his teeth and Echo could see the contempt he felt for her at that moment. When she arrived for this visit, she had no idea which direction their conversation would take but she wasn't sorry for the ruthless bantering. It was opening her eyes to clearly see a narcissist sitting before her; not the friendly neighbor she thought she once knew. She now believed Russell was incapable of remorse and consideration for anyone other than himself and his family. It was clear. The Sycamores were mere inanimate objects without significance.

Echo no longer cared to walk on eggshells for fear of hurting his feelings. She was naive when she started on this journey, and his character, his integrity and the values he held dear were not known to her.

Suddenly, she began to realize that Tom was just a boy back then and couldn't have formed sound opinions about the veracity of an adult neighbor that he enjoyed hanging with on the porch in the wee hours of the morning during the dead-dog-days of summer.

Echo's anger boiled to the top. "You have no right to be upset with them when it's they that have every right to be mad as hell at you and your son."

"Well, I'm angry with you right now because I don't believe the murder of Daniel Sycamore is any of your business. Yet, you seem to have inserted yourself right dead center in the middle of it all. And sitting here listening to you today, I'm very leery as to whose side you're really on!"

Echo chuckled in sarcastic hyperbole.

"First of all, it's good to finally hear you speak Daniel's name. It sounds so much better than 'that boy'. Secondly, let me set the record straight. It was your son, Geoff, who called me at your behest, asking for a favor. Consequently, it was you who placed me right dead center in the middle of it all. And finally, just to let you know, I have always been on the side of accountability, forgiveness and healing for everyone involved."

"Ha! That's funny coming from you. Seriously, don't talk to me about forgiveness when you haven't done that yourself. Really, even a blind man can see the hate you harbor for Lyndon Johnson. You haven't forgiven him for Tom's death. So, I think you should practice what you preach. Why don't you try plucking the beam out of your own eye before you attempt to remove the splinter from mine?"

The room grew quiet. Echo sat stunned at the stinging diatribe. Only the rhythmic sound of the fan could be heard drowning out the beat of her racing heart. Tears were building in her eyes. The meeting had disintegrated into a vitriolic volley between them.

"You know," Russell said, "When I asked Geoff to reach out to your family, it wasn't an invitation to talk about a murder that's been over and done with for many years now."

Echo felt ire rise within her. "Over for who? You, maybe; but not for those of us who don't have our loved ones with us any longer. Maybe, it will never be over for us!"

"Touché," he conceded with a half-smile. "Still, I've made no secret that I would like to spend the rest of my days at home with the family. So, I used you toward that end."

"Oh, you didn't do anything to me that I didn't allow you to do, Russell. I haven't been wearing blinders and I know what time it is."

"Nevertheless, if it weren't for the clemency and parole hearings, I wouldn't have had these discussions with you in the first place. Don't get me wrong, I've enjoyed seeing you again. It's just that hashing over painful memories was never a part of the plan."

"What painful memories? You claim you don't have any

memories. You possess one-sided recall; that of the pain your family endured."

Russell stared stone-faced at the table top and shook his head from side to side. In exasperation, Echo looked up at the ceiling and exhaled loudly.

"I just don't know what else I can say to you other than I really need to leave before we both say anything further that we might regret later. Echo stood from the table and motioned to the guard. She teetered on the verge of bursting into tears.

"You'll have to wait just a moment while we take the inmate out first," the guard said.

Just then another guard entered the room, and Russell James stood from the table. "It was good to see you again, Echo." He spoke somberly, failing to look directly at her, as the guard escorted him through a side door. He would be searched once again before being sent back into the belly of the prison.

A female guard led Echo through another door into the yard and over to the sally port where she was allowed to return to her car on the parking lot. At no time did Russell ask her to return for another visit.

She unlocked the car and hurried inside. Her bottom lip quivered. She laid her head on the steering wheel and the flood gates to her soul broke as tears flowed from her eyes.

It was over. She would never satisfy her aspirations to write the book for which she possessed such passion. She wagered he'd want to do the right thing but she sorely lost the gamble.

Her tears weren't so much for the book she'd never write but for Russell's stinging diatribe. He hit the proverbial nail on the head when he spoke of Echo's unforgiving hardened heart toward Lyndon Johnson. She was so angry she could have spit nails. As she sat in her vehicle, her mind raced with thoughts of his cutting rhetoric.

What was he attempting to do anyway, switch the tables on me? My circumstance is completely different than his. I haven't harmed anybody like he has. Instead, my family's position runs parallel to the Sycamores. What right does a murderer have to criticize a victim for her lack of forgiveness? Did Lyndon Johnson ever ask for it?

Echo snickered at the absurdity of it all. Yet, her wounded

spirit wasn't laughing. The legitimacy of his words cut her to the quick and stung with the melittin of five bumble-bees. Still, her mind refused to consider the message.

CHAPTER 26
Jimmy's Sharp Eyes
1970

Lois Ryan and Rosie Shepherd didn't notice the yellow Ford Fairlane parked at a meter in front of Ryan's Jewelry Store, in Durham. They were running a little late, and it was close to 9 a.m., the start of business, on January 2. The ladies still had set-up work to do before their first customers began arriving.

Lois placed the master key inside the deadbolt and unlocked the door. Yet, she failed to lock it behind her once the ladies entered the store. Both women walked to the back into a little break room where they hung up their coats and placed their purses on a shelf.

Rosie talked a mile-a-minute about the New Year's Eve party she and her husband attended, and how good it felt to have New Year's Day off to re-cooperate. Lois said she and Frederick, her husband, spent the holiday quietly at home with their children and grandchildren stopping by.

The two women continued chatting, oblivious to their surroundings. Lois walked into the main room and now noticed through the storefront window, two men leaning against a yellow car parked at a meter. The sight caused no alarm. She walked behind the counter and placed a key into a display case.

Rosie came out of the back room just as the two men entered the store and locked the door behind them. The older man walked up to the counter and drew a .38-caliber revolver from his jacket.

"Okay, ladies, we don't want any trouble here. If you'll cooperate nobody's going to get hurt." The older man's voice was stern and threatening.

Lois raised her hand to her neck in surprise. "What's going on?"

"Just hurry up, open the safe and we'll be out of here in no time."

Rosie hurried, fear-struck, to where Lois stood and burrowed closely into her friend and employer.

Lois, co-owner of the jewelry store, was shaking in fear. "I can't do that. I don't know what the combination is. My husband is the only one who knows the numbers, and he isn't here yet!"

The younger man took the revolver from the elder, very strikingly similar-looking man. He viciously placed the barrel at Lois' left temple.

"Let's go into the back room, ladies. Right now!" His voice demanded compliance, as he flailed the weapon in the direction they were to go.

"What are you going to do with us?" A frightened Rosie Shepherd tearfully pleaded to know as the two women huddled together.

"Just shut up, do as you're told, and no one will get hurt."

The women held tightly to one another and entered the back room. The gun-yielding thug followed closely behind and with his right foot, dressed in a shiny black alligator shoe, kicked the door closed behind him. The loud bang caused the women to gasp aloud.

He ordered the ladies to sit on the floor. He tied their hands behind their backs with rope he brought with him for his dirty work. Then, he tied the ladies back to back, double-looping the rope around their waists. The young criminal put the gun on top of a cabinet, grabbed Lois's purse and rifled through it. He took twenty-seven dollars from her wallet.

"Why don't you take what you want and just leave us alone?" Lois pleaded as Rosie whimpered. The young man took a roll of masking tape from his coat pocket and roughly slapped it over their mouths and wrapped it around their heads.

When finished, he hurried back into the main room and handed the pistol to the older man who took it and stood guard at the window.

The ginger-haired, younger and slightly taller man began emptying the glass jewelry cases, loading the contents into a cloth bag he'd brought along for this purpose.

Suddenly the elder man spoke in a highly excited voice. "Hey. Hey, quiet down. Someone's coming!" Lois could hear the conversation up front and realized it was time for her husband's arrival. Surely, they were speaking of him.

"Please, dear God, don't let them hurt Frederick," she prayed aloud. Just as her husband reached for the handle to open the door, the older man opened it for him. He brandished the gun, demanding, "Get inside here!"

But Frederick Ryan was no fool. He didn't know what would happen if this man got him inside behind closed doors. And he didn't want to find out. He'd rather take his chances in broad daylight on North State Street.

He understood if he could raise someone's attention, he could get some help; not only for himself but for his wife and Rosie as well. The two women were trapped inside by a possible maniac having a gun with a hair-trigger, for all he knew.

Quickly turning away from the doorway, he noticed a passerby walking up the street. "Help. Robbery. Somebody, call the police!"

The two thieves now forgot all about the safe as the younger thief picked up one more handful of jewelry.

The ginger-head shouted to the older man as he passed through the threshold onto the sidewalk. "Let's get the hell out of here."

The two men jumped into the yellow Fairlane. The younger man quickly started the car and shoved it into gear. Watching his speed so as not to attract attention as he made their get-away, he drove the car over to W. Gordon Street.

***

Jimmy Paige, a twelve-year-old from the Gordon St. neighborhood was playing on the sidewalk in front of his house. He noticed two men fooling around with the rear license plate on a yellow car parked in front of his neighbor's home.

"They were folding it over from top to bottom like they wanted to hide the numbers," he later told the police.

"I saw the older guy put a shiny gun in his coat pocket. Then, they ran up Andre's driveway and went into his back yard. I ran to see what they were doing, and I saw them enter the back porch."

A street-smart kid from a rough neighborhood, Jimmy learned early to recognize trouble when he saw it and he thought these two had trouble written all over them. He ran into the house as fast as he could.

Jimmy's voice was high-pitched with excitement as he burst through the back door. "Mom, I just saw two white guys going into Andre's house!"

Monique Paige was stupefied as she noticed her son's widened eyes. Jimmy ran to the kitchen window to see if he could spot them again. His mother sat confused at the table. "What white men? What were they doing over there?"

"Boy, come over here and have a seat. You need to take a breath, slow down and tell me exactly what you saw the two white men doing."

After Monique heard her son's breathless tale, she quickly dialed '0' for the operator. "I need the police department immediately!" Now Monique's own voice was shrill with panic.

***

Frederick Ryan made an emergency call to the Durham Police Department as soon as the two men made a b-line for the door and fled the scene. A squad car was dispatched to take down the witnesses' statements. Crime scene technicians would soon be busy collecting evidence.

When Monique contacted the Durham Police Department with her son's story, their antennas piqued immediately. Law Enforcement was already at the scene of the armed robbery. They believed little Jimmy Paige's sharp eyes had honed in on their suspects.

CHAPTER 27
A Most Liberating Accomplishment
1996

Echo and Don arrived for dinner at the Sycamores at 6 p.m., sharp. Shari and Patrick Reilly had also been invited.

"Is there anything I can help you with?" Echo asked Addie.

"Yes, please, I need water and ice in the glasses on the dining room table."

Echo walked toward the freezer just as the doorbell rang.

"Oh, that must be Shari," Addie said. "Come on in," she hollered at the door.

Shari meandered into the kitchen. "Hi everyone."

Echo walked to the tall lady and extended her hand. "Hi, Shari. I'm Echo and I'm very pleased to meet you."

"Likewise," Shari responded.

"Where's Pat," Addie asked?

"He's parking the car, but he'll be in momentarily."

Addie had prepared a delicious meal. It consisted of homemade macaroni and cheese, garden salad, baked ham, green bean casserole, rolls, and coffee or tea.

Shari introduced Patrick to Echo, and he sat down at the table next to her.

A couple of conversations were going on at the same time. Patrick placed his salad in front of him and began gently massaging it with his fork.

"Echo," he whispered, leaning into her so as not to be heard by the others. "Do you know what kind of lettuce this is? It looks funny to me. There's stems on it!"

She turned toward Patrick and saw he was as serious as a heart attack. Echo looked at the content of his salad plate and then struggled to stifle a raucous laugh. She leaned toward him and whispered, "It's spinach, right from the garden."

"Really? I've never had spinach like that before in my life."

"Are you joshing me?"

"No," he retorted. "I don't eat salad, let alone spinach salad."

Echo chuckled. "It's good for you. You should try it. You'll like it."

Dallas looked up from his plate and planted a smile on his face, remembering the recommendation of the parole board.

"So, Echo, how is the murderer doing since his parole was denied?" Echo looked up and saw all eyes were resting upon her. The room fell silent.

Addie cried out, mortified. "Oh Dally, don't be rude to our guest,"

"I'm sorry, Echo, I shouldn't gloat. I hope you understand I agree wholeheartedly with the Parole Board's recommendation. But I don't want my satisfaction to make you uncomfortable in any way."

"Nothing adverse taken. I think he's resigned himself to believing he'll never get out of prison."

"Maybe it would be best for him, then, if he would just stop fighting it. Resign himself to his tiny cell as Danny is forever relegated to a 3' x 8' rectangular space inside the ground. It's not as if it's a unique idea. We've all had to resign ourselves to the consequence of his actions. I'm just wanting a little justice for my brother, that's all." Silence pervaded the room before Dallas spoke once more.

"You know, when I learned of Danny's death, I think I went into shock. I remember being rocked to my core by its suddenness. The finality of it devastated me. And I was stumped as to why and how the incomprehensible brutality occurred."

"And then when the Jameses were arrested for his murder all I could think of was they were breathing the very air they stole from my brother. I saw no justice in that. My anger boiled in me. All I wanted was for them to have to suffer what they forced us to endure."

"Back then, if I could have, I would have taken justice into my own hands. I would've done to them ten times over what they did to all of us. And in my dreams, I already have. I wanted them dead. It's the old eye for an eye and tooth for a tooth.

"You know, we eventually learn to live with the death of a loved one, but the lack of equity in a system that considers only the rights of the criminal leaves a foul taste in the mouths of the victim's survivors. And that's the thing that lingers."

"These murderers were sentenced to death. Yet, they were given a reprieve. I used to cry my eyes out asking God when Daniel was going to get his reprieve. I had no peace, no matter how I tried."

"You wouldn't have liked me much back then about fifteen years ago before I realized I needed help. The guilt I felt over being the one brother that survived caused me to spin completely out of control."

"I was dying, inch by inch on the inside. Daniel's murder was taking a toll on me. It seemed I turned the power to affect change in my life over to demons that kept me locked in bondage."

"It was back in 1981. I guess Danny had been gone twelve years, and I was still living back on that day the murder happened. I couldn't allow myself to do otherwise. It didn't seem fair that I could move forward when Danny's life had ceased forever. So, I allowed the cruel and brutal murder to imprison me in a vice grip of guilt that tightened down to the depth of my soul without a way to break free."

"Addie and I were married less than a year when I started drinking heavily after Danny was killed. Addie would call mom, and she would call Don to drag me out of the tavern and bring me home. Many times, Don found me on that bar stool crying like a baby. And my tears were always over Danny -- missing him so badly – longing to spend one more day with him. I would have agreed to die just to be able to see him again."

"And once I'd get started talking about Danny to another patron, rest assured the very next subject was centered squarely on the Jameses. Once that happened, I couldn't shut up. I'd murder them over and over again with every vile epithet that spewed forth from my mouth!

If I had the opportunity, I wouldn't bat an eye before I'd blast those animal's blood all over the place. I'd laugh as they drew their last breath."

"I hated them with a passion that only survivors suffering in the same manner can understand. The depth of my hate was frightening. And the people that loved me were very concerned."

Dallas reached to his left and squeezed Addie's hand and she smiled up at him.

"Of course, Don would come to the bar and he'd talk me into going home but I'd repeat the procedure all over again in the next day or two. My dad was blessed to have this good man as his best friend and every one of us benefited from their association."

Don blushed. He smiled and leaned back in his chair. "The person you are today has made it all worthwhile."

"I didn't appreciate just how long-suffering Addie was to put up with all my drinking. I'm grateful she didn't throw in the towel and walk away. She was at her wits end!"

Addie looked at her husband compassionately. "It was a tumultuous time, and I was on the cusp of leaving forever. I love Dally but he was self-imploding before my eyes. And I didn't want to witness the final collapse." Addie spoke as if the memory pained her still. "He was messing up at work, not going in when he was supposed to."

"I think it was the hangovers that were responsible for that," Dallas said, lightheartedly.

"Of course, when his mother passed away it only intensified the anguish of Danny's murder. Dally believes she died before her time because the Jameses murderous actions took her desire to go on without Daniel. And when she was diagnosed with brain cancer, she just gave up the fight."

"Now, I don't know if all that's true. I think she fought as good as she could but sometimes it's not worth the struggle when the outcome is the same either way." Addie grabbed a Kleenex and blew her nose.

"There was an incident, however, that shined a light on the dark hole my husband had crawled into and without professional help, I believe he'd never be able to crawl back out again."

"I went to a video store and picked up the movie, "Death Wish," starring Charles Bronson. It was a snowy afternoon. The roads were becoming slippery, and I knew once Dally came home from work, we wouldn't be going out again. So, after supper, we settled into the family room to watch the movie."

"But as the brutal crime unfolded on the television, Dallas went into a maniacal rage. The fire in his eyes, the taut doubled-up fists shaking in unearthly rage, the clenched teeth, the screaming vile language that he spewed at the actors performing the dastardly deed frightened me. I never heard anything like that ever cross his lips. My mouth dropped wide open in shock and unbelief."

"Dally, what is wrong with you?" I cried as I witnessed the

rage crescendo and then slowly dissipate before my eyes. So, I rushed into the kitchen, picked up the telephone handset and called Pastor Sorenson. "We need help," I told him in no uncertain terms, making an appointment for 6:30 p.m., the next evening."

"And what my lovely wife didn't know back then," Dallas interjected, "is that my visceral reaction to that brutal movie scared the hell out of me, also. I had no idea the depth of rage inhabiting me or that it could resuscitate at the perusal of a fictional murder scene on the television."

"Paul Kersey, the main character whose wife was murdered and daughter assaulted, killed criminals as he saw crimes being committed. And I would howl with elation that came from my core at the death of those animals. I literally jumped from my chair laughing, cheering, which scared the daylights out of me!"

"I began to question my sanity. The scene unfolding on the screen assailed my sense of safety and security. I was grateful Addie made the appointment for us to speak with Pastor Sorenson; someone I could trust with my innermost feelings and emotions."

"I told my wife, "maybe he can explain to me how the good Lord could let Daniel be murdered and explain, too, how God allows bad things to happen to good people."

"You know, I gave Addie a heads-up, though, that if our pastor was going to preach things like, 'it was God's will,' 'God called him home,' or 'he's better off in heaven,' I would walk out and never go back to church again! I wasn't about to take that garbage inside me."

"I don't believe He wills for us to die like Danny did and I think that's the very reason why my parents and I never lost our faith throughout that tragic time. We never blamed God for the actions of the Jameses."

"I've known Pastor Sorenson all my life. He baptized me. I just wish I had sought his counsel sooner than I did. I could have avoided scars from many self-inflicted wounds. I suppose it took that long to recognize I needed help."

"Through many counseling sessions, Pastor guided me through the process of acknowledging and accepting Daniel's death. He helped me see no matter how much I wished otherwise; Daniel wasn't coming back."

"Of course, I knew that in my head. Still, from time to time

I'd see a tall stranger walking down the street, and I'd do a double take to make sure it wasn't him. In those times, Pastor counseled me to return to the casket that held Daniel's body until I couldn't deny the obvious any longer."

"He helped me understand I put my feelings about Danny's murder on hold, suppressing them while I tended to my heartsick parents. He explained when a person puts off their own grief process, they can carry the pain and heartache for the rest of their lives. I lost myself in my parents, grief, failing to take the time for my own healing. I recognize it now but I didn't then."

"Best of all, Pastor helped me find a place in my heart for Danny where he would be safe, sheltered, protected and never forgotten. When I placed him in my heart, I knew I was finally able to move on, no longer guilt-ridden for having survived."

After our counseling sessions, I was persuaded to forgive Steven and Russell James for what they did to Daniel and my family. But not for their sakes. You see, when I hated them, they had power over me, but once I truly forgave them, I took my power back. When I finally understood how they owned my yesterdays, I refused to give them any more of my tomorrows."

"Now, that doesn't mean I don't want them in prison for the rest of their lives because I do. Justice and forgiveness are two different things. But I wish them no ill will in their current circumstances."

"Who wants coffee?" Addie asked. "I'll serve it in the sunroom. Why don't we head back there?"

"Oh, none for us, thank you," Patrick said. "Our son has a high-school wrestling match this evening, so we're going to have to be leaving."

"How is young David doing on the wrestling team?" Addie asked, smiling.

"Not bad. His record is 12 and 1."

Shari and Patrick stood to leave. "Good to meet you, Echo. Good to see you, Don," Patrick said.

"Likewise," Echo responded.

Shari smiled kindly. "Echo, I'd love to share with you some of my memories of Daniel, if you'd like to hear them. I was his girlfriend, and Patrick was his best friend."

"I'd like that very much."

"C'mon, I'll show you to the door." Addie put her arm around Shari's waist as the two-walked side by side.

Echo took the plates from the dining room table into the kitchen and took a seat on a comfortable padded wicker barrel chair positioned under the window and in view of the sparkling aqua swimming pool.

Dallas spoke softly, filling his words with compassion. "Forgive me if I'm out of line, Echo, but I see so much of myself in you. Not the drinking or loss of control I experienced, of course, but the deadening toll of hate from grief deferred. Maybe you were just too young back then." But Echo wasn't having any of it.

"Oh, I don't know, Dallas. What is proper grieving for a thirteen-year-old?" Echo's tone was defensive and sardonic. Her question represented more a statement rather than an inquiry. She looked perturbed. It was obvious that Dallas' observation wasn't sitting well with her.

"It seems so funny to me -- almost ironic -- how the last time I saw Russell James he, too, felt the need to let me know his perception of my unforgiving nature. All I know is my parents' tears affected me terribly. I admit I was young and sheltered the day the soldiers came knocking on the door. Up until then, my family hadn't suffered a loss like that. So, it's quite probable I didn't fully grieve as I should have."

"Yet, I am not the one who sent over 500,000 of America's finest into harm's way for my own political gain. Nor did the incompetent snake ever ask for my forgiveness!" Echo's ire bubbled to the surface for all to witness with every word that flowed from her mouth.

"Why are you turning the tables on me? You have just criticized me with the very same sentiment Russell did the last time I spoke with him. Frankly, I am at a loss to comprehend what you distinguish in me that I'm not able to perceive in myself. All I know for sure is this was never supposed to be about me."

Echo could feel the ire rising within her. "It appears I'm being lambasted from both sides. Maybe there's a lesson for me somewhere in all this. But I certainly don't know what it is."

"Forgive me, Echo. If what I said doesn't ring true, please just let it go. I'm not the kind to preach what you should or should not do. I only wanted to share with you what gave me back my life and my wife."

"No, I'm sorry, Dallas. I've become defensive and I never meant to do that. I appreciate all you've shared with me. Your opinions are important. I want to hear what you have to say, and all that you would like for me to know. Please."

"Well then, the bottom line is I had to rid myself of the angst before it got rid of me. Forgiveness was my last hope for change. If it didn't work, I'd be lost forever. But I'm here to say it was the most freeing project I've ever undertaken."

He reached for Addie's hand and held it, smiling warmly. The two had survived so much together and were stronger for having weathered the storm.

"Forgiveness is like a powerful counter punch to the injustices in our lives. Once I understood I wasn't betraying Danny by forgiving Russell and Steve James, I was ready for it. It cleared out the rubbish that stained my heart, allowing me to make a home for Danny there. Today, I take him with me wherever I go. It is truly the best thing I've ever done for myself. It is my most liberating accomplishment."

CHAPTER 28
The Perfect Patsy
1970

Andre and Aretha Tinsley were next-door-neighbors to the Paige family. The saxophonist with the Smooth Notes by night was a custodian by day for the Durham Public School District.

That morning, Andre reported for work on his regular 7 a.m. shift. He was working at the South Shore Grade School when the intruders entered his home. Aretha and the children were there but they never heard a thing.

At approximately 10 a.m., Officers James R. Thomas and Brent Newby of the Durham Police Department, responded to the information provided by Jimmy Paige and his mother. They rang the front doorbell at the Gordon address. Aretha Tinsley answered the door.

Officer Thomas maneuvered his way into the living room. He spoke softly and quietly. "Hello, Ma'am. We got a report that two men entered your house through the back door."

The officer's eyes scanned far and wide as he cautiously made his way toward the kitchen, never asking the homeowner for permission. He drew his gun and held it in front of him. Officer Newby remained close to Aretha, keeping an eye on her every move.

Aretha was shocked and dumbfounded. She was becoming more frightened with every passing second. "What men? There isn't anybody here but me and the kids."

"We received a call that two Caucasian men were seen entering your home at the rear of the house," Newby said.

"What?" Aretha looked stunned. The hair on the back of her neck began to rise.

"We need to check out the situation and secure the premises. Do you have any objection?"

"Not at all. Please do."

The children ran to their mother and threw their arms around her. "It's going to be okay," she told them softly.

* * *

The two robbers entered the enclosed back porch and picked up a duffel bag from under a skirted chair that contained two sets of clothing. They went directly to the basement where they quickly disrobed and changed their clothes. Now ready to make their move, they could hear the conversation taking place above them. As Officer Thomas drew closer to the steps that led down to the basement, the two men decided to make a run for it.

They were not aware the house was surrounded by personnel from the Durham Police Department and the Macay County Sheriff's Office. Running up the stairs, they pushed the back door open and ran into the back yard.

"Halt!" Officer Thomas had his gun trained on the backs of the suspects. Both men came to a standstill and lifted their arms in the air. Guns were pointed at them from every direction.

"Lie flat on the ground," they were commanded, atop a four-inch blanket of fresh fallen snow. Officer Thomas secured each suspect with handcuffs. He brought the two men back inside the house for identification. They didn't put up a fight. They were brought into the living room where Aretha stood hugging her frightened children close to her.

Aretha was shocked to learn two men had indeed entered her home without her knowledge. She was equally shocked to learn their identity because they were in her home just the day before. They talked about saxophone lessons for the younger one and just a week prior she served coffee to the older man and his wife. On each of those occasions, however, they had been invited in. Not this time.

"What in the world is going on," she wondered?

The suspects were frisked for weapons. While officers searched the car, Thomas and Newby searched the basement. They found the duffel bag that now contained the clothing that was worn by the robbers as described to the officers by the two women at the jewelry store. It didn't, however, contain the weapon used in the robbery. Still, they knew it had to be around there somewhere.

Officers outside noticed the folded-over license plate on the

Fairlane. They opened the trunk and found watches, rings and other jewelry stuffed in a pillow case. They went over the car with a fine-tooth comb but could not find the weapon.

The suspects were hauled off to the station for questioning and Aretha, frightened as she had never been before, was taken down for questioning also. Law Enforcement suspected she may have abetted in the criminal activities of the two suspects. At the time, there was no other explanation that made sense as to why two white men would enter a black man's residence without the two being in collusion. Aretha would be questioned strenuously.

Afterwards, Officer Thomas created an arrest report on the James men and forwarded it to the State's Attorney for possible prosecution. The report summarized the events leading up to and including the arrest of the suspects. They carefully documented the date and time of the incident, as well as the site where the incident took place. Little Jimmy Paige was listed as a witness along with Rosie Shepherd and Lois and Frederick Ryan.

* * *

Andre received a message from the South Shores School secretary. "Your neighbor, Monique Paige called and said you need to go home right away!"

"Why? What's going on?"

"I don't know, Andre, but she sounded really upset to me."

The time was close to 11 a.m. "I'll take my lunch break and run home to see what's going on."

As a rule, Andre generally went home for lunch. He'd have only half of an hour in which to eat and return. This day, however, there would be no going back to work. Neither would there be a hot lunch awaiting him. His children were excited and afraid when he entered the house.

"Daddy, the cops took Momma to the police station!"

Andre was becoming a little agitated by all the confusion. "What for?"

"The men came into the house and went down into the basement."

"Wait a minute. Slow down. You're talking all at once. I can't understand what's going on. Tyrone, you tell me what happened here today." Andre looked straight-faced at his eldest child.

"Those two white men that were here yesterday came into the house, went into the basement, and the cops came and took them and Momma away. Daddy, you got to go get Momma. They got her down at the police station."

Andre talked to Monique Paige who was watching his children since Aretha was hauled off to the station. She explained all that little Jimmy saw but Andre became more confused by it all.

"Can you stay a little longer while I go to the station to find out what is happening to my wife?"

"I'll take the kids next door to my house, so I can make them something to eat."

"Thank you, Moni. I'm very concerned for Aretha. I just don't understand why they have her down there." But Monique was just as confused as he.

When Andre arrived at the station, he was led into a room and was questioned separately. Like Aretha before him, he was shocked and confused. He couldn't figure out why the Jameses would sneak into his home.

"Aretha don't know nuthun' about no robbery," Andre told the officers. "What she knows is Steven was going to take saxophone lessons from me and she would have let them enter the front door if they'd only knocked." Andre was incensed by the audacity of the two white men.

Aretha was questioned for about three hours before Andre was allowed to see her. She was frightened and in tears. Her eyes were swollen and red. Her statement was clear and unchanging.

She could not offer one iota of an explanation as to why those men would enter her basement covertly and the detectives were now beginning to believe her story.

In a few hours, her statement would be corroborated. Each of the James men, separately and of their own volition, admitted the Tinsley's had nothing to do with the robbery. Indeed, they had no inclination of the Jameses criminal shenanigans. With no evidence to hold her, the officers allowed Andre to take his wife home. The time was 3:30 p.m.

* * *

Back at the house, Andre went directly to the basement. He struggled to fathom why the Jameses would be in his cellar. He wondered what they had been up to down there. He walked around, looking for just what he wasn't sure.

He found himself straight back from the stairs in the area of an old coal bin that had been converted to a natural gas furnace. Something shiny above it caught his eye.

Moving closer, a revolver came into focus. He didn't allow guns in his house and instinctively knew it had to belong to the men who entered his home through the back door uninvited. He ran back upstairs and called the police.

He excitedly told the sergeant working the front desk, "This is Andre Tinsley. I live on Gordon Street and you guys made an arrest at my house this morning."

"Yes, Mr. Tinsley, what can I do for you, sir?"

"I found a gun in my basement that doesn't belong to me, and I want you to send someone over here to get it out of my house. I want nuthun' to do with it! I know it belongs to the Jameses that robbed the jewelry store today. They're the only people that have been in my basement." Andre was dogmatically opposed to weapons of any kind.

"Alright, Mr. Tinsley, have you touched the gun or picked it up in any way at all?"

"No, sir, I found it on a rafter above the old coal bin, and I left it there, ran upstairs and called you."

"That's good sir, just leave it right there. We'll send the officers back to the house to pick the weapon up."

After hanging up the telephone, Andre called his children into the kitchen. "I don't want any of you going down into the basement."

"How come, Daddy?" Tyrone wanted to know.

"There's something down there that can hurt you, and the police are coming to take it away; but until they do, you are forbidden to go downstairs. Now is that clear to everyone?"

"Yes, but what's down there, Daddy?"

Andre looked at each of his children. "Don't trouble your mind about it. Just be sure you do as I say."

After promising to obey, the children scattered to different sections of the house. Andre and his wife sat down at the kitchen table with a pot of hot coffee and waited for the police to arrive.

"I'll tell you one thing, Aretha, I'm glad I had the good sense not to touch that gun. That's all they'd need -- a black man with his fingerprints all over that thing. They'd make me out to be the mastermind."

Officers Thomas and Newby arrived at the Tinsley home at 4:45 p.m. Andre led the officers to the northeast corner of his basement and opened the door of the coal bin. Lying on a rafter above the door was a shiny, chrome plated revolver with a black handle. Thomas picked it up with his pen through the trigger guard and placed it in a plastic bag.

The pistol was taken back to headquarters and given to Detective Roger Davis, who, using latex gloves, opened the weapon, inspected the gun and removed three bullets from the five-round revolver.

Roger noticed the serial number had been removed. He placed the weapon back into the plastic bag and attached a Durham Police Department's property slip to it.

Aretha and Andre sat sipping coffee at their kitchen table. "You know, I think the James boys were trying to set me up. I think the whole story about Steven wanting saxophone lessons was just a ruse. They wanted to befriend a black man so that his house could be used to store a duffel bag over night and hide a gun used in a robbery."

"If they got caught, well, all the evidence would be found on that black man's property and who do you think the cops are going to believe? A black man over two white men? I don't think so. Yes, I'm sure of it. They were hoping to make me their perfect patsy."

CHAPTER 29
Unfulfilled Dreams
1996

Echo and Don climbed the steps to the front porch on Celeste Court in Piedmont at the home of Patrick and Shari Tyner. Don rang the doorbell.

The Sycamores were invited but weren't able to attend. Their twenty-five-year-old, pregnant daughter, Daniella, went into labor. They called Shari and Patrick Tyner with their regrets and rushed to the hospital.

The seven pound, six-ounce, healthy boy that Daniella and her husband, Ben Hennessey, named Daniel Benjamin, was the Sycamore's first grandchild.

The baby's father beamed like a pixel on Freemont Street in Las Vegas when Dallas and Addie entered their daughter's hospital room.

***

Patrick answered the door bell and invited Don and Echo into the cozy living room. Bonbons were spread on a platter sitting on the coffee table. Shari entered the room and greeted her guests. She hugged Don and then hugged Echo.

Shari Tyner is statuesque, standing five feet, ten inches and is as thin as a toothpick. When she was in high school, she used to pull her dark brown perfectly straight hair up into a bun. Everyone recognized the uncanny resemblance she possessed to "Olive Oil" of the Popeye comic fame. In spite of her gangly appearance she possessed a warm and friendly personality. She was infectiously happy, and everyone wanted to be her friend.

Echo was no exception. She liked Shari from the moment

she first met her; felt she had known her all her life. Shari and Patrick were the parents of two children.

"It's good to see you both again. Please sit down and make yourself at home. I'll bring out a fresh pot of coffee." Shari said, warmly.

Patrick followed his wife into the kitchen and returned with sugar and creamer bowls. After pouring the piping-hot liquid into each cup, Shari and Patrick sat down on the sofa.

Shari looked at Echo for guidance. "I don't know where I should begin. Is there specific information you're wanting for the book?"

Echo never told anyone the bitter details of her last bitter encounter with Russell or her regret that the book might never see fruition. She hoped she might find another angle through which to tell the story, without Russell's input.

"I want to understand who Daniel was as a person. So, I'd be grateful to hear any information you are comfortable in sharing."

"Then, I'll start with our freshman year. I met Daniel on the first day at Piedmont High School. He was a big kid, standing six feet, two inches tall and weighing one-hundred-eighty-five pounds. He had an athlete's build, high-cheekbones on a handsome face and a mop of light brown hair neatly coiffed in a Beatles' haircut."

"He was a standout in track and field, among the best 440-yard-dash runners in Sturnus County. Although he loved to pull schoolboy pranks on classmates and teachers, he was a decent young man, possessing empathy and compassion."

"Daniel asked me to Homecoming, and our friendship blossomed. Throughout high school we were inseparable, building a bond of shared interests and mutual respect that was impenetrable by outsiders."

"Whenever you saw Daniel, you saw Shari," Patrick chimed in with a smile. "They were two peas in a pod. If Danny and I made plans to go fishing, it was understood that Shari was coming along."

"That's true," Shari giggled. "But I remember an incident when I wasn't with Danny. It was his first experience with death, up-close and personal."

"During high school, Danny worked at 4 p.m. at the Texaco Station. Ron English, Harlan Vernon's brother-in-law, would then relieve him at 10 p.m. and work the overnight shift."

"Well, on a Tuesday evening in November 1967, Ron arrived at the station a few minutes earlier. The guys exchanged a few pleasantries, and Danny retrieved his coat from the back of a chair and put it on before heading toward the door. The two said their goodbyes, and Danny exited the station."

"You be careful out there," Ron hollered after him. "There's ice patches. Watch the bridges and overpasses."

"Danny raced to his car, unlocked the door and climbed inside, starting up the engine to get the heater going. He then climbed out, scraper in hand, and began the chore of relieving the windows of their ice build-up."

"In a few minutes, he was ready to pull off the apron. At the stop sign, Daniel turned south onto Route 66 and drove one mile to the Route 114 exit, and navigated eastward for the five miles into Piedmont. But as he drove under the Route 66 overpass, he noticed a set of high-beam headlights shining in the distance."

"The beams appeared to be out of place and positioned in an area well off the traveled portion of the highway. And he could hear through his rolled-up car windows, the piercing incessant sound of a car horn blaring louder the closer he drew near."

"The horrific sight of a single car accident startled Daniel as it came into view. He slowed his vehicle, pulled over onto the shoulder and quickly assessed the scene."

"It appeared the westbound car slid on a patch of ice, left the highway from the north shoulder and slid approximately 100 feet before slamming broadside into an oak tree about 50 feet off the shoulder. The accident must have occurred just moments before because Daniel was the first person on the scene."

"Hurriedly he turned on his flashers, grabbed a flashlight from the glove compartment and rushed down the shallow ditch and up the other side to the mangled metal and steel that used to be someone's vehicle."

"He reached the front passenger door first, but couldn't pry it open. Shining a light into the car his eyes fixed on a macabre scene."

"Just then another car pulled up, and Danny hollered out to the guy to drive to Sully's Gas Station and call for police and paramedics."

"The two women in the front were dead. Their eyes were

wide open and fixed. They were later identified as thirty-five-year-old Marissa Delavan and Honora Piccard, Marissa's sixty-five-year-old mother."

"Danny told me the body of Honora, the front passenger, was twisted in ghoulish distortion. The heel of her right foot lay atop the steering wheel, now in an awkward crumpled position to the right and down toward the lap of the driver."

"The lower portion of Marissa's body was completely hidden from view by the twisted mangled wreckage. The side of her head lay heavily on the car's horn that blared incessantly."

"It would take rescue squad personnel over two hours to free the bodies of the two ladies from the carnage that trapped them."

"Suddenly, Daniel heard a weak and fearful voice crying out from inside the rear of the vehicle. "Mommy, Mommy, -- I want my Mommy."

"He immediately raced to the back-passenger door, gripped tightly and with all his might pried the door open."

"Inside on the floorboard, lay three young children, two males and one female, wrinkled in a heap. Each was on their backs facing the rear window. They were the children of Marissa Delavan. None seemed aware their mother and grandmother had expired."

"Daniel climbed onto the back seat. The older boy didn't move and appeared unconscious, but the younger boy and girl were now crying and calling out for their mother."

"I want my Mommy. Mommy. Mommy!" "The little girl's inflection pleaded for a response. Yet her mother's reply was not to be."

"Instead, Daniel took the little girl's right hand and placed it into the left hand of her brother. He brushed the light blonde hair from the little girl's face and as comforting as he could he spoke to the children."

"Hold on tight to one another. I'll be right back in a flash!"

"He climbed out of the wreckage, sprinted over to his car and retrieved a green wool military blanket from the trunk, hustled back to the frightened children and placed the blanket over them. Then he took the little girl's left hand and held it in his."

"Hold my hand, honey," Danny said to her. "He guessed the little girl's age was approximately eight years."

"You're going to be okay. Help is on the way."

"He looked at the young boy, estimated to be ten years and saw fear in his eyes.

"You're going to be alright, buddy. Just try not to move. Lay as still as you can until help arrives. I'll stay right here with you!"

"Daniel reached down and grabbed the little boy's right hand, rubbing it gently with his thumb.

"You're very brave." he told the children in a soothing voice, "and you must be brave for a little while longer!"

"Suddenly, Daniel said his ears perked up and he asked the children, "Listen, can you hear it? Daniel told me he'd never heard a more beautiful sound in all his life!"

"Emergency vehicle sirens grew louder as the distance between them dwindled. The third child, estimated to be about twelve years of age, began moaning and moving his head from left to right."

"Danny climbed from the wreckage to allow the paramedics to reach the children."

"The youngest boy's name was Mark Delavan, of Peoria. He was placed on a stretcher and wheeled across the frozen turf to an awaiting ambulance. He was crying, so Daniel bent over the stretcher and brushed the boy's hair with his hand. Mark threw his arms around Daniel's neck and sobbed bitterly."

"We were headed home to Peoria after visiting Aunt Viola when we ran off the road and hit the tree. I think the road was too slippery for us to drive on. Will you please come with me to the hospital?"

Danny said he felt awful telling the child he'd have to go alone. He said, "I'm sorry, I'm not allowed in the ambulance. But I'll come see you tomorrow after school."

"Mark was listed in fair condition with a possible concussion. The older brother, William, was freed and whisked away from the scene. He was admitted to St. Jonathon's Hospital Trauma Center, Intensive Care Unit, in serious condition with a concussion, multiple fractures, and lacerations. The girl, Jocelyn, was listed in fair condition with facial lacerations, a broken right arm, and a possible concussion."

"Daniel's heart ached for the young children who just lost their mother and grandmother."

"Do they know the condition of the women in the front

seat?" Officer Sam Schuster, Piedmont Police Department, asked as the third ambulance sped down the highway.

"I don't think so. We never discussed it. I didn't have the heart to tell them myself."

"Life is cruel sometimes," Danny told me. "He said his worst regret was not hopping in his car and driving to the hospital. He said he didn't know what to do but was afraid he'd impede the doctors and nurses working on the children's injuries."

"That was the character of Daniel Sycamore. He was a decent human being who was caring, loving, kind and warm."

"Early the next day, the children's father, Reilly Delavan, a large gregarious balding man with a rip-roaring laugh, had already arrived from Peoria."

"Reilly had a zest for life that would buoy his children in the dark days ahead. He arrived in the early morning, heartbroken, but determined to hold his family together. Reilly was the one person with the unenviable task of informing his children of the deaths of their mother and grandmother."

"Daniel stayed in touch with Reilly until the day he died, exchanging letters, birthday cards, and phone calls, following the progress and growth of the children." Shari smiled warmly in recollection.

"I had the horrible task of telling Reilly about Danny. We cried like babies for about an hour on the telephone. Reilly often said he was sorry the tragic accident occurred but was grateful to God that it was Daniel who came along to comfort and support his children."

"You were their beacon on that dark traumatic night, and I am forever grateful," Reilly told Danny.

"So, I kept the birthday and Christmas cards going until the children were grown. I did it for Daniel because I think that's what he would have wanted me to do!"

CHAPTER 30
Weapon Tagged
1970

Detective Roger Davis placed the plastic bag containing the revolver into a cabinet behind his desk at the Durham Police Station. Standard operating procedures for the recovery of any weapon required the notification of surrounding law enforcement jurisdictions.

Accordingly, Davis sent a telex to the State Police and to the neighboring Sturnus County Sheriff's Office, the Starling Police Department and to law enforcement agencies in all of the surrounding counties.

ARMED ROBBERY
RYAN'S JEWELRY STORE
DURHAM, IL
ARRESTED - TWO MALE STURNUS COUNTY RESIDENTS
RECOVERED - IVER JOHNSON .38 CALIBER REVOLVER
SERIAL # ERADICATED FROM WEAPON

***

Dominic Kenney, a nineteen-year veteran of the state police, was sitting at his desk when the teletype began printing. He rolled in his chair to the machine and began reading the incoming information.

Kenney was at the Texaco station on December 19 and witnessed the lifeless body of Daniel Sycamore lying on the concrete storage room floor. He picked up the phone and placed a call to the Investigations Unit of the Sturnus County Sheriff's Department to speak to Don DeLario.

"Dominic, how are you doing?"

"Good, Don. Have you seen the telex from the Durham Police Department?"

"I just saw it," Don responded.

"I've been assigned to drive over there to retrieve the revolver for the crime lab, and I was wondering if you'd like to ride along. Maybe you could talk to these guys about the Sycamore case."

"You bet I would. I was just thinking about taking a drive over myself!"

"It will be about half of an hour before I can pick you up." Dominic relayed.

"That's perfect for me. I'll be waiting for you. See you then." Don placed the phone back in its cradle.

* * *

The two law enforcement officers arrived at the Durham Police Station at approximately 3:30 p.m. that afternoon. They were escorted to the south end of the second floor where they entered the Detective Unit. Russell was taken from his jail cell and brought there into an adjoining conference room. After introducing himself and Kenney to their suspect, Don began questioning Russell James.

"Would you give us your name and tell us where you're from?"

"My name is Russ James, and I'm from Starling."

"What is your age, Mr. James?"

"I'm forty-two years old."

"Are you married, sir?"

"Yes, I am. What is this all about?"

Don pulled out a laminated card from his billfold and began reading the suspect his Miranda rights. This would be the last shot the detectives would ever have to speak with Russell James.

Over the ensuing days, Miranda rights would be read to Steven James every time he was questioned by Sturnus County authorities. Each time the suspect responded 'yes' when asked if he comprehended those individual rights.

"We're here today to speak with you about a murder at a gas station that occurred in Sturnus County." Don's voice was smooth and cordial.

"Okay, but why do you want to speak with me about a murder? I sure as hell didn't kill anyone! How in the world can I contribute to a conversation when I know nothing about it?"

"Mr. James, in reference to the murder of one Daniel Sycamore at a Texaco Gas Station near Glenrose, do you recall your whereabouts on the early morning of December 19, 1969?" Don looked at the suspect for any sign of nervous sweat or flushing on his face.

"I can't recall that far back. I really don't remember where I was. I don't remember what I did yesterday let alone two weeks past. I think what you need to do is ask Steven. He's got a better memory than me. Maybe he'll be able to tell you our whereabouts. What I know is that I didn't commit a murder. That's for damn sure! I tell you in no uncertain terms I'd sure as hell remember something as horrible as that and it wouldn't matter how much time had passed!"

"We don't know you, sir. That's why we have to ask these questions." Don reflected a face of stone, betraying no hint of what he might be thinking.

"I do recall reading about that murder in the newspaper, though, and hearing about it on the radio. Steve and I were discussing it because we used to work with a Sycamore kid about three years ago and wondered if this might be him. I sure hope you boys can catch whoever did it."

Don responded with confidence and determination "Oh, we will. Be assured of that. Now, Mr. James, how many weapons do you own, how many are there at your residence and what caliber are they?"

"I don't own any weapons and there are no guns of any kind at my residence."

"Then, where did you get the gun you brandished today and used in the Ryan's Jewelry Store robbery?"

Russell's face flushed, and his jaw dropped open as Don pushed forward with his questioning.

"What about any shotguns you may have in your possession or at your residence?"

"Like I said before, I don't have any guns, shotguns or

otherwise, in my possession."

"If I told you that a young man by the name of Herschel Johnson has come forward to say that you gave him a shotgun in late December, would that help refresh your memory?"

Russell never hesitated. "I never gave a shotgun to Hersch. Perhaps Steven gave him one and so he'd be the person you need to talk to about that, now wouldn't he?"

"Mr. James, would you be willing to take a polygraph test concerning the armed robbery and murder of Daniel Sycamore?"

"No, I will not." Russell's tone was obstinate and unwavering.

Don wasn't surprised. From the first sight of him, he felt that Russell would never agree to a polygraph test that might reflect poorly upon him. Still, he had to ask.

"I'm sorry, gentlemen, I'm just not able to be of any help to you boys at all. It seems to me you're trying to pin your unsolved crime on this poor schmuck so you can have another notch in your belt. Well, I'm not your ladder to the top. I didn't do what you're asking me about. I don't think I want to discuss this with you anymore. If you intend to question me further, then I would prefer to have an attorney present."

"Very well Mr. James. We'll get an officer to take you back to your cell."

Kenney got up from the table and opened the door of the conference room. The jailer, standing just outside the door, looked over at him.

"We're all finished with this one. You can take him back now."

The jailer entered the conference room and walked over to where the suspect sat. He placed his hand under Russell's arm and gently lifted him out of his seat. "Let's go, buddy."

As they were preparing to leave the room, Russell turned to look at the Sturnus County officers.

"Is there anything else you'd like to say, Mr. James?" Don asked.

"Well, I was wondering if you could talk to Sheriff Jason to see what arrangements could be made for my wife to come over from Starling. She doesn't drive a car."

"She can ride over with us sometime in the next couple of

days. I'll try to make some arrangements for you. Does that sound fair enough?" Don was not without compassion for Mrs. James whom he considered a victim herself.

"That's more than fair and I appreciate it."

The two visiting officers watched as the jailer and the robbery suspect made their way through the door and down the hall. The detectives knew they had no choice but to stop all questioning. Miranda prohibited further inquiries.

Don looked at Dominic Kenney and smirked. "Did you notice how he pushed everything off on his son, like when he said, ask Steven where we were and maybe it was Steven that gave Herschel a shotgun? How does a decent father do that?"

Dominic was at a loss to understand the self-absorption of the man they just interviewed. "Yes, I got that same impression. You know, if my instincts are correct, we could be witnessing a set of circumstances that are unique to this entire area. In all my career, indeed my entire lifetime, I never heard of an armed robbery and murder committed by a father and son team -- at least not around here."

"I haven't either," Don responded matter-of-factly.

Don was glad the jailer was escorting Russell back to his cell rather than showing him the front door. All of their efforts would now be centered on Steven whom his father seemed to serve up on a silver platter. "There's something stinking in Sturnus County, and I've got a hunch the stench originates with Russell James. That man was way too defensive, way too soon for my liking. I know he's dirty, even though instinct is all I have to go on."

* * *

Steven was brought down next, and the inquiries were repeated with him. He, too, feigned ignorance. But unlike his father, he didn't invoke his right to have an attorney present during questioning. Don didn't want to push the issue. There would be no good-cop, bad-cop tactics from the detectives, at least not at this early stage. They'd have plenty of time for that later. The younger James was returned to his cellblock.

Don hoped this meeting with Steven today would increase his anxiety. He wanted the young man to understand Sturnus County had its eyes on him and were looking into his recent activities. If he and his father were guilty, Don was determined to take them down.

After seeing them for the first time, Don was surprised by the Jameses diminutive stature. Although looks can be deceiving, they appeared incapable of harming a fly. Just one glance and Don knew they would never have been able to stand up to Danny without a gun in hand.

Don and Dominic exited the conference room and entered the Investigations Unit. They walked up to the first officer sitting just inside the doorway. "We're here to see Detective Roger Davis, please."

"Right over there. He's the guy on the telephone."

"Thank you." The two law enforcement officers stood silently by his desk while Davis ended his telephone conversation. "Any luck with the suspects, gentlemen?" Davis took a sip from his coffee cup.

Don responded. "No, not at this time. We'll be back again tomorrow, though, to have another go at the younger one."

"You're here to take that gun over to the crime lab in Starling, aren't you?"

"Yes, sir, I'll be taking it back with me," Trooper Kenney said.

Roger Davis wheeled backward and opened the file cabinet behind him. He reached in and pulled out the tagged plastic bag containing the revolver and placed it on his desk. Dominic Kenney picked it up.

Davis handed the Trooper a departmental chain of custody receipt. Kenney signed the form and placed his initials on the plastic bag that contained the weapon.

"Thank you for your cooperation," Don said.

"Anytime, fellas."

It was well after 5 p.m. when the officers left the city of Durham. The crime lab in Starling was now closed. The revolver would remain in the possession of the State trooper for the duration of the weekend.

On Monday, January 5, 1970, Trooper Kenney rode the elevator to the second floor at Duffy Tower. There, he turned the gun over to Anita Alexander, Cecilia Dempsey's replacement. Alexander placed her initials on the tag for chain of custody. Soon, she would prepare the weapon for shipment to the crime lab in Joliet, where all recovered weapons were sent for testing and storage.

CHAPTER 31
The Speed of Light
1996

    Shari's memories of time spent with Daniel were bittersweet. "All through high school, Daniel was a starting center on the varsity basketball team, and I attended every game I could. My girlfriends took turns sharing the driving duties during away games. Daniel wasn't allowed to ride with us. School rules required the team travel together on the bus; but we followed right behind them, to and from."

    "I attended all his track meets too, and what a wonderful experience in his junior year when he went all the way to State in the four-forty-yard dash. He came in an impressive second place finish to the runner from Sandwich. I was there unabashedly cheering him on. I was focused on Daniel unaware of anything else around me. I told him I was so proud of him. I felt my heart could leap from my chest. Heck, just a few seconds faster and he would have won."

    "Still, Daniel would never return to State level competition again. In his senior year, he made a lay-up at a late-season basketball game and came down on the side of his right foot, severely spraining his ankle and rendering him out of competition for the rest of the year."

    "At graduation, Daniel and I walked together into the auditorium. Happiness beamed on all of our faces until the finality of our high school days hit us. Kathy Barber, a classmate of ours, sobbed as she reached up and hugged Daniel. "I'm going to miss you," she told him before turning toward me."

    "She said, "Shari, can you believe we made it?"

    "I told her, yes, but I'm going to miss Daniel when he moves to Bloomington to attend Indiana University."

    "That's when Kathy said something that stabs me every time I think of it. I know the words were intended for comfort, but they haunt me even to this day. She said, "Oh, I know, but he'll be home on holidays, at Christmas time and spring break."

Shari's heart filled with sorrow as her mind rolled back to that fateful day in late, 1969. "Home for the Christmas holiday, -- that's exactly what happened. Sweet Daniel was home from college on Christmas break."

"He called me that last morning. He said he was going for a run and had to work that night at 10 p.m. We made plans to go to Starling in the early afternoon to have lunch at the Snug Puppy."

"I told him to be careful on his run because it was slippery out and foggy as well. Sometimes drivers can't see joggers until it's too late. I told him to be alert. I said you don't want to get hit by a car and be killed.' And in light of what happened, I've never been able to get that memory out of my mind. It, too, rattles me just by recalling it."

"Who would have known in less than 14 hours Daniel would be taken from us and at the hands of a vicious father and son who cared nothing for the man whose life they snuffed out."

"Daniel was going places, studying criminal justice. He was doing what he was supposed to do for his future; our future. He had his whole life before him."

"Those thugs were hell-bent and determined to rob and kill. And in doing so they ripped our aspirations from us, with no consideration given to their own long-term goals and hopes for their future."

"It simply blows my mind just how many people have suffered because of their brutal and deadly actions. And for what? What good came from it?" Shari unfolded the Kleenex in her hands and dried her eyes.

Echo's heart ached for the young woman. She, too, knew the absolute wastefulness of murder. Unlike Shari, who appeared more saddened than anything, Echo could feel her indignation rise.

"Daniel picked me up at about 12:30 p.m., that last day in his orange 1969 Pontiac GTO, Judge, and we went to lunch. It was awesome cruising Route 66 in that car. It was the cream of the crop for muscle cars back then and to be sure, we got a lot of approving glances."

"Danny worked and saved what he could for a down payment. After he was murdered, Dallas kept up the payments and eventually paid it off but he never drove it. Not one time, ever. I know he and his wife still have that car stored in the pole barn at the corner of their property, covered and protected for all these years."

"Anyway, at lunch, Daniel ordered four corndogs, an order of fries and a large coke. And I had a corndog with a cherry coke."

"Daniel loved those dogs. He could eat a dozen of them, I swear. He would load them with mustard on one side and catsup on the other so he'd have a taste of each condiment in every bite. I can still see him sitting in that booth smiling broadly, and my heart aches all over again, for him, for me, for his family, friends and the dreams we shared."

"I can remember very little of what we talked about although God knows I've tried to hold and cherish every moment of that final day in my heart. It seems it was the usual playful banter Daniel was good at. He was the proverbial clown and always made me laugh; sometimes until my sides hurt."

"I do recall a solemn moment from that afternoon. It happened after we finished eating and were sitting back finishing our sodas. Out of the blue, Daniel seemed to turn subdued, and it struck me as odd."

"He said, "Shari, do you know how much you mean to me?" Danny was so serious that it completely altered the jovial mood of just moments before."

"Yes, I think I know," I responded, wondering where he was going to take this. It wasn't so much what he said, but rather the way he said it. It seemed so inappropriate at that moment. I mean, to go from laughing, painting pictures on his plate with catsup and mustard while using a French fry for a paintbrush, to such a shift in his disposition. It surprised me."

"He said, "Do you, because it's important that you understand just how grateful I am to have you in my life. I've even thanked God that your father accepted the job offer that moved you here our freshman year. Had that not happened I would never have met you."

"I responded in all sincerity, "I do understand, Danny, and I feel the same about you. He took my hand and squeezed it lightly. "Then promise me that no matter what happens you will always remember the love and friendship we share at this moment."

"So, I told him straightforward, Daniel, I'm not likely ever to forget. And we have an entire lifetime in which to grow that love and friendship. We're like two peas in a pod, and we'll always remain that way. He nodded his head when I said that and a smile crossed his face. But I still wonder about that conversation to this day."

"Did he have a premonition of what was to come in a few short hours? Did he need reassured that I would never forget him? He was so solemn; as if he knew. Maybe the Lord showed him, I don't know. Certainly, it's torture not knowing Daniel's mindset at that moment, and time passage has granted no reprieve."

"Afterwards, we went downtown to Sears to buy his mother a Christmas gift. It was an easy task because all she ever wanted was a bottle of Cierra perfume. It was her favorite, and Daniel purchased it for her every Christmas."

"By this time, Daniel had returned to his normal self; joking, laughing, cutting up and clowning around. He'd leave me bent over in stitches; laughing so hard tears streamed down my face."

"He was doing his best John Wayne impression on the sales clerk behind the perfume counter. However, he was lousy at impersonations and the sales clerk looked at him as if she had some crazy lunatic on her hands. I can still conjure that picture in my mind of her curled upper lip and tilted head as she struggled to understand the incorrigible customer. We had so much fun that day."

In an instant, Shari's smile faded into a grimace with every heart-stabbing recall. Patrick put his arm around her in an effort to comfort his distraught wife. His own eyes were now teary and moist.

"It's hard on Shari and me to recall the precious moments we spent with Danny. They're so intimate and personal and all we have left of him." Patrick focused on a spot on the floor to camouflage his reddening eyes.

"I'm so sorry for your loss, and I truly understand how you feel. The memories of my brother are all I have left of him as well. And only heaven proffers amnesty." Even the walls seemed to feel the sorrow in the room.

Don looked at the two ladies compassionately but was rendered helpless to ease their grief. He understood the danger of revisiting the past and stirring old and painful memories. Patrick stood but remained otherwise motionless.

"Patrick and I are sorry for your loss as well, Echo. Even after all these years you seem to wear the pain on your sleeve. I never had a brother in Vietnam myself. But no matter where violence and death happen, -- be it at a service station, or in the service of an incompetently executed war, -- the outcome is always the same."

Shari's sincerity was evident. "You know, it's strange how just one brutal act can change the course of a person's entire life forever. Sometimes it happens at the speed of light."

CHAPTER 32
The Right to Appeal
1970

On that same Monday, an informational hearing was held. Steven James and his father were taken to the court room of Judge Terese E. Cato by the sheriff of Macay County.

"This hearing is to inform you that you are being charged with the crime of armed robbery. Do you have a copy of the information detailing those charges?"

Both suspects responded in unison, "Yes."

"You have a right to trial by jury and to a preliminary hearing. You have a right to bail and a right to counsel at the time of arraignment. If you are found indigent and cannot afford an attorney, one will be selected for you. Bail is fixed at $6000 each." Cato brought her gavel down and adjourned court.

Neither of the Jameses could afford to post bail, and both were taken to their new digs at the Macay County Jail and placed in separate cell blocks. Steven James never received those saxophone lessons he was to begin that Monday. Instead, a grand jury was impaneled to determine whether there was enough evidence to bring an indictment against him and his father.

* * *

On Tuesday, the Sturnus County Chief Investigator, accompanied by his top Detective, Lewis Morell, arrived in Durham at 2 p.m.

They went directly to the Macay County Jail where the Jameses were transferred after their court appearance on Monday. The officers entered a small conference room that was set up for them. Steven was brought in.

"Are you married, Steve?"

"Yeah, but I'm in the process of getting a divorce."

Don had one more question he wanted to ask. He hoped it would have just enough punch to get under Steven's skin, causing stress and anxiety to rise in the suspect. He hoped to observe even the slightest reaction to confirm what he believed to be true. Don's question was built solely on a hunch, based on Herschel Johnson's word alone.

"Mr. James, can you tell me what happened to the twelve-gauge shotgun you took from the Vernon Texaco Station the morning you robbed it and murdered the attendant?"

Steven let out an audible, "Oh my God." His jaw tightened. He rubbed his temples with his visibly shaky hands. Sweat beads were developing on his forehead and upper lip.

"This is ridiculous. I don't know anything about a shotgun. And I told you before that I didn't murder anyone. So, why do you continue to ask me stupid questions like this? Are you trying to wear me down with this harassment, so I'll confess to something I didn't do? I wasn't there. You got it?"

Don felt satisfied to have provoked the reaction he witnessed. He had definitely hit a nerve. Now he knew he was on to something. "Okay then, that'll be all, sir."

Don planted seed for thought, and he hoped Steven would do a whole lot of thinking in the days ahead; wondering just what it was the Sheriff's Department of Sturnus County knew.

* * *

The Macay County Grand Jury returned 16 true bills of armed robbery and presented them to Judge Cato who convened the arraignment the next morning.

"Mr. Russell James, approach the bench, please. Do you have an attorney present or will you be retaining one?"

"No, ma'am, I can't afford an attorney, and I'd like the court to appoint one for me."

Judge Cato, seeing the defendant hadn't filled out an Affidavit of Indigence, assigned a deputy clerk to assist Russell in doing so. Meantime, the court would move forward and appoint an attorney for him but Cato made it clear that the attorney would be relieved if the Affidavit didn't support his claim.

The judge then handed a copy of the indictment to the bailiff and asked him to hand-pass it to Clay Slaughter, the Public Defender, standing at the defendant's table. "As to that charge of armed robbery, Mr. Slaughter, what is the defendant's plea?"

"Not guilty, your honor."

"All right. The record shall so reflect."

Judge Cato looked at the desk calendar in front of her and slotted the case for jury trial on February 16 at 9:30 a.m. When finished, she was prepared to accept all prosecution and defense motions.

Samuel Searcy, Assistant State's Attorney filed a request for Notice of Alibi Defense on behalf of the prosecution. The defense filed a motion for a list of all witnesses and to produce any confessions.

Judge Cato ordered the people to answer the defense motion within ten days. Likewise, she ordered any other pretrial motions to be filed before February 1."

With nothing further, Cato asked the elder James to return to his seat and proceeded to call Steven before the bench where the procedure was repeated with him. When asked, he too pleaded not guilty.

***

On February 2, the Court was petitioned by the public defender to determine Russell's competency.

Judge Cato suggested using a Durham psychiatrist since it would be easier to transport the accused locally, rather than having to take the defendant into Starling. A no-nonsense judge, Cato didn't like wasting time. The case was set for trial two weeks hence, and she wasn't about to change the date. But Slaughter insisted.

"Your honor, we prefer Doctor Bernard Sheridan of Starling rather than a local psychiatrist because he does the testing that is needed. This doctor is familiar with Russell James' psychiatric history."

Cato let out an audible sigh. "Are there any objections, Mr. Searcy?"

"No, your honor"

"Alright, but I am not changing the trial date. Let the record show Doctor Bernard Sheridan is appointed to examine Russell James and he is ordered to submit his report to the Court."

***

Russell was taken from the Macay County jail and driven to the psychiatrist's office. He was given a battery of psychological tests. He obtained an IQ rating of ninety, placing him at the bottom of the average range of intelligence. The doctor saw no indication of a schizophrenia. He did believe; however, that Russell manipulated his answers to make the results veer in the direction he wanted. His scores at those times went over the top.

In his report to the court, Dr. Sheridan found the patient has a psychopathic personality with depression; lacking remorse and empathy. He said the patient's responses were typical of this type of personality.

"He is a manipulator. He is audacious and is quite egotistical. He understands the nature and purpose of the proceedings against him and is able to assist in his defense."

Dr. Sheridan further wrote in his report. "Russell James' psychiatric involvement began in 1965 when he came to my office, and I prescribed medication for depression. In 1967, I recommended he be placed in Hope Memorial Hospital for six weeks to be given electroshock therapies."

"However, he didn't seem to improve at that time, and I had him transferred to a state hospital in Jacksonville. He was there for three days and wanted to leave. I told him that if he left, he was doing so against my medical advice. Still, he checked out, but continued his regular visits to my office until September 1969."

"During that period, he told me that various and strange peculiarities were happening to him. He claimed blackout spells, depression, trances and sundry of other things. Then, during the last part of 1969, Mrs. James asked me to examine her husband at the

Sturnus County jail. He was put there on a drunk and disorderly reported to the police by his son, Geoff."

"When I arrived at the jail, the patient was highly agitated and, I determined, was sick enough to be admitted to a State Hospital. He signed the papers for admittance, but he never followed through. His wife bailed him out of jail and that was the last time I saw him until today."

"He relayed to me that sometime in November he applied for voluntary admittance into the Veteran's Hospital in Danville. He told me he was having re-occurring chronic depression along with what he described as a 'stupor.' He told me the only reason he robbed Ryan's Jewelry Store was so that his family would have some money while he was at the veteran's hospital."

"I don't believe that's true. He is a manipulator and a poor actor as well. I feel that if he did make application to enter a veteran's hospital, it was for only one purpose; to cover his tracks in a robbery in case he was caught."

Dr. Sheridan's report further stated that if he was called to appear at trial, his testimony would reflect that of his report.

Having read the Doctor's statement, Russell directed his attorney to withdraw his request for a jury determination of competency. A new motion was entered to withdraw his not guilty plea. Russell wanted, instead, to plead guilty to the crime of armed robbery as charged in the indictment.

Judge Cato explained the consequences of such a plea and made certain the defendant understood he had a right to a trial by jury. Still, Russell insisted on pleading guilty anyway.

Steven James then followed suit.

The guilty pleas were accepted by the court, and the defendants signed waivers giving up their right to a jury trial.

Steven filed a petition for probation, and Judge Cato referred it to the Probation Office for investigation. She would delay his sentencing until the probation officer could consider and file his report back with the court.

Russell, however, stood ready for his punishment. He waived his right to present any mitigating evidence, and the State's Attorney waived the people's right to present aggravation evidence. With nothing further, the judge sentenced Russell on the spot.

"Defendant Russell James is sentenced to the State

Penitentiary for an indeterminable term of not less than four years minimum and not more than fifteen years maximum imprisonment, or until otherwise discharged through the legal process."

"The defendant is remanded to the Sheriff of Macay County with instruction to deliver him to the Department of Corrections to carry out this sentence. You have the right to appeal."

Russell stood stoically throughout. If being sentenced to prison for the first time in his life caused the little guy to become fearful; his face never showed any evidence of it.

CHAPTER 33
The Bitter Price of Unfulfilled Dreams
1996

"Patrick and I attended the trial every day and sat with Danny's father. Dallas was in the service stationed in San Diego and couldn't attend. His mother chose not to."

"Janice didn't want to hear the forensic testimony or see the graphic pictures shown to the jury. She didn't want the memory of Danny lying dead to assail her senses in the years to come."

"She would call me every night, and we'd talk about the murderers. I would fixate on their appearance, what they did or what they said and how they reacted to each bit of testimony proffered. I was preoccupied with it as if their image, mannerisms, and words might lend an explanation for their inhumane act. I kept trying to comprehend how two ordinary looking people appearing mentally competent, could do such a thing. I searched every inch of them looking for horns, fanged teeth and flesh-tearing claws, anything to show their true nature. But they looked like everyone else."

Echo nodded her head with understanding.

"Had it been a crime of passion, hatred, love, whatever, I think I could have at least understood something like that. A person in a marital argument, for example, loses his temper and in one fell swoop the violent act is done and there's no going back. But that didn't happen here. These men didn't know Daniel."

"They snuffed out the life of a complete stranger, -- someone who had never caused them harm, -- and for a measly $500 dollars. Why? I asked myself over and over again. What kind of animal does that? No, my apology to the animals, for they take care of their own."

"So, for me, not counting the loss of Daniel and all the grief and suffering since, it was the agonizing 'whys' that persisted long after the trial was over."

"I couldn't comprehend the murder, knew in my heart it didn't have to be. I mean, if they wanted to rob the station, why not cover their faces so they're unrecognizable and rob the station."

"Why end a life that will ultimately cause forfeiture of theirs when caught? It just doesn't make any sense. Daniel, me, Daniel's family, his friends, the murderers and their family; all lives altered and for what? Why? Why did they have to do it?"

Shari grabbed a Kleenex and daubed her eyes again. Echo lowered her head as her heart filled with sadness. For she understood all too well the anguish of the 'why's' that will never be answered.

"Why couldn't they have tied Danny up, taped his mouth so he couldn't holler, grab the money and simply flee the scene. Why did they have to take him from us?"

"The suddenness and the finality almost took my breath away. I had no chance to say goodbye. All that was left was the longing to go back and somehow reverse the tragedy but with no recourse or power to do so."

"Eventually, I came to realize that I was dedicating all my thoughts, energy and attention to the two murderers while Danny was ebbing into the recesses of my mind. So, I made a conscious effort to ban the killers from my brain. I wanted only to concentrate on the good, on Danny, and cleave to the memories I had of him. After all, who cares to waste a moment on them when Danny was lost to us forever."

"I tried desperately to repress the memory of the method in which his death occurred and to grieve instead for the loss of Danny's love, and the dreams that will never be fulfilled. I guess I handled the situation the same way I chose to handle my diagnosis of breast cancer ten years back. I pursued treatment like a dog after a bone. I wasn't cavalier. I understood the seriousness of the predicament I was in and I devoted all my thoughts, prayers and energy to healing."

"I resolutely refused to give the disease a place in my life. Just because it had infiltrated my breast, I saw no reason to turn the rest of me over to it. I avoided referring to it in possessive terms, such as 'my', 'I have', or 'I'm sick' with cancer. It was my way of fighting the condition with everything I could muster without acknowledging the disease itself."

"And that's what I did with the murder of Daniel. I grieved his loss and suffered his absence with excruciating pain. But I refused to give the two sickening cells that caused his death a place inside myself. Only Daniel belonged in my heart. There was no space left in me for them."

"You know, I lost my faith for a moment, and I never thought I would ever be happy again. It was hard but I had to arrive at a place where I could acknowledge and accept the reality that Danny was dead. I didn't want to carry the pain for the rest of my life. I had to come to terms and adjust to a life without him. I believe having my daughter helped me to do that."

"There was new life ushering in; a happy and fulfilling time. We named her Danicka! She has the first three letters of Daniel's name and the last three letters of her father's name. The letter "a" at the end is added for gender."

"And as I watched her grow over the years I often envisioned Daniel in that cloud of witnesses looking down from heaven watching over and cheering on his namesake. And that has always made me happy."

"Thank you for sharing that with me, Shari. But remember, he's in that cloud watching and cheering you and Patrick on, too."

Shari smiled at the thought. "Would anyone like more coffee?"

"Oh, no thank you. We really must be leaving."

Don stood as if on cue.

Echo smiled affectionally. "Thank you so much for your hospitality. I feel I've gained two new friends today."

"Likewise," Shari responded. She reached out to hug the much shorter Echo and had to bend over to accomplish it.

"My goodness, you're no bigger than a minute!"

Echo chuckled. "Yes, I'm still waiting for my final growth spurt."

As Shari walked her guests out to Don's car parked on the driveway, the two made a vow to stay in touch. Echo couldn't help but feel the entire gamut of Shari's loss and the bitter price of dreams unfulfilled.

CHAPTER 34
Like a Deer in the Headlights
1970

The court was dismissed and the defendants were taken back to the Macay County Jail. Russell needn't have concerned himself with the possibility of being immediately placed in a penitentiary.

Sturnus County had a hold order on both the father and son. When the time was right, Don planned to take the duo back to Starling where the State's Attorney would charge them with armed robbery and the first-degree murder of Daniel Sycamore.

In a few hours, Sergeant DeLario and Lewis Morell arrived at the jail. Making the trip over with them was a young black man. He sat quietly in the back seat, speaking only when spoken to for the entire thirty-minute duration of the trip. Steven James would be interrogated for nearly three hours. This time the officers had a little surprise for him.

Don removed glossy black and white pictures of the crime scene from a manila envelope. Intentionally slow and systematic, he spread them one at a time, before the young suspect.

"Would you care to take a look at these pictures, Mr. James?"

Don spoke in a tone of voice dripping with disgust at the sight of young Daniel's lifeless body sprawled out on the concrete floor. The pictures were stark and gruesome depicting a river of crimson, Daniel's own life's blood, leaving his body and streaming to the drain on the floor beside him.

There was silence in the room. The two law enforcement officers glued their eyes upon the suspect, watching intently as they witnessed all the color drain from the young man's face.

Steven sat grimacing at the carnage sprawled out before him. He stared, apparently mortified by his own actions of recent days past, transfixed by recollections the snapshots evoked.

He pushed the gruesome pictures across the table toward Don. He either would not or could not look at them any longer.

Steven's hands were visibly shaking.

"I'm going to tell you right now, I don't know anything about the murder at that gas station, and you're not going to pin it on me. I wasn't there!"

Once again, Don could see Steven beginning to sweat. His countenance took on that of a trapped and caged animal. His jaw was tightened and fixed. His eyes were wide with fear as if he were expecting a death blow at any moment.

"Steve, do you know a boy by the name of Herschel Johnson?"

"Yes, I do."

Steven flashed a surprised look across his face. Don rose from the table and walked over to the door. He motioned to someone standing in the hall and opened the door wider so he could enter the room.

"Steven, do you recognize this man as Herschel Johnson?"

"Yes, that's Hersch."

"Did you give Mr. Johnson a shotgun back in December?"

"Yes, I did."

"Alright, Mr. Johnson, that's all for now. If you'll take a seat out in the hallway there, please."

Herschel reached for the door knob and took one more look back at Steven before exiting the room.

"Steve, I asked you yesterday what you did with that shotgun. Now, we both know that you passed it along to Herschel. Will you tell us, sir, how that shotgun ended up in your possession in the first place?"

The suspect didn't answer. He stared at the floor, fraught with worry. The smell of his own fear infused his nostrils.

Don plunged forward, feeling confident the suspect was teetering on the precipice of a confession. The detective could feel it in his bones. The young James boy was just moments from spilling the beans.

When Don again spoke, he made sure his voice took on a more ominous and intimidating tone.

"Steve, we've traced that shotgun back to you. To go back any further with it, we'd end up at the Harlan Vernon Texaco in Glenrose where we'd find it standing behind the door of the storage room; because that's where you first saw it. You picked it up, shot the attendant and took it with you when you fled the scene."

Steven's voice quivered out his denial. "No, that isn't true!"

"You better tell us where you got it then because if you don't, you're going down for this murder!"

Don couldn't have known at the time that the crime lab in Joliet was but a few days away from tying the revolver, recovered from the basement of the Andre Tinsley residence, to the murder scene as well.

"We're not playing games here, Steve. We've got you dead to rights with that shotgun and you know it!"

Still, the suspect did not respond. His jaw clenched as if he was grinding his teeth. The detectives could envision the wheels turning in his brain. Surely, he was plotting a story he hoped would get him out of the mess he was in.

"Look, Steve, I'll tell you what I'll do for you. If you cooperate with us, tell us what you know about that weapon, I will make a promise to you right now that I will do all I can to verify the veracity of your statement. I'll follow every lead, look in every nook and cranny, go above and beyond to give you every impartial consideration. You will have the benefit of my twenty-years' experience. But you are going to have to tell us everything you know about that weapon first."

"Alright, I'll tell you everything I know about that shotgun. But I just can't do it right now. My head is pounding, and my stomach feels like there's a war going on inside it. We'll have to do this later. I just don't feel well. I think I have the flu. You need to understand one thing, though. I didn't commit that murder. I wasn't there. The only reason I didn't tell you about the shotgun before is because I was told the gun was hot."

Don didn't want to end the questioning. He believed Steven was ready to crack but didn't want to press the suspect into invoking his right to have an attorney present during questioning. He was grateful the Jameses were separated and couldn't compare notes.

"Okay Steve, we'll bring the secretary from the State's Attorney's office over with us tomorrow. She will take down the statement you have volunteered to give us about that shotgun."

Don walked over to the door and stepped out into the hall to signal the guard to escort Steven back to his cell. Herschel nodded as the two made eye contact before Steven was taken away. Just moments before, Herschel had successfully found a vending machine and sat waiting to be taken back to Starling with a Coca Cola in his hand.

Morell and DeLario walked toward the office of the Macay County Sheriff where their winter jackets were hanging on a coat rack. Don was clearly disappointed. "I thought we had him for a moment, Lew. I worried he'd invoke his right to counsel. At least this way we'll get another shot at him. Tomorrow will roll around soon enough. Maybe he'll sing then. In the meantime, that young man out there has been sitting for hours. What do you say we take him to the Wits End for a hamburger? He has to be hungry by now, and then I must get back to the office to finish a few things."

A hamburger sounded good to Lew who was beginning to feel the day's first hunger pangs. "Yes, I could stand to eat something myself."

Don removed his coat off the rack and Lewis followed suit. They exited the sheriff's office and Morell turned out the light.

* * *

At 8:30 a.m. the next morning, a Sturnus County deputy knocked on the door of the James' residence. "Hello young man, may I speak to Mrs. Russell James, please?"

"Just a minute." Geoff raced into the kitchen where Margaret was preparing breakfast for herself and the children that Saturday morning. "Mom, there's a Starling cop at the front door."

Margaret's heart began to pound. "Good Lord, now what's happened?" She picked up a kitchen towel and dried her hands. Nervously, she made her way to the front door where the officer waited.

"Won't you come in from the cold, sir?" Margaret stepped aside to allow the officer to enter.

"Okay kids, I want you to go upstairs to your rooms to play, and I'll call you for breakfast in just a few minutes."

Bryce and Michelle protested audibly. Bryce complained, "No, I don't want to." Melissa followed his lead. "I don't either. I'm hungry."

Fortunately, Geoff intervened.

"You two better get yourselves up those steps and do what your mother told you or I'm going to see to it that you don't come out of your rooms for the rest of the day." As he approached the children, they scurried off in a mad dash for the stairs.

"I'm sorry for the interruption, officer. Now, what can I do for you?"

Margaret seemed to hold her breath for a moment, not knowing what part of the sky was going to fall this time. Geoff came over and stood beside his mother.

"Oh, that's all right, ma'am. Those are a couple of good-looking children you have there."

Margaret remained polite while retaining that apprehensive worried look on her face. "Well thank you, officer."

"Mrs. James, Sergeant DeLario asked me to stop by to inquire if you would like to ride over to Durham with him around 11 a.m., to see your husband and son. Mr. James informed Sergeant DeLario that you didn't have transportation."

"Oh, yes I would like that very much!"

"Alright ma'am, I'll let him know to pick you up."

The deputy stepped back onto the front porch, exited the steps and walked over to his squad car parked on the driveway. Margaret returned to the kitchen.

Geoff wanted desperately to see his father. "Can I go too, Mom?"

She placed her hand on Geoff's shoulder. "I don't think so, honey. I really need you to watch the children while I'm gone. Kids, come on down. Your breakfast is ready, and it's getting cold."

Margaret looked at her second-born son sheepishly, and winked. "Oh, my goodness. Geoff, is there a herd of elephants in this house?"

"No, that was just Bryce and Melissa running down the stairs; knowing they're not supposed to."

"Those two little dainty things causing that entire racket?" Margaret sounded shocked while placing both hands on her hips. Melissa and Bryce roared. Their mother's reaction was the funniest thing they ever saw.

After breakfast, Margaret went to shower and dress. She opened the closet and retrieved her winter coat and placed it over a chair in the living room by the front door. The time was now after 11a.m. She took a seat in the living room where she could look out the window. At 11:20 a.m., an unmarked Sheriff's car pulled into the driveway. Margaret stood, put on her coat and kissed the children before heading out the front door.

Don got out of the driver's seat and opened the rear driver-side door for Margaret. Lewis Morell sat in the front passenger seat. Betty Rapps, a legal stenographer with the District Attorney's office, sat in the back seat behind him. When Margaret entered the car, the ladies exchanged cordial hellos but did not speak beyond that.

The car pulled up at the Macay County jail just in time to see Bonnie James preparing to enter the station. The two James women didn't speak to one another. Steven and Bonnie were involved in a bitterly contentious divorce.

Steven was allowed to talk to his wife in the sheriff's office. Margaret was placed in a conference room where she would have to wait to see her husband and son. A female jailer searched her purse and patted her down before exiting the conference room. Margaret sat silently by herself; nervously fidgeting with her handkerchief.

Although she wasn't given a reason, Margaret James waited for approximately forty-five minutes before her husband was brought in to see her. Don led the suspect down a long corridor. He opened the door and stepped back into the hall, allowing the husband and wife about twenty minutes of privacy.

Margaret rose from the table and ran to Russell throwing her arms around him. She began to cry. Her world was shattering, and there was nothing she could do to stop it.

"How could anyone believe my husband and son were capable of such a horrible crime," she thought to herself as she clung tightly to the father of her children.

It would be several minutes before she allowed Russell to gently pull her from him and lead her back to the table where the two sat down. A considerably longer time would pass before Margaret would gain her composure.

Russell asked how she was doing and asked about their three youngest children.

"Are they holding up okay?"

"Geoff is having a bad time because all the kids at school are talking about the robbery, and now he thinks everybody's looking down their noses at him. It's terrible. He's hurting so bad, and I have no ability to make it better for him."

A compassionate woman, Margaret's heart was breaking for her children; more so than for herself. Russell reached for her hand and held it. She wiped the tears from her eyes and asked how he was and how their firstborn son was doing throughout all this.

"Well, I'll tell you one thing. I'm not doing any talking until I get an attorney. I just wish I could get the word to Steven that he shouldn't be doing any talking either!"

Russell could feel in his gut the full strength of the Sturnus County Sheriff's office tightening their grip around his neck. It was just a matter of time, he knew.

Don opened the door and stepped inside the room. "I'm sorry, your time has elapsed. You'll have to come with us now."

Russell put his arm around Margaret's waist, and the two walked out into the hallway. The convicted armed robber was taken back to his cell, and Margaret was escorted back into the conference room.

She would wait another forty-five minutes before the jailer brought her eldest child in to see her. The officers from Sturnus County wanted a word or two with Steven first. He waited for them in Sheriff Jason's office.

* * *

The time was 2:05 p.m. Betty was already seated at the table in the Sheriff's office. Her duty today was to take shorthand dictation of the suspect's statement, transcribe and prepare an official document for Steven James' signature.

Don spoke slow and steady for Betty's sake.

"We have discussed with Steve James the details pertaining to a sawed-off shotgun. He has agreed to give a statement on how he came to have this shotgun in his possession, where and when he obtained it and from whom."

Don read the suspect his Maranda rights, and Steven affirmed that he understood what was read to him.

"Betty, I will try to remember to speak slowly for you and

Mr. James, I'll ask that you try to be aware of Ms. Rapps' efforts to take down your spoken word and speak as clear and steady as you can, please, sir."

"This is Sergeant Don DeLario, Badge #3657, in the Macay County Sheriff's Office. I'm here with Detective Lewis Morell, Badge #2762, Ms. Betty Rapps, a stenographer in the DA's office and with Mr. Steven Wilbur James."

"Steve, at this time do you wish to give us a statement concerning your knowledge of this weapon?"

"Yes."

"Would you tell us please, all the details leading up to and after that weapon came into your possession? Dates, times and circumstances will be most appreciated. Just start at the beginning and take us right through the time you gave it to Herschel. Whenever you're ready, sir, just go ahead."

"My father and I went to St. Louis in the late afternoon, around four or five, on December 18. I believe that would have been a Thursday. Anyway, we had two purposes in mind for going."

"I was in the service with this guy from Lovejoy who had a Pontiac Firebird for sale. We wanted to go down there to check out the car to possibly buy it from him. But we couldn't locate his house. Also, with the holiday just around the corner, we planned to do a little Christmas shopping the next day."

"So, since we couldn't find the house, we decided to check out some of the bars to see what kind of live music they had playing there that night. We had some drinks and were enjoying ourselves. And when the taverns closed, we picked up two bottles of wine from a liquor store and headed for East St. Louis and found a room at the Holiday Inn."

"I don't know why I did it but instead of using my own name, I registered under the name of Tom Middleton. He's this guy from the neighborhood we knew who was recently killed in Vietnam, back in October. He'd been on my mind in recent days with what happened to him and all. And so, I just used his name and his old address on Matheny Avenue when I signed the registration card. I did write down my correct license number, though, which would be on a 1969 plate BN 1124."

"I believe it was a few hours or so after the taverns closed that we checked into the hotel and we checked out around noon the next day. We left there and went to a restaurant to get something to eat. After that, we drove into downtown St. Louis which brings us up to the time when I first saw the shotgun."

"When we got to St. Louis, I drove onto Market Street down there by the Arch. I parked the car, and my father plugged the two-hour meter. We started walking around, looking for some stores where we could Christmas shop. I'm not sure which street we ended up on but it wasn't too far from where we parked. Well, like they say it's a 'small world,' because I ran into Jesse Harris. He's this fellow I was stationed with in Granite City in the early part of 1969. We both said how good it was to see one another again."

"Anyway, when I was talking with him, I was approached by another fellow that identified himself as Bud, who said that we went through basic training at Fort Leonard Wood together."

"Harris began to walk away, but he was still approximately ten feet from us and I am sure, in all probability, he would be able to identify Bud. Anyway, I really didn't recognize the guy. He looked completely unfamiliar to me, so I can't say that I knew him. I mean, after all, there was just so many people on that military base."

"So, he approaches me and says, "Hi, Red," and asked me if I remembered him. I said, Yes, I believe so," just trying to be friendly. During the conversation, he asked if I wanted to buy a shotgun. I told him no because I didn't have any reason for one."

"He said I could buy this one cheap at forty dollars. I told him I didn't have that much money and that's when he said, "Well, the shotgun is hot, so I'll sell it to you for $15. That's when I agreed to buy it."

"We walked over to his car, a 1965 white Pontiac Grand Prix coupe that was parked just across the street from where we were standing, and he took it out of the trunk. He placed it under his trench coat, and we walked over to my car that was parked about two and one-half blocks away. I unlocked the trunk for him, and he placed the shotgun inside."

"I gave him the money for it, we shook hands and my father and I finished our shopping. I bought a pair of shoes, a shirt or two, and a couple of forty-five records. I believe my father bought a couple of shirts for himself."

Don DeLario's interest suddenly piqued, recalling the cat's

paw print that had been planted on the storage room door.

"Steve, do you remember if you would have worn those new shoes back home? And if so, what did you do with the old pair?"

"I wore the new shoes home and threw the old ones in a dumpster in St. Louis because my old pair lost a heel. I remember I didn't wear any of the shirts, though, until we came home. It was in the earlier part of the evening that we drove back to Starling; I would say approximately 6 o'clock."

Don looked at Lewis. Both men believed they now knew who put the print on the storage room door but they would never be able to prove it.

"When we got home, I wrapped the shotgun in a dirty old blanket and placed it up in the rafters in the garage."

"Then, on December 26 when my father, Hersch Johnson and I were sitting at the kitchen table after being at the Red Ruby, Hersch made the comment that he wanted to do some hunting. So, I went into the garage to retrieve the shotgun, a hacksaw, and a file."

"I sat down at the table and proceeded to cut off the double barrels. I don't know why I sawed them off, but I did. I handed it over to Hersch, and that's the last time I saw it."

"I know it's illegal to saw off the barrels of a shotgun, so if you want to charge me, I'll go ahead and plead guilty to that. But I will not plead guilty to a murder that I didn't commit."

"Steve, are you sure you didn't saw off those barrels so the weapon wouldn't be as easily identified?"

"No. That is not true! I don't know nothing about what went on at that station. I'm going to tell you for the last time, I wasn't there. And that's all I'm going to say on the matter."

"Okay, Steve. Now, everything you say in this statement that you have given us, you say is true and correct?"

"Yes, it is."

"Are you giving us this statement of your own free will?"

"Yes, I am."

"Do you acknowledge the only promise I've made to you is that I will do all I can to verify the truth of your statement; that I will go to St. Louis and try to locate the subject from whom you say you purchased the shotgun?"

"Yes, that's true," Steven responded.

* * *

The probation officer's report on Steven ordered by Judge Cato was now no more than wasted time and energy.

On the following Monday, Don, accompanied by Sheriff Roland, entered the Macay County jail. On this trip, though, they had no intention of questioning either of the admitted armed robbers. Now that the City of Durham had completed their proceedings against the two men, they turned the father and son over to law enforcement officers from Sturnus County.

All of the transfer papers had been prepared earlier that morning. Don signed the documents, and the prisoners were taken to the waiting squad car. The two didn't speak to one another. Their hands were secured behind their backs by a set of handcuffs.

The Jameses were on their way back home to Starling but not to the house on 12th and Miller Streets.

They were taken to the Sturnus County Jail on Jackson Street where they were booked on a charge of first-degree murder and armed robbery. The father and son were fingerprinted, and mug shots were taken.

They were searched and ordered to remove their civilian clothing. Jail-issued orange jumpsuits were provided for them. The processing took about forty-five minutes to complete.

Father and son were separated and placed in different cell blocks. Over the weeks and months that followed, Steven would find a friend and confidante in someone that shared the same cell block with him. His name was Ricky Carpenter.

CHAPTER 35
Sins of his Father
1996

Echo had just returned from church that Sunday when the telephone rang. She had changed from her dress and quickly pulled up her jeans before answering the ring. The caller was Geoff James.

"They've scheduled my father's clemency hearing for this Thursday at 9 a.m., at the James R. Thompson Center in Chicago."

"Oh, good. I was beginning to think the Governor had forgotten all about it."

Echo was genuinely surprised by Geoff's phone call. She thought she would never hear from him again after the altercation with his father. However, it soon became apparent that Russell hadn't spoken to Geoff about it, and she was grateful for that. Otherwise, she might not have received the call to learn the date and time of the hearing.

Echo wanted to attend and looked forward to seeing the odyssey through to its final conclusion. She believed if clemency wasn't granted, then Russell's chances of dying in prison were pretty much assured. She was curious as to what had brought the clemency matter to the forefront in the first place. So, she asked Geoff for an explanation.

"There's a group of law students who have taken on a project started by a University of Chicago law professor. The Aging Convict Program," Geoff said, "is a support group for older inmates who cost more to incarcerate, largely for health care reasons, and who, because of their age, are at a lower risk for committing new crimes."

"My father received an indeterminate sentence. His incarceration length was to fall between the minimum and maximum parameters with the parole board making the determination on the length of incarceration. The inmate is at the board's mercy."

"It's unfair to keep these people in a sort of limbo not

knowing when or if ever they're going to be released. An indeterminate sentence has no light at the end of the tunnel; it comes down to an issue of fairness."

"Today, there are over six-hundred inmates with similar sentences in the prison system. They are all C-numbered."

"The Walnut Justice Center from which the law students are affiliated, looked into the records of the C-numbered inmates and found seven prisoners they felt were excellent candidates for executive clemency due to age and prison records."

"My dad was one of them. The seven men are all convicted murderers, ranging in age from sixty-five years to seventy-three years. Most have been behind bars since the early to mid-1970s. My dad, as you know, was convicted in June 1970."

* * *

Echo reached for the phone and placed a call to directory assistance and received the phone number of the Bismarck Hotel. Geoff told her he would be staying there because of its proximity to the Thompson Center on Randolph Street.

"Would you like to ride up with me?" he asked, but Echo declined.

She told him that her niece, Jennifer Kiddy, was visiting from Seattle. "We might want to shop after the hearing and may stay over until Friday."

The animosity between Russell and Echo created a fission. And with Geoff unaware of it, she felt most uncomfortable without full disclosure. Echo certainly didn't want to be the one to tell him. After all, blood is thicker than water and she could stand to lose.

Echo was glad Jennifer was back visiting and would accompany her to the Windy City. She could legitimately offer Jennifer's presence as her excuse for not riding up with Geoff.

Echo made reservations for the two of them. She planned to arrive in Chicago while it was still light in order to do a little window shopping along the Magnificent Mile.

She hurried home from work that Wednesday and loaded the car. The sun was shining brightly, and the temperature was warm. It was a perfect day for a long drive. Jennifer had her bag packed and was ready to go.

Echo tossed her car keys to her niece and climbed into the passenger seat. "How would you like to drive my car?"

"Sure, you know I would." Jennifer jumped into the driver's seat before her aunt had a chance to change her mind.

When they eased onto the highway, Echo proceeded to tell her the long story of her connection to both parties in this sad and tragic case. She shared with Jennifer that she had written a letter to the Governor on Russell James' behalf.

"I did it for Tom because I think he would have done the same, had he been called by Geoff. I tried to convey what he might have said, had he been able to."

Jennifer was curious, not knowing what to expect. "I've never been to anything like this before. Will we have to stand and say something?"

Echo tried to assure her. "Neither have I, but we will be observers, nothing more. It won't be our place to speak. All we'll do is sit back and listen to those that do. You needn't concern yourself about that."

Echo turned her head toward the passenger window and lowered the back rest on the seat. It felt good to relax for a while. She'd been on the go since 5 a.m. She closed her eyes and thought how wonderful it was to have Jennifer with her. Always upbeat and fun, Echo hoped the seriousness of the hearing wouldn't put a damper on her bubbling personality or take the enjoyment out of her visit.

Echo told her they would have dinner at Carson's, and window shop on Michigan Avenue before turning in for the night. Jennifer, an avid shopper, would surely enjoy Water Tower, and Echo hoped it might help to ease the weightiness of their trip into the state's largest city.

Jennifer gently shook Echo's left arm. "Wake up, we're here."

Echo's eyes popped wide open, and she sat up in the seat, raised the backrest and looked around acclimating herself to the surroundings. "Jennifer, I'm sorry. I didn't mean to fall asleep like that."

"Oh, that's alright. But you have to tell me which way to go now."

"Start moving into the left lane. Randolph Street intersects at the next traffic light."

Jennifer navigated the left-hand turn, and two blocks later she pulled up to the curb in front of the Bismarck Hotel. Echo looked to the right and noticed the James R. Thompson Center at the corner of the block.

The parking valet opened Jennifer's door, and the women retrieved their backpacks and made their way inside. They checked in, put their bags inside the room and decided to take a walk. As they made their way through the lobby, Echo wondered if Geoff James had already arrived.

The ladies found themselves window shopping at Water Tower. As late afternoon approached, they headed over to Carson's on Orleans Street for dinner and arrived back at their hotel room around 8:45 p.m.

Echo looked to see if the message light on the telephone was flashing, thinking that Geoff might have called to see if they had arrived safely. He hadn't.

"Jennifer, would you like a drink from the vending machine?"

"Sure, I'll take the ice bucket with me, too."

Echo grabbed her purse and removed three dollars in change from her wallet. "I'll shower while you're gone so take the key with you."

Jennifer grabbed the swipe card and headed out the door, looking for a soda machine.

* * *

Echo emerged from the bathroom pajama clad, with a towel wrapped around her shampooed head.

Jennifer's eyes were wide with excitement! "You should have seen the guy at the soda machine."

Echo looked at her niece curiously and removed the towel from her wet hair. "Oh really, what about him?"

"I don't know, it was weird. He was standing there looking

at me funny-like."

"Well, what happened? Did he say or do anything?"

"No, it's just the way he was looking at me."

"Well did he scare you?"

"No, not at all. It was more like he wanted to speak but wasn't sure if he should or not. I don't know, maybe it was all in my head."

"Just so long as he didn't enter your personal space or put his hands on you. Right?"

"No, it wasn't like that. It was as if he thought he knew me but just wasn't quite sure."

Still, Echo knew there was no way that anyone in Chicago should know her niece. Jennifer was twenty-six years of age and had lived in Seattle for twenty-three of those years.

"Did he look familiar?"

"Oh no, I've never seen that guy before in my entire life." Jennifer was sure of that.

* * *

When morning rolled around, Echo and Jennifer climbed out of bed and prepared for the day. They went to the Medallion Room off the hotel lobby for a breakfast of eggs, ham, and toast before making their way up the block to the James R. Thompson Center.

The hearing would be held on the second floor. The duo walked up the steps, entered the hearing room and took seats in the back.

A long table stood in the front of the room and twelve men and women, who collectively formed the State's Prisoner Review Board, sat facing the gallery.

Another much smaller table with three chairs stood in front of the long one. The chairs at this table faced the board members. Attorneys from both sides would sit there as they pleaded their client's cases. A microphone sat perched on the smaller table.

The Prisoner Review Board consisted of one chairman and eleven members. There were nine men and three women, the majority of which were Caucasian, with the exception of one black male and one Latino male.

They were all highly educated professional people consisting of teachers, lawyers, journalists and government workers. The majority of them had extensive background work within the Department of Corrections.

Their homes are in Starling, Marion, Kankakee, Chicago and other towns across the state.

In the year before Russell James' clemency hearing, there were two-hundred-eighty-four petitions for clemency filed. Commutation to time served was granted in just five cases. Pardons were granted in forty-four cases, and the number of cases denied was one-hundred-eighty-four. By the end of the year, there were forty-six petitions for executive clemency pending.

Echo looked around for Geoff but didn't see him in the room that was filled to capacity. A gentleman sat directly in front of her, five rows up, and she thought that might be him, although she couldn't see his face. A woman who appeared to be an attorney with her legal briefcase sat next to the man.

The board chair, Mr. William Kettering, a retired police chief from Naperville, spoke for the group, welcoming everyone to the clemency hearing.

"Attorneys on both sides, for the limited time you have to speak here please refrain from reiterating what is stated in the documents and letters which the Board already has in their possession. Of course, this is your time, and you may go over all of it if you'd like, but I assure you, we have the files and all documents will be reviewed thoroughly. Just a brief summary is really all that is necessary. Now, without further delay, the Board will hear the first case." And with that, the hearing began.

Four cases were heard before the board took their first break. The first case was that of a sixty-eight-year-old, Cook County black man named Emory Allison, who murdered his wife of twenty-four years in a domestic violence dispute.

Then came the case of a seventy-three-year-old, Lake County, Caucasian named Heath Eggleston, who raped and murdered a young mother of two. Those children, now adults, were present and sat eagerly listening to the State Attorney's argument to keep their mother's killer behind bars. The attorney spoke of their pain and the anguish this hearing was causing them to experience all over again.

The third case was that of sixty-nine-year-old Caucasian, Andre Hoyt, from Cook County who robbed and beat to death a twenty-nine-year-old homeless man in a dark, dingy alley. The victim had been panhandling on Rush Street in Chicago. The metal cigar coffer that was recovered at the scene in the hands of the murderer, contained a whopping sum of fifteen dollars and thirty-seven cents.

The fourth case involved the kidnapping and murder of a ten-year-old Madison County school girl. Her body was found in a cornfield, but evidence was discovered in her killer's car. Blood and fingerprint analysis were indisputable and secured his conviction. The sixty-five-year-old Caucasian, Delbert McDevitt, a participator in the Neighborhood Watch program, lived in the same block as his victim. Like Russell, he was originally sentenced to death but his death sentence was overturned by the Supreme Court in 1972, and he was re-sentenced.

With the finish of the fourth case, a much needed thirty-minute break was taken. Jennifer and Echo left the room to grab chips and a drink from the cafeteria. Returning, they sat on the green metal folding chairs located outside the hearing room for the few minutes they had left.

The gentlemen that had been sitting five rows in front of Echo walked out of the room into the hallway and headed toward the restrooms. Jennifer recognized his face from the previous night.

"Oh, that's him. That's the guy from the soda machine at the hotel last night!" Echo looked as he passed by.

"That's Geoff James. He didn't see us sitting here, or he would have come over to say hello. We'll catch up with him on his way back inside."

The two ladies were still in the hallway when Geoff rounded a corner and began to make his way down the hall toward them. A smile of recognition lit his face as he walked straight up to Jennifer and extended his hand.

"You're the young lady at the soda machine last night."

She smiled cordially, extended her hand toward his and nodded in the affirmative.

"Hello, Geoff, it's good to see you. This is Jennifer, my niece. She's here from Seattle visiting her grandparents."

"Well, you certainly didn't have to tell me Jennifer is related to the Middleton family. You possess those strong Middleton traits, like all of your uncles and aunts. I recognized the similarity as soon as I saw you last night. I almost spoke, but you appeared leery, and I didn't want to frighten you. Still, I'd have bet money on who you were at that moment."

Jennifer smiled politely and sat back down in the green folding chair.

"It's good to see you again," Geoff said to Echo.

"How are you feeling about the way the Clemency hearings are going?" she asked.

"Oh, you can never tell about these things. I've been to a lot of parole hearings where I thought the board was going to rule in our favor but it never happened. So, I've given up trying to read their faces and body language. I've been wrong too many times in the past. I've learned to be patient and try not to second-guess them."

"Well, how long do you think it will take for the Governor to make his ruling?"

"First the Board will make its recommendation. Then your guess is as good as mine as to when we might get word of his decision. He has the final say, and there's no time frame he must adhere to."

"He will most likely review each case individually, which will take more time to complete than to review them under the same blanket. I've just made up my mind not to get myself worked up over it. We've already been warned by the attorneys not to raise our hopes because it's only a small percentage where the Governor has granted clemency. So, this could all be for naught. Still, I guess anything is possible."

"Looks like they're heading back inside now," Jennifer said, seeing some of the board members taking their seats at the long table in the front of the room.

She noticed, also, the attorneys from the Walnut Justice Center ushering inside. One of them went up to the smaller table. The party she was representing was the first one scheduled after the break.

"Excuse me," Geoff said cordially, "I must get back inside there."

Echo watched as he made his way up to the smaller table and sat next to the woman who was sitting beside him earlier. She and

Jennifer quickly entered the room and took new seats up front by the smaller desk, directly behind Geoff and the smartly dressed attorney. Echo wanted to hear clearly the conversation that would commence momentarily.

Attorney Stephanie Cohen, representing Russell James, spoke first. She talked about Russell's age of nearly seventy years, his glaucoma and his suffering from arthritis of the spine.

"Mr. James has spent twenty-six years in prison for the murder of Mr. Daniel Sycamore during a robbery at a service station in Sturnus County" she began.

"Now that's longer than most spend in prison for the same crime. But since he was sentenced under an old state law, he has no idea how long he must remain behind bars."

"Mr. James is deserving of release based on the length of time he has already served. In our opinion, he should have already been paroled years ago, especially when you take into consideration his clean institutional record over all these years."

"Additionally, older prisoners such as Mr. James cost more to care for and are statistically at a lower risk than other inmates for committing new crimes."

"Mr. Geoff James, Russell James' second-born son, will address you in a moment. But first I'd like to read a letter you already have in the file before you from a young lady who knew Mr. James before his imprisonment."

Echo sat, stunned, as the letter she wrote to the Governor was read before all present. Geoff failed to tell her it would be used at the hearing in this matter.

Maybe he just didn't know, she thought.

Russell wrote a letter to the board also but it wouldn't be read openly. In his letter, he said, "I'm so very sorry for what happened. I can't fathom that I had anything whatsoever to do with it, although I do take full responsibility for it."

"In 1969, I was in and out of a veteran's hospital suffering from deep bouts of depression. There's just so much that happened back then that I have no recollection of."

No one from the Sycamore family was present at the hearing but a slew of letters written by family, friends, and neighbors beseeched the Governor to stand strong on the side of justice for Daniel.

"Daniel isn't able to begin a new life. Why should Russell James be allowed to?" Much of the correspondence in Russell's file, conveyed the same sentiment that was found in Dally's letter.

Geoff James now addressed the board members. If he was nervous or fearful, he didn't show it. His voice remained strong and unwavering throughout.

"If my father should be granted clemency, he will come to live with me, my wife and our two children. We have a spare bedroom that is ready and waiting for him. We live in rural Sturnus County, approximately ten miles outside of Starling, and my wife has a huge vegetable garden that my dad will be of assistance with. We have chickens and two horses that need fed and cared for. So, he will be kept busy and he will be happy there. I can say with one-hundred percent certainty he will never hurt another human being ever again. I know this because it isn't in him any longer."

"I'm not attempting to minimize the crime, but truly my father has suffered, and he has served a prison term well beyond what today's standard deems reasonable. My father is in failing health, and he deserves a second chance. The person I am today is a direct result of what my father instilled in me before he took the life of an innocent young man. I just want my children to know their grandfather's love as I knew it; the love that's back inside him now."

"I certainly sympathize with the Sycamore family and all the pain they've had to endure. Keeping my father in prison isn't going to bring Daniel back. Unfortunately, there's just no way the effects of this crime can be reversed. All we can do is move forward and care for the living," he said.

"My father is alive but is withering away in a prison. He has served his time exceptionally, with no disciplinary marks on his record, and has earned your recommendation for clemency. Thank you for your attention."

Echo sat back in her chair. Her heart filled with compassion for Geoff. His love for his father was apparent in the words he spoke. For a moment, she wished she had the power to grant clemency. Not for Russell, but, rather, for Geoff, who had so richly forgiven his father yet was powerless to find a clemency to erase the pain of his father's absence for over twenty-six years of his life. It was another consequence of the sins of his father.

CHAPTER 36
We the Jury
1970

The Jameses were indicted by a Sturnus County Grand Jury on March 29, 1970, on six counts of murder of various degrees of intent and one count of armed robbery each. Jury selection began June 19.

Judge Wilbur Chambers informed the prospective jurors that the State intended to seek the death penalty. Many potential jurors stated they would not be able to pass that sentence due to various personal reasons. Several were excused because of their opposition to it.

After three full days; one lasting well into the evening, four women and eight men were selected to hear the case. Additionally, two females were chosen as alternates. The jury would be sequestered for the duration of the trial. The courtroom filled to capacity with spectators and news media. Defense Attorneys, Jenna Wells and Edward Aultech, had been secured by Margaret James to represent her husband and son.

Assistant state's attorneys, Hobart Richards, and Benson Bradley, represented the people.

In his opening statement, Hobart told the jury the State will prove that Daniel Sycamore was killed with an Iver-Johnson pistol owned by the defendants and was wounded by a New Elgin shotgun kept at the service station.

The prosecution built its case through the intensive investigative work of Sergeant DeLario and his team at the Sturnus County Sheriff's Office.

Testimony began Tuesday, June 23. Brian Redmond returned to Starling to attest to the grisly discovery he made in the early morning hours of December 19.

Then, Herschel Johnson took the stand to identify the weapons he saw in the James possession prior to and after the murder of Daniel Sycamore.

Herschel was adamant. "I know it's the same shotgun they gave me because if you look at the handle, you will see HVT. Those letters were right there in that exact spot when the Jameses gave that gun to me."

Jeremy Summer was sitting in the courtroom next to Harlan Vernon. He looked at his boss and gave a thumbs-up. "I could picture Danny placing the hangman's noose around the necks of those two scumbags with the identification of the letters he carved on that weapon. For me, it was the most satisfying testimony of the entire trial."

Harlan had to admit that the same thought had crossed his mind as well.

Herschel was excused from the witness stand, but before he exited the courtroom, he shot a quick glance at Steven and Russell James. The animosity the father and son felt for him at that moment was palpable.

Steven glared at his old friend, shooting daggers like torpedoes to assail the one whose damning testimony could hurt the defendants the most.

Russell sat scowling at the young man who had dined at his own supper table on far too many occasions to count. He wondered how he ever trusted the guy he now knew was wholly turning against him.

Russell fumed as he thought to himself. *He might just as well have shaved our heads and attached the electrodes, for all the good his testimony did for us.*

His abject ire couldn't be contained. As Herschel passed by the defense table on his way out of the courtroom, Russell was heard saying, "You'll get yours, you double-crossing, back-stabber!"

Susan Kingsley, Crime Laboratory Analyst with the State Bureau of Identification, was called to the stand after Herschel. The forty-two-year-old raven-haired portly woman had a Bachelor of Science Degree from the University of Illinois.

She was trained in the field of tool marks and firearms identification. Susan was no stranger to courtrooms, offering her expert testimony in hundreds of other cases. Her present duties included the examination and evaluation of evidence; particularly that of comparative microscopic analysis.

Hobart Richards walked up to the witness stand. "Ms.

Kingsley, will you tell us a little bit about your job responsibilities?"

"Basically, I attempt to ascertain if a particular bullet was fired from a particular weapon."

"How is that done?"

"I fire a weapon in the laboratory using standard bullets. Then I look at the bullets under a microscope to see if the weapon I used reproduces consistent markings on the bullets. If it does, then I will compare one of the laboratory test-fired bullets to the bullet in question. The striations, which is the patterns or markings on the test-fired bullet, must line up with the majority of striations on the evidence bullet. If there are sufficient similar markings, I will conclude the bullet in question was fired from the weapon."

* * *

The Iver Johnson revolver had been shipped to the crime laboratory in Joliet in January 1970, along with eight other recovered weapons. It was requested that Kingsley compare them with the two projectiles recovered from the Sycamore murder that she received three weeks earlier.

First, she examined all the weapons to determine if they were operable, making several test-fires for comparison.

The two bullets from the Sycamore murder had been logged and placed in the open file for future testing. Susan now retrieved them. One of the two had been removed from the plating between the walls at the Vernon Texaco service station; the other was taken from Daniel Sycamore's brain.

* * *

Hobart first questioned Susan about the projectile found on the plating between the walls at the station.

She determined it was a .38 caliber projectile whose nose was far too damaged for comparison. The striations were nearly wiped away, and it was impossible for her to make an identification of the firing gun.

Richards then asked about Kingsley's findings when comparing the test-fired bullets to the bullet removed from Daniel's brain.

She determined that this projectile contained five lands and grooves with a right-hand twist like the Iver-Johnson revolver. When she compared it to test bullets fired from the Iver-Johnson, she found matching striations. She concluded that this projectile was fired from the .38 caliber revolver in question."

"Did anyone else examine this projectile?"

"Yes, sir. I asked my manager to look at it under the microscope to verify the match; and he did so verify"

* * *

On June 24, the defense presented its case. "Ladies and gentlemen of the jury," Edward Aultech said, crossing the floor to the jury box to present his opening statement. "The evidence will show the defendants weren't in possession of the shotgun or revolver until December 23 1969. The evidence will also show that the defendants were in St. Louis in the early morning hours of December 19 and not in Glenrose committing a murder." When Aultech finished with the opening statement, Judge Chambers asked him to call his first witness.

"Your Honor, I would like to call the defendant, Steven James, to the stand." Don, who was in the courtroom, nudged the sheriff sitting next to him and whispered, "I've been waiting for a long time to hear this."

The sheriff chuckled. "It'll be interesting to hear. He's had some time to think up a good story."

Aultech retrieved the revolver and the New Elgin shotgun from the evidence table. He approached Steven. There was no question that both weapons had been used in the murder of Daniel Sycamore.

Handing the weapons to the witness, Aultech asked Steven if he ever saw them before, and if so, when and where and how they came to be in his possession?

"Yes, on the afternoon of December 23, in Chicago."

"Why were you in Chicago?"

"Leroy Drake asked me to give him a ride home. So, on December 22, we took him up there and spent the night. The next afternoon my dad and I were getting ready to head back to Starling. We piled into the car, and I started up the engine to get the heater going. Leroy told us not to take off yet because he had something that he wanted to show us. He ran back into the house, and we sat there until he came outside carrying the weapons."

"He asked me if I wanted them. I told him I wasn't buying because I didn't have any money, but Leroy placed the shotgun in the back seat of my car anyway and handed the pistol to my father. He said he wanted us to have both of them as payment for taking him home to Chicago."

"Steven, is this the first time you ever saw the shotgun?"

"Yes, it is."

The defense attorney then returned that weapon to the evidence table.

"Directing your attention to the revolver. Did you ever see that weapon before the afternoon of December 23, 1969?"

"Yes, I saw it once before. It was at the Red Ruby on the night of December 21st."

It, too, was returned to the evidence table. "Steven, please tell the jury how you came to see the revolver on December 21."

"My father and I met up with Leroy Drake and his lady friend, Rose, on the sidewalk outside the Ruby. And just before entering the tavern, Leroy handed my father that pistol. Later on, when a fight broke out between Leroy and Joe Wright, my father took the pistol out of his pocket and broke up the brawl. When Leroy calmed down, my dad gave the gun back to him."

"Did you witness this?"

"Yes, I did."

"And did you ever again see that particular weapon your father handed back to Leroy Drake?"

"Yes. It's the same pistol that Leroy gave my father before we left Chicago on December 23. It's the same pistol you have in evidence today."

"Now Steven, tell us your whereabouts from the late hours of December 18 into the early hours of December 19."

"I was in St. Louis. We went to visit a friend who has a Pontiac Firebird for sale. We wanted to take a look at it, but we couldn't find the street where he lives. We did a little bar-hopping and then we stopped at a package liquor store and purchased two bottles of wine and headed for home."

"We got approximately ten miles this side of St. Louis when I became too tired to drive any further so we returned to the Holiday Inn at East St. Louis."

"What time were you at the package liquor store?"

"Approximately 1:20 a.m., to 1:30 a.m."

"Were you drinking earlier in the evening?"

"Yes, but we weren't drunk if that's what you mean."

"Thank you. No further questions." Aultech looked over at the prosecution table. "I pass the witness."

* * *

Hobart Richards stood from his chair. When asked, Steven stated his check-in time at the Holiday Inn was approximately 4 a.m. He said he paid for the room upfront. In answer to questions from the prosecution, Steven said neither he nor his father were employed at the time of their arrest. His wife worked and supported Steven, but he didn't know how his father supported the family.

He stated he was stationed in the service at Granite City approximately five miles from St. Louis. He traveled twice a week from Granite City to Starling while in the service from January until May 1969, when he was discharged. He admitted becoming quite familiar with the route. He said he drove the normal speed limit, with a few exceptions."

Hobart Richards took exception. "Mr. James, haven't you stated to a Mr. Ricky Carpenter that you can make that trip in sixty minutes?"

"No, I never said that. In fact, that's the exact statement he made to me!"

Carpenter was called to the stand and was asked about a conversation that had taken place at the jail in the evening on May 24.

"We were standing in the cell block, and I told Steve that I drove down to St. Louis once and I looked at the speedometer and I was doing a hundred and ten miles an hour. He asked how long it took me to get there, and I said I didn't know. I told him that I never timed the whole trip. Steve said he could make it in sixty minutes' flat. That fast. He said he did it all the time when he was in the service and was never stopped by the State Police for speeding along Route 66."

"Have you been promised anything for your testimony?"

"No, I have not."

"Have you been coerced in any way?"

"No, I have not."

Lemar Joiner, owner of Lemar's Package Liquors of St. Louis, testified that Steven purchased two bottles of wine at approximately 1:30 a.m., on December 19.

Bonnie James, Steven's now ex-wife, testified that when he returned from St. Louis at around 8 p.m., on December 19, something serious had happened to his right foot. It was severely swollen and causing pain for him to walk. She testified that she never saw his old shoes again.

Simon Drake was called as a rebuttal witness; taking the stand to testify that his father, Leroy, passed away from a massive heart attack on March 13, 1970, in Sacramento California. His funeral was held in Starling. Drake, to the James' good fortune, would no longer be able to confirm or refute the testimony Steven gave.

CHAPTER 37
Wedding Bell Blues
1996

Echo's voice was oozing with frustration. "C'mon, Cassie, help me, will you? I only have three hours remaining before the wedding, and I've yet to complete the finishing touches for the reception. And we still have to dress and make it to the church on time!"

"Sure, whatever you need me to do. Just let me know; but you've got to stop stressing and start relaxing a little. Everything looks beautiful. You've done a fine job pulling it all together."

"I hope so, but if I don't get these last-minute tasks done, I'm not going to be able to make the wedding."

Cassie was home visiting from Gadsden, Alabama. She returned to attend the wedding of her niece, Tia Marie. Echo and Trudy, Tia's mother, planned every detail and had worked diligently for months. Echo wanted perfection for her brother's only daughter when she walked down the aisle at 2 p.m.

Cassie smiled gleefully. She and Echo stepped outdoors with their arms full and entered the reception tent. "Isn't it wonderful for Tia; becoming a bride today? I'm so happy for her and Phillip. She's almost twenty-seven now and so fortunate to have found someone like him."

"Yes, and that's as it should be," Cassie responded.

The bride-to-be waited a long time for this day to come. Always smart, Tia put her priorities in order at a young age. Her best friend and maid of honor was Sheila Barrington, whose father owned a fish cannery in Alaska.

From the time the girls were freshmen in high school, they spent their summers there, cleaning the fish and putting them on ice. They worked hard and made good money working long hours, six days a week. On Sunday they would wander about touring the area on their bicycles. Tia Marie saved almost every dime she earned for her college tuition. She had established a goal for herself and was determined to become a nurse.

After high school, she was accepted into Hope Memorial School of Nursing and lived at home with her mother. She was frugal and single-minded in her efforts to obtain her nursing license.

Quickly, Echo and Cassie set to the task. White ironed and starched tablecloths and autumn floral centerpieces were placed on each of the tables set up on Echo's freshly cut and manicured backyard, underneath the large white tent she rented for the occasion.

The back deck and patio were decorated with pumpkins, gourds, haystacks and corn stalks. Banisters and handrails were wrapped with a string of silken leaves of gold, green, amber and brown, containing every color of the fall season.

It was not elaborate I but rather earthy, seasonal and exactly what the bride wanted; Mother Nature's paint brush to set the ambiance at her reception.

The weather was cooperating fully. October 5 was a bright sun- soaked, seventy-two-degree day with barely a stitch of humidity in the air. A 'feels-like-fall,' slightly cool and gentle breeze counteracted the heat rays of the sun.

Tia Marie met thirty-two-year-old Doctor Phillip Prentiss when she assisted him in the operating arena at Hope Memorial. The patient was a sixty-five-year old male, overweight pipe-fitter undergoing triple bypass surgery. Phillip was tall, blonde and blue-eyed. He was the most kind and gentle man that Tia had ever known.

"He reminds me so much of you, Grandpa," Tia told Marshall Middleton the day she brought Phillip over to the house to meet her father's parents. After getting to know him, Marshall couldn't tell which one was luckier, Phillip, or his precious son's daughter.

Over the ensuing years, Phillip became a vital and loving part of the family. Today's ceremony only served to make it official.

*　*　*

Echo hollered up the stairwell. Having finished their tasks, the ladies quickly showered, groomed and anxiously dressed in their finest clothing. The time was quickly approaching. "C'mon Cassie! Let's get a move on. We've got to go now!"

"All right, all right." She scurried down the steps like a herd of wild horses.

"How many times have I heard your mother tell you not to run down the steps? I swear you haven't changed your ways since high school. Do you want to fall and crack your head wide open?"

Cassie laughed out loud. "Girl, you're beginning to sound just like mom."

"That's alright. I'm proud to sound like her."

The two hopped into Echo's Prelude and traveled to St. Joseph Catholic Church. Their seats had been reserved on the pew with their parents.

***

Everyone stood and all heads turned toward the back, anxiously awaiting Tia's entrance from the vestibule. Echo smiled as her niece entered the church dressed in an eggshell white form-fitting Italian lace gown, with cap sleeves, a swooping neckline, and an empire waist. The cathedral train trailed eight feet on the floor.

Tia's blonde hair was swooped in a bun with thin pieces of her curled mane hanging down to softly frame her face. She looked beautiful but as Echo looked at her niece, she was suddenly struck by the likeness Tia bore to her father. The likeness was nothing new, but on this occasion, it set off a series of emotions that pushed open a bastion of grief that spewed forth like water down a mountainside. This unexpected surge of emotion hit her like a ton of bricks.

The wedding ceremony had awakened the beast that laid dormant within Echo for all these years without her comprehension. Now, it stirred to the vanguard of her intellect. She had no idea a modest wedding for her niece would become a time of reckoning for her.

Seemingly, from out of nowhere came the realization of all that Tom had been denied. In an instant, Echo's spirit cried out within her, *My God, where is my brother on this special day?* Her heart ached as her brain pounded from the overwhelming reality of her family's loss.

Marshall Middleton walked his granddaughter down the aisle in her father's stead, along with her maternal grandfather, Delbert Reardon. It was the way Tia wanted it -- to honor the man who assisted Trudy in raising her and to honor the man who raised her father. This was supposed to be a happy occasion but Echo's eyes filled with tears, and she fought valiantly to suppress them.

She wondered if her mom and dad were feeling pangs of grief? She locked her eyes upon her dad as he escorted Tia down the aisle, and all she could see was happiness etched all over his handsome face. Echo turned back around to see her mother beaming like a spotlight, smiling broadly from ear to ear.

Nothing but joy for Tia should have encompassed Echo. Yet, the bitter reality of Tom's death assailed her senses without warning or mercy. It rolled over her with the full weight of an eighteen-wheeler careening out of control on a Blue Ridge Mountain downhill slippery slope. She wanted so much to run away to where she might find a quiet spot to be alone and cry with abandon.

Tom had never held his baby's hand, never kissed her cheek, never wiped her tears, and now Tia was becoming a bride. In a few years, she would have children of her own, and Tom would become a grandfather without ever knowing. It felt so unfair, miserably unjust and wasteful. Echo wondered if her heart might shatter into tiny pieces.

She knew the time for her grieving had arrived but she was hesitant to open the door to it. She was hosting a reception and could not afford to be an emotional wreck.

This was Tia Marie's day, and Echo refused to spoil it with the sorrow she was feeling on this happiest of occasions for her niece. Tia Marie would never understand Echo's quandary; she would have no conception of the loss we had all suffered. How could she? He was already gone months before she was ever born.

Echo struggled to smile for Tia's sake and struggled more to maintain a happy appearance. Somehow, with God's grace, she knew she had to succeed.

***

At the reception, Tia opened wedding gifts. One, in particular, drew a lot of approving gasps from the big gathering.

It was a large oak case Tom picked up for his mother when he was on R & R in Taiwan a few years before his death. It contained three levels of gold-plated cutlery with delicate mahogany handles. The sugar bowl, creamer, salt and pepper shakers were gold plated.

Mariah used the set once at Thanksgiving the year before Tom was killed. When Tia was born, she stored it away to pass down to her granddaughter.

"Oh my," was all Echo could muster in her fragile state. The sight of the case sent more waves of emotional grief flooding her weighty spirit once again. The reality that even the box of beautiful cutlery outlasted him was not lost on her. Her spirit was laden with pathetic downhearted melancholy.

Tia kissed her grandmother on the cheek, and Trudy walked over to Mariah and put her arms around her. "I know how much that cutlery means to you, Mom," she said with tears gleaming in her eyes.

Echo felt as if she were going to start screaming if she didn't get out of the reception tent for a while. She was on the verge of sobbing and fought desperately to withhold the tears until she could exit unseen by the happy family and friends of the bride and groom.

Their joy stood out in complete contrast to the horrific ache Echo was feeling. Understanding she was in full-blown grief, it felt as if she'd never have reason to smile again.

Echo looked around at the happy faces of the wedding party and guests and realized it was as good a time as any to make her exit. She ducked out unseen, and ran across the street to a little park-like setting at the tennis courts. She sat alone on the picnic table and let go a guttural cry. Her tears sent her eye makeup streaming down her cheeks but that didn't matter; she desperately needed to relieve the build-up of an agonizing emotional day.

When Echo returned to the gathering, she was composed. Tia was still occupied with the couple's wedding gifts. She hadn't noticed Echo's absence. It didn't appear as if anyone had.

***

That night Echo couldn't sleep after all the guests went home. She tossed and turned on her bed with Tom settled heavily on her mind. She got up to get a glass of water, retrieved a pillow and blanket from the bed and went to the family room sofa.

She turned on the television, but it didn't hold her attention. Her mind was determined to drift back to a time so long ago when life was innocent for her but full of harsh realities for her older brothers.

Echo wanted desperately to telephone her dad. She knew he might be able to explain why she felt so heartbroken now. He was full of what she called Godly wisdom that was derived from years of studying the bible.

Marshall always made the solution to any problem seem so obvious, and Echo needed to talk to him now but a call at 2 a.m. would only disturb her parents, who were surely sound asleep at that hour.

Echo lay supine on the sofa. Somehow in the wee morning hours, she managed to fall asleep because she found herself being awakened by the ring of the telephone. To her chagrin, the morning had not dissipated her sorrow.

The caller was Marshall Middleton.

"That was a beautiful reception you had for Tia Marie." Marshall's voice was upbeat, and Echo felt confident that neither he nor her mother had noticed her emotional frailty of the day before.

"Oh, Dad, I'm glad you called." The simple sound of his voice lifted Echo's spirit. He was her rock, her safe harbor as he was for his entire family.

"Were you up or did I wake you? You sound like you're half asleep."

"Oh no, I've been up. I'm just a little-tired still, that's all." Echo changed the subject swiftly so as not to betray her attempts to hide her sadness. "Dad, do you know if mom still has the letters Tom wrote while he was in the service?"

"Oh, I'm sure she does. Why do you ask?"

"Well, I just wanted to read them again, that's all." But the tone of Echo's voice betrayed her.

"Are you alright, dear?" Marshall Middleton's inflection exposed his concern. She attempted to sound lighthearted as she fought back tears. When all she really wanted to do was run into her father's loving arms and cry her eyes out over the loss of her brother.

"Sure, I'm fine, Dad."

"Alright then, I'll ask your mother to drag them out, and I'll bring them to you this afternoon."

"Oh, thank you. I'll be right here waiting." Echo's eyes were burning with bitter tears but she didn't have the heart to burden her father. Besides, how could she ever explain the retching grief that was gripping her now after all the time that had passed?

She realized just as she wasn't able to alleviate his pain and sorrow when the loss was fresh, her father wouldn't be able to take away hers now. There would be no more hanging on to her dad's shirttails, not on this one. Grief is so terribly personal.

Marshall pulled into the driveway a little past noon, and Echo met him at the door. He carried a large pillow case that Mariah converted into a bag by sewing a zipper onto its open end. Marshall handed it to Echo. She unzipped it and dumped its contents onto the dining room table.

A large pile of envelopes covered the tabletop. Hundreds of sympathy cards and every letter Tom sent home lay mingled in that pile, as well as all other correspondence in relation to his untimely death.

Echo sat down, ready to pour into them. The pain she was feeling must have shown on her face.

Marshall looked at her lovingly. "You know, dear, there's a period of mourning and there comes a time when we have to put it down and go on. Let the dead bury the dead. We still have living to do. And we have the comfort of knowing we'll see our loved ones again. Believe it. Let it build you up in confidence and don't let the past rob you of your future."

Now the flood gates opened and tears began to flow. Echo could no longer hold them back. She glanced up at her dad and noticed concern etched on his face.

She addressed him with a quivering voice. "I know, Dad, but I really don't believe I ever truly mourned Tom's passing. My tears back then were caused by yours, and Mom's and Grandma's and Grampa's. I think I was too young to understand."

He reached out and placed his hand on Echo's shoulder. "Alright dear, that's fair enough. We all have to grieve sometime. If you need me you know where I'll be. Call me anytime."

Echo raised her arm to her shoulder and placed her hand on top of his. She looked up at him and managed a slight smile through her tears. "Thank you, Dad."

"Have a blessed day," he told her and off he went, exiting through the kitchen and out the back door where he saw the men from Armbruster Tent Makers taking down the reception tent and folding chairs. He waved cordially as he rounded the driveway and entered his vehicle.

Now she was alone, just her and the correspondence spewed out on the dining room table.

***

Echo created three different piles. One pile contained the sympathy cards, another contained all official correspondence, and the last held all the letters Tom wrote while in the service.

Once she had the sorting completed, Echo collected two large rubber bands and carefully bundled up the first two piles individually and placed them back into the bag. All that remained on the table were Tom's letters from Camp Pendleton where he took basic training, to the last letter written, penned somewhere near the demilitarized zone on the top of a C-ration box top.

Echo took the letters and sorted them by the month, date and year stamped on the postmark. She placed them in chronological order from the earliest to the latest.

Finished, she was ready to read, to follow a soldier's trail, her brother's own. She hoped to discover his thoughts, his insight into the anguished scourge of war that would lead to his final resting place at Camp Butler National Cemetery.

She didn't know what she would find, only that she felt no peace in Tom's passing and longed to discover something good, something invaluable to cling to that would forever assuage the grief that encompassed her.

She knew so much more about the war than she did back

then but that knowledge only served to make Tom's death all the more difficult to accept.

A memory of an incident that happened several years before, around 1980 or 1981 flooded her recall. It had been stored in her memory bank and now had found its way to the front line of her consciousness.

She went to the cemetery to place flowers on Tom's grave and the grave of another soldier from her Catholic Parish who had lost his life in Vietnam by 'friendly fire' a little more than a year and one-half before Tom lost his.

Echo visited her brother's grave first. She bent down and placed the silk floral arrangement into the ground and stood up for a moment of silent prayer. As she did, she heard a moaning sound that seemed to be coming from the bowels of the earth.

She looked around and saw no one. Her eyes scanned the headstones that were lined up all around her; rows and rows of them. Over to her left was Matthew Adelman's tombstone and situated further back but in the same section was the headstone bearing the name of Franklin Greeley.

Echo looked across the street and knew somewhere in the midst of all those fallen comrades lay the body of young Willy Moffatt. People whose funerals she had personally attended. They were her brother's friends, who, having gone to Vietnam were now back home and together again, ensconced forever in the prairie soil.

It seemed as if everywhere Echo looked the headstones read 'Vietnam.' The groan seemed to be coming from the graves that were marked in that manner. As the seconds flew by, the moaning became louder as more and more fallen Vietnam casualties joined in the outcry.

Justice and unity were their gut-wrenching groan. "Don't let our deaths be for nothing," was their simple plea.

Echo had not heard this groaning with her physical ears, but rather it had come from the core of her inner being, and it frightened her.

Quickly, she made her way to the Adelman gravesite and stuck the remaining flowers in the ground. She didn't stop to say a prayer but walked as fast as she could to her car.

When she returned home, she phoned her dad and they talked about the incident. They understood that 'justice' and 'unity,' were the essence of what Echo needed for a successful resolution to the devastation caused by Vietnam.

Justice for all who fought there and for those who lost their lives needlessly by the incompetence of the nation's leader. And unity for the nation's people that were torn apart by the scourge of Vietnam through that same incompetence.

This incident showed Echo there was unfinished business she needed to address but time marched on, and it became but a memory without any further attempt to understand it. Now, that memory was back again in full force, and she would not be able to turn her back on it so easily this time.

Tom's letters originated in January 1967 and depicted the thoughts of a happy seventeen-year-old boy having not a care in the world. From boot camp at Pendleton, California, he wrote: "All this week we've been firing artillery, grenade, 3.5 rocket launchers, bazookas and a large variety of rifle grenades. We spent three days and two nights this week on field bivouac. That was really a lot of fun."

As Echo sat reading, she began to realize the preparations that were being made to turn him and the other soldiers like him into fighting machines. They would stem the red tide, fight back Communism. They knew it had to be right; their government said so.

Tom continued in his early correspondence: "The place where we bivouac is really beautiful." Now, as Echo read the words, herself being older and wiser and with the benefit of hindsight, she wondered if her brother had any conception of where his training would lead.

She wondered if her brother understood that he was being developed into a highly skilled infantryman, taught to be gung-ho in the service to his country. Did he understand he was systematically being broken down to be built up again as a United States Marine, ready and willing to die for the principles the unprincipled leader of this nation espoused? If he did, did he expect that leader to be honest and forthright with him and his fellow soldiers? Did Tom have the right to expect that honesty and support?

"You better believe you did, my brother!"

She could feel her anger rising. Tears blurred her eyes, and she couldn't see the writing on the stationery. She had not known the bitterness she was feeling back in 1969 when the wound was fresh on her heart. She was younger then and ignorant of the world outside her own little universe.

She put the correspondence down on the table and went to retrieve a tissue. She hurt so badly for the horrible loss her family and many others suffered. The letters were painful to look at, even after all these years. Somehow, they managed to bring Thomas Middleton back to life again, if only in Echo's mind, and she ached to see his handsome face and to hold his hand. She could still envision him saying and doing the things he wrote about, feeling happy, smiling and carefree.

As she read Echo returned to the past at Fifteenth and Matheny Avenue. It was her first Holy Communion day. Her mother had the video camera out. Tom picked his sister up and placed her on his lap, as the two clowned for the camera.

Echo remembered, also, the times when Tom would chase his sister, Cassie, out the back door and around the long grapevine the Middleton's had in their back yard.

Cassie would make two loops with Tom in pursuit, and then veer off in a mad dash for the back door. She'd quickly lock it so that he couldn't get inside. He'd bang on the door, and Mariah would have to let him in as Cassie made a b-line for the front door.

The ritual only involved the two of them. Cassie would lay in wait for Tom to come home, run to the back door and holler, "you can't catch me," and no matter what, Tom would begin the chase.

"Here we go again," Mariah Middleton would say as she flailed her arms in hopeless jest.

Tom loved chasing Cassie, and she loved the challenge of beating him in a foot race.

"If I catch you, you're going be sorry," he'd threaten. Cassie would laugh heartily knowing Tom would never catch her, because she knew he never really tried.

Echo found herself smiling through tears as bittersweet memories flooded her senses. It hurt to read those first letters from him, so filled with childlike innocence. The problem was she had learned so much more about the war since her brother's passing.

Now, her sorrow was intertwined with raw anger at a president that would send over 58,000 of America's finest to their slaughter in a land so far from home with no instruction or knowledge of the plan to win the conflict.

The soldiers were betrayed and deceived along with their parents and the entire nation. She believed they were murdered by the incompetence of the power that sent them there in the first place! It isn't hard to spot a Vietnam Veteran. They are the guys with white hair and homeless in every major city in the nation. Their faces are haggard, and they appear older than their average 50 years. But they have Echo's heart.

Although not a tall kid, Tom was handsome, charming and loved to sing. Dion and the Belmont's was his favorite vocal group and although Echo couldn't recall his voice, she could still envision him climbing the steps to his bedroom singing, "The Wanderer."

He was happy-go-lucky without a care in the world, holding it all in the palm of his hand. He needed money all the time as it seemed to burn a hole in his pockets.

In a letter postmarked February 25, 1967, Tom enclosed his W2 statement for the calendar year 1966. He wanted his dad to fill out the 1040 form for him.

"I could sure use a little extra money," he wrote. "I hope I don't end up owing the IRS anything." His total wages for that year were $934.07 and Federal taxes withheld amounted to $45.50.

Tom purchased his clothing at pricey Robert's Brothers. The day Tom's obituary appeared in the State Journal-Register; the Middleton's received a call from the owner. He expressed his sympathy and assured Tom's parents that his debt, somewhere around $300 had been wiped clean. "That's the least we can do. We're so very sorry for your loss."

Echo will never forget the kindness extended to her family and the compassionate gesture of the good store owner.

In his final letter from Camp Pendleton, California, Tom wrote, "We have but ten days left before graduation. After my leave, I'll be going to the 3rd Bn., 7th Marine Division. We've been told we will be Okinawa bound and be there for an 18-month tour of duty. Okinawa was, you know, the last major offensive action for the Marine Corp in World War II."

In closing, he wrote, "You never spoke the truth more, Mother, when you said I'd miss home when I left. I hope Cricket still remembers her big brother. She almost forgot the last time." 'Cricket' was the nickname Tom affectionately attached to Echo.

Happy and carefree, his letters stirred her memory of the youthful boy she knew and loved. The one constant in every correspondence was his concern for his brother, Shawn. In letters not dated, but postmarked February 1967, he wrote, "How is Shawn doing lately? Things seem to be getting worse over there." Shawn Middleton was also serving his country in the United States Army.

Then the letter the Middletons never wanted to receive made its way to the house. Tom had dated this one 3/15/67.

"Dear folks," it began. "Well, we've finally made it to Vietnam for whatever it may be worth. I don't want you to start to worry about all this. I'll be just fine. I'll tell you what's been happening. It all started nine days ago. It was a Wednesday afternoon when we received word that we were moving out in the next few hours. No one took it seriously, but before we knew it, we were boarding transport planes at Kadena Air Base."

"We landed early Monday morning at Da Nang. The whole battalion was set in around the air strip. A few days later we were moved into fortified bunkers. Since then we've been working to improve our positions. We've been fired on the last few nights by snipers, but that's about all. We have a little well in the back of our bunker for showers. It's really bad news. I'm looking forward to taking a real shower someday."

In the next post-dated letter, he stated: "We lost seven men a few days ago when the Viet Cong ambushed one of our platoons on a recon mission. Just a few days earlier I was transferred to another squad. I had been attached to that platoon for several months. I was lucky again."

On 26 July, 1967, from Da Nang, "I'll have no trouble in coming home on leave, with plenty of money. I have not yet decided whether to bring my clothes home from Pendleton. I'll probably bring a few suits with me. I shall have from thirty to thirty-five days' leave."

In that same letter, he wrote, "I was taken aback a little when I read your letter stating that Shawn asked for $20. I don't know about that guy. This is war!"

Echo couldn't help chuckling on that one. Tom was always asking for money; always wanting just a little more. Yet, that must have been the first and only time Shawn ever had to borrow anything as he could make a dollar last an entire month.

His first trip to Vietnam had apparently not scarred Tom terribly from the sound of his letters. He remained upbeat and youthful. His hand writing was smooth, and he still maintained clean legible penmanship.

"Give my love to everyone. I should be home in about seventy-five days, somewhere close to the first of October."

After Tom's first trip to Vietnam, he was stationed at Okinawa and Camp Lejeune, North Carolina. Sometime before he came home on his final leave, he was issued new orders that would send him back to Vietnam, so close to the DMZ and undergoing such intense fighting, that he had not experienced on his first trip.

His mother and father didn't know for several days that Tom's leave had expired, and he was now AWOL. Russell James came to the house, and they joined him and Tom on the back porch, encouraging Tom to head back before he sunk into deeper trouble. Tom was up for a Lance Corporal promotion, but his chances of achieving that were now out of the question although that didn't bother him so much.

He was more concerned about bombs and grenades going off in every direction. He was young and wanted so desperately to live, to have a future, to grow from a boy to an old man.

Echo knew her brother would have preferred to watch his daughter develop into the woman she is today. The weight of the situation must have borne down on Tom like a drill pounding through asphalt.

Echo could only imagine the turmoil that assailed his brain as he pondered what course he would take. The first trip over had been a learning experience but this was different. He'd been in that hellhole and knew exactly what awaited him on his return.

Echo saw Tom's turmoil as a 'damned if you do, damned if you don't' situation he'd have to reconcile within himself. She understood it clearly through a metaphor. She pictured her brother in a house that's ablaze. He falls to the floor, and he crawls on the ground, feeling his way through the house because he can't see through the heavy black smoke that is beginning to overtake him.

Somehow, Tom finds the front door and makes his way onto the porch and down the steps to where the air is clean and the flames and smoke are behind him. He thinks to himself, *Thank God, I made it out of there!* He realizes just how close he came to the possibility of losing his life.

Yet, just when he's made that sigh of relief, someone with power and authority says, "No, you're not done yet. You have to go back in." That's when his chances of survival have been drastically reduced. Because he's already exhaled and let his guard down.

Echo suddenly remembered an incident that happened while Tom was home from his first trip to Vietnam. Although she couldn't understand it then, she came to recognize it as a direct result of Tom having been there.

He hadn't been home but a few days and was sitting at the kitchen table one morning as Mariah was frying bacon at the stove. Tom was reading the morning paper and Echo sat with her head resting on the table waiting for breakfast to be served.

Their youngest brother, Teddy, awakened and made his way into the kitchen. He was but a teenager at this time, probably no older than fourteen.

"Sit down, honey," his mother said, "and I'll bring you some bacon."

"No, Mom, I just want cereal," Teddy told her. So, he went to the cupboard to retrieve a bowl. He attempted to place it on the table top, but it fell to the linoleum floor and shattered.

Startled, Tom jumped across the table with a flying leap and grabbed his younger brother by his pajama top around the neck. He backed him up into a corner and had his hand in a fist, wadded up in the pajama top, at Teddy's throat. The upward pull forced the young teenager to his tiptoes.

Mariah shrieked in horror. "Thomas Michael!"

She put the fork she was holding on the stovetop and hurried to where her two sons were. Teddy's eyes were huge with fear, but he never said a word or cried a single tear. Echo realized he was too afraid to speak and too stunned for any other immediate reaction.

Mariah grabbed Tom's hand and tried to break the hold he had on his little brother's pajama top.

"What do you think you're doing? Let go of him right now!" she commanded.

Tom seemed to have been somewhere else in the few seconds it took him to leap the kitchen table. Echo never witnessed him doing anything like that before. Fortunately, he never took a swing at Teddy, and he did loosen his grip as his mother commanded.

Teddy went back upstairs having totally lost his appetite. He had been shaken to his core. At the time, Tom never proffered an explanation. Echo became angry and she wanted her mother to punish Tom harshly. If her thoughts could have affected anything, he wouldn't have gone back to Vietnam, for he wouldn't have been able to walk or fire a weapon. Echo would have torn him apart limb by limb! After all, it was only a bowl.

It was hard to believe Tom attacked his kid brother because he happened to drop and break a bowl. The truth is, Tom didn't attack Teddy because of a bowl that broke. The loud shattering of that bowl, however, sent him back to a place ravaged by war and separated from the present by only a few days, where loud noises such as bombs, grenades, and gunfire sent fear traversing through him.

Tom reacted to that sound in the only way he was trained to react; ATTACK! Echo was convinced he didn't mean to frighten his brother and she now knew that Tom's fear far exceeded Teddy's at that moment.

Mariah understood as it was happening. When Ted walked back up the stairs, Tom returned to his seat at the kitchen table. His mother followed him and stood beside him as he sat down. She looked as if she wanted to say something, but she waited until he looked up at her. When he did, she placed her hand on his shoulder and bent over to speak to him.

Her voice was soothing and motherly. "You're home now, honey, and you're safe. Everything is going to be all right. You'll see." Mariah's eyes were glassy with tears of concern for her third-born child.

"I'll see to it the children don't make so much noise, so that you can relax a little better," she promised him.

He responded gratefully, "Thank you, Mom. It's the loud noises that make me so jumpy. I didn't mean to," but his mother didn't let him finish.

"I know, dear. I know you didn't mean to hurt your little brother. It's going to be all right," she assured him again. She kissed the top of his head and walked over to the stove and removed the bacon from the skillet. She turned off the burner and made her way up the stairs to speak to her youngest son.

***

The letters from his final trip to Vietnam began in that same innocent boyish fashion. Tom was on the verge of emerging into a fine upstanding adult, one that could not only fight the nation's battles but would soon be endowed with another kind of weapon, the right to vote. Before the end of this tour and the end of his life, a grown man would emerge having seen enough death and destruction to fill a lifetime.

On 4 August, 1969, he wrote: "Sorry it has taken me so long to write but for the three weeks that I've been here we have really been kept busy. Could you send me a care package if it isn't too costly? We are really hurting for chow over here."

"Send some packages of iced tea and Kool-Aid. Also, will you put in some bottles of hot sauce? We use it in the field for our C-rations; anything that will help the taste of them. Also, some champagne. REALLY! We can have these things as long as we don't buy them from the local populace because a lot of it has glass or poison in it."

Toward the end of that letter, he said, "I was thinking the other day and did you know that this Christmas will be my twenty-first birthday?"

Now, tears streamed down Echo's cheeks once again, and she could no longer see to read the words on the paper. Tears caused by the loss of a life so young and promising flowed like raging river waters rushing over a mountainous cliff.

It was an ironic twist of fate. Tom wasn't able to buy an alcoholic drink. He couldn't even vote for the man that sent him to Vietnam in the first place. He wasn't old enough. Yet, his government thought he was quite aptly aged to fight a war that Lyndon Johnson, and a civilian military advisor were running.

Tom's handwriting seems to have lost some of its legibility. It appears that his hand may not be as steady as before. Maybe it's because he is in the field and doesn't have anything solid on which to place the paper as he writes.

From 16 August, '69 he writes, "Trudy and I are doing quite

well. As far as I'm concerned, Mom, she is the only girl for me. As it stands now, the wedding date is 18, June, '70, just ten months away. Thanks a lot for the prayers. I really need them."

This letter seems to be the last upbeat correspondence from Tom. It would appear he's reached a turning point in the general tone of his communication. Now Tom has a little over two months to live, and his letters seem to reflect the thoughts of a grown man beyond his youthful years with real concerns and fears.

"Dear Mother," he began in a letter not dated but postmarked September, 1969. "I'm sorry that I haven't written sooner. I've been in a rut, you might say. I just couldn't get in the mood to write. I've been so depressed for the last few weeks. I'll try to write more often."

Continuing, he said, "We have been on numerous patrols and have captured a total of five Viet Cong. We run into heavy sniper fire on all of our patrols."

"We have taken about fifteen casualties in the last three weeks, several from small arms fire, two from land mines and the remainder from punji traps. There have been several people that I went through boot camp with that have caught a bullet."

He asked his mom to send him some home-made fudge, explaining, "When we go on these patrols for two and three days at a time we absolutely starve. We're issued one meal a day. Sometimes, if we're lucky we get two. What makes it worse is that we're constantly on the move. That chocolate would really come in handy. Send it air mail if you will."

In ending this letter, Tom said, "They're planning a beach party in a few days. I'm really looking forward to that. It will do us good to get off this hill for a few hours."

"I love you, Mom and Dad. Tell the brothers and sisters I love them too. I want you both to know that I'm sincerely sorry for all the disappointments you've suffered on my account. I'd like to apologize to anyone I have ever offended. I wish I could tell them all myself, in person, but I don't know when or if ever, I will have the chance. Keep the prayers going, Dad. I've never needed them more!"

From his letter written 29 September, 1969, Tom wrote, "We just arrived at Dong Ha this morning. It's a distance of some seventy kilometers from Phu Bai. We are roughly about ten miles from the DMZ and the North Vietnamese border. BOY, WHAT AM I

DOING HERE?"

From a later dated 4 October, 1969, "The fighting here has been very heavy these last few days or so, but our company has been really lucky as far as casualties go. I hope it remains that way!"

"I must cut this short as we are going out real soon. Give all my love to the family. And please pray for all of us here. I've been doing so much of that myself lately."

Tom's letter written 9 October 1969, caused Echo's eyes to fill with tears, and she had to take a break from her reading. Her tears blurred the words on the paper, and she could no longer see them clearly. She felt such heavy sorrow as she came to understand the fear her brother suffered just before his death. She wished she had been there to put her arms around him to comfort him, to shelter him, somehow.

Wiping her eyes, she picked up the letter again to resume her reading. "Dear Folks," the letter began. "This is going to be short. We're waiting for a chopper to bring in supplies and then we're moving out again. I'll give this letter to someone in the chopper to mail for me."

"Yesterday, we were so close to the DMZ we could see over into North Vietnam from the mountain. That's really getting close, wouldn't you say so, Mom? Sometimes, when you and Dad go to church, say a few prayers for me, will you, please? "I could really use them."

"I don't mind telling you that I'm scared, I'm really scared. Quite a few times when things got thick and the fighting got heavy, I said a few prayers myself. I've been doing a lot of that lately."

"Several of us had a prayer meeting a few weeks ago, and I openly confessed that Jesus Christ died for my sins and was raised to life. And I said aloud that I trusted him as my Savior and asked that He guide my life and help me to do His will."

"So, I want to thank you, Mom and Dad, for my Christian upbringing. It taught me where to turn when the problem was bigger than myself. When I feel alone and you can't be near, I've called out to Him and He has seen me through some harrowing situations. Keep praying, please. We need them desperately."

Now, tears drenched Echo's cheeks. Her poor brother, afraid and all alone. She hurt so badly at the thought of it and couldn't contain the emotions she was feeling. She got up from the dining room table and threw herself down on the sofa in the living room where she began to cry with abandon.

Echo wondered what it must have been like for him those last few minutes and seconds before his death. Did he want his mother and cry out for her as Echo was sure she would have? What were the last words he spoke? Her heart felt sick and broken.

The house was silent but for the sound of Echo's sobs. She closed her eyes and lay prostrate on the sofa. Her shoulders shook from bitter sobbing. Then, a thought, a revelation knowledge, caused her to gasp aloud. She ceased her bitter crying and lay perfectly still as she pondered its meaning.

When it came to her, she gasped. "Oh, my gosh," she said aloud before rising from the sofa. She walked over to the letter lying open on the dining room table.

I'll never know what his last spoken words were, but here before my eyes are the last penned words sent home to his family. Maybe they are saying everything I really need to know, she thought.

She picked up the letter and slowly began to read it again. The words written on the yellowing parchment now caused her spirit to leap inside her.

As a kid, Echo thought anyone who laid down their life fighting communism, received an automatic pass into heaven but she knew differently today. She never really questioned before where Tom might be, taking for granted that all good people go to heaven, but she'd learned that good works weren't the key. And so, dying for some idealistic noble cause, -- Vietnam was no such thing, -- wasn't going to buy him a place in heaven. Oh, but prayer. Now that was something substantial, she knew.

Her Bible instruction taught her that anyone who confesses that Jesus is Lord and believes that God raised Him from the dead will be saved and right there in that letter, Tom was telling his family he had done just that.

Echo's tears now flowed like a river, but they flowed from gratitude on learning that indeed her brother was safe and had not died all alone so far away from home. And once she came to understand that, it made all the difference in the world. There was nothing she could do about his death. Tom was never coming back but she found peace in the certainty that she would see him again.

Tom's last letters showed Echo his heart during the last

weeks and days before his death. A large part of the torment surrounding his demise had been replaced with a joy that begged to shout boldly, 'O death, where is thy sting? O grave, where is thy victory?'

Echo learned that day that her brother was taken away from all the turmoil and travail his government had placed upon him. She began to feel like a kid in a candy store, excited and happy. She had not set out to learn this but was grateful for the disclosure.

When she began this project, filled with pain and sorrow, Echo had no idea she would find peace in its wake. Her brother was in heaven. His last words assured her of it.

Echo began to recall the times Tom was home on leave and wouldn't go to church with the family on Sundays.

"I'm too tired, go without me," he would say.

"You should get up and go with us," Mariah would fire back.

"No, I can't go. I'm an atheist, I don't believe in it."

"You're not an atheist. What you are is lazy!" Tom's mother hit the nail on the head. He was lazy, but he had been raised in a Christian home and those values had taken root deep within him. At the peak of his strongest adversity, his true nature revealed itself.

With a smile on her face, Echo wondered if there will be a grapevine in heaven. Oh, how she would love to hear her mother tell Tom one more time, "You might as well forget it, Thomas. Cassie's already out the front door." He'd always smile at his mom when she said that. The two of them had a shared knowledge that he had once again let his younger sister escape his ferocious wrath.

Thomas was a wonderful big brother and now Echo knows with biblical verity the opportunity will come when she will be able to tell him all the things she feels in her heart at this moment.

Echo picked up the phone and called her father. She wasn't surprised to learn he had already discovered for himself that which was revealed to her now.

"It's wonderful how the burden lifts by simply knowing he's safe in heaven," Marshall told Echo when she mentioned those last letters of Tom's from October 1969.

"Yes indeed!" Echo responded, awestruck at the lightning-quick change that had taken her from the depths of sorrow to euphoria. When she ended the conversation with her father, she returned to the final two letters she had left to read; one written on a piece of cardboard, a C-ration box top.

On Thursday, 16 October, 1969, Thomas Middleton wrote, "This place has really been battered. B-52's have dealt a devastating blow, relentlessly for the last several days. Their bomb craters seem to be big enough to hold an averaged sized home."

"The hills and mountains are pocketed with smaller holes from our own weapons and even in this war-ravaged place, your prayers have kept us going. Please keep sending them up for all of us. I send my love to each and every one of you."

After his signature, he wrote, "P.S. Tell Dad when I get home, I'll take him into any place of his choice and buy him a beer. I'll be twenty-one when my birthday rolls around this Christmas."

Tom has ten days to live. He will not see his twenty-first birthday. His last correspondence, a makeshift postcard having no paper on which to write, arrived long after the news of his demise. The postmark was October 22, 1969, A.M.

On the box-top, he wrote, "Tomorrow we leave to start Operation North Carolina, a little closer to the DMZ than our present position. I still can't make any sense out of what we're supposed to be doing here. I predict Americans will look back on this endeavor one day and recognize the total waste of it all."

It was accompanied by two unopened letters, one sent from Mariah Middleton and the other from Tom's youngest sister, Annalisa, who helped her mother make fudge and cookies to send to Tom.

Fortunately, the care package is not returned, and the family is left to hope that the boys in Tom's platoon will find some much-needed energy from the fudge while on their patrols.

Echo picked up her mother's unopened, returned letter. She sat back down at the dining room table and began to read it aloud.

"I'm sending a package. I made some cookies, -- mincemeat by the way, -- and I stuck a batch of fudge in, too. It is packaged in popcorn to help keep it moist. I hope it works. Keep me posted."

"You mentioned being scared. I imagine you have lots of company, Thomas. I think it is terrible that our boys have to be there fighting for their lives. If the Americans are fighting communism over there, I think they ought to lay it on and finish it."

"The reason I got started on this is that last week I saw on the television where the Quakers wanted to send bandages and other things to North Vietnam."

"This I can't imagine. It makes one fighting mad. I'll be as happy as you when your time is up over there. Maybe it won't be for long."

"We are all praying for you, anyhow. And as you know your dad is ALWAYS on his knees. You can depend on that. Take care and don't forget your own prayers at all times."

"We all love you and keep you constantly in our thoughts. Stay safe. Love always, Mom."

CHAPTER 38
Final Arguments
1970

On Monday, June 29, final arguments were heard. Benson Bradley spoke first. He stood and walked over to the jury box. He began by taking the jurists over all the testimony again, meticulously weaving facts together to leave no lingering reasonable doubt.

"Ladies and Gentlemen, how convenient for the defense to place both weapons into the hands of a dead man who can no longer speak for himself. The defense knows we can't pull Leroy Drake from his grave to testify any more than we can raise Daniel Sycamore to confirm what hideous falsehoods these are."

"I ask you to think long and hard about it, ladies and gentlemen because there's a pattern of operation with the defendants that attempts to pin something like this on the dearly departed. Remember, this isn't the first time. Think back on Steven James' testimony. Why do you suppose they registered at that hotel under the name of Thomas Middleton, a young man who lost his life in Vietnam? I suggest they did because, if caught, the trail would lead to Camp Butler National Cemetery where Mr. Middleton wouldn't be able to say, "I wasn't there!"

"I think you folks are smart enough to see through their flimsy diatribe because the State has clearly laid out for you how both weapons have been brought full circle to Russell and Steven James."

"A terrible thing happened at that station. Daniel Sycamore was brutally executed there. And these two defendants have his blood on their hands." Benson Bradley turned swiftly from the jurors to point his finger directly at the defendants. The room grew silent as the jurors took in the poignant scene. When he spoke again, he didn't turn back around to face the jurors. He kept his eyes glued on the defendants.

"No one will forget Daniel Sycamore. He was a vivacious, nineteen-year-old. He had his future before him, passing from a child to a man. He was a college student with a bright and promising future. He was a human being with air in his lungs. Blood flowed in his veins. That is until these two defendants decided to put a bullet in his brain, and all for a measly $500!"

Bradley's voice dripped with disgust. He looked squarely at the faces of both Russell and Steven James, then turned to face the jury.

Bradley's voice was filled with emotion. "We want the death penalty badly!"

The prosecutor glared once more at the defendants. Contempt showed on his face. "Think about the painful anomaly of murder, folks. The victim lies in his grave, while the guilty are alive to walk the earth. The Jameses came like thieves in the night to steal, kill and destroy. Daniel Sycamore lies in his grave because of that!"

"Ladies and gentlemen, justice will be done when you return guilty verdicts against the killers along with the recommendation for their deaths. Thank you for your conscientious attention during this most solemn trial."

The defense was now ready for their closing argument. Jenna Wells walked over to the jury box. She thanked the panel for their participation and for their patience over the past eight days.

She began as she pointed her finger at the empty chair that stood beside the Judge's desk, affixed atop an elevated platform. "Ladies and gentlemen, most of the testimony you heard from that witness stand throughout this entire trial is irrefutable."

"The defense agrees with all those prosecution witnesses who testified that a murder occurred at the Texaco Station. There's no question about that."

"We don't disagree with the folks who testified that they saw the Jameses in possession of the revolver two weeks after the murder. In fact, you heard Steven James testify that he and his father, indeed, possessed both weapons as soon as two weeks after the murder."

"And we don't take issue with the State's witness who is an expert from the State Crime Laboratory. The defendants trust her knowledge and expertise. They have no disagreement with her findings."

So, out of everyone that testified from that witness stand, there is only one person that we have contention with. It is only his testimony that we cannot abide. This witness was at the Red Ruby Lounge on December 21, 1969. And that, ladies and gentlemen, is Mr. Herschel Johnson."

Jenna Wells looked at each juror directly before speaking. She quoted former President Lyndon Johnson, "Come now, let us reason together."

"Herschel was clear across the room during a fight in a dark bar when Russell intervened with a revolver. Yet, Mr. Johnson was positive it was the same gun he saw in the Jameses kitchen on December 6, 1969. Now think about this. The gun was shoved into Joe Wright's face and he couldn't identify it. Ladies and gentlemen, isn't that reasonable doubt?"

"Is it reasonable that on December 26, the defendants would lay a murder weapon on a kitchen table in front of a witness who could identify it? I don't think so, folks. Would they give the shotgun taken from the station to someone knowing it could be traced back to them, -- with all the identifiable markings this one has? Is that reasonable? Hardly."

Jenna Wells stood silent for a moment allowing her words to soak into the brains of the jurists.

"Now, let's consider the sworn testimony of the package liquor store owner from St. Louis. He placed the defendants in his establishment at approximately 1:15 a.m. Remember, Dr. Grant's testamony that death occurred not more than an hour before the body was found around three o'clock. You heard that the overpasses were hazardous and slippery. So, is it reasonable to believe that in those conditions a person could drive from St. Louis to Glenrose in just forty-five minutes time?" Jenna Wells smiled at the twelve jurors and shook her head from side to side. "There's nothing reasonable about that."

"Ladies and gentlemen, the defendants are not required to prove their innocence. The State has not met the burden of proving its case beyond a reasonable doubt as required by law. I am confident you will follow the court's instructions and return a verdict of not guilty.

"Jurors have a solemn responsibility. I wish you God's wisdom as you consider all the testimony and evidence admitted during this trial. Thank you, ladies and gentlemen."

Jenna Wells turned and made her way back to the defense

table. Since the State has the burden of proof, it is allowed to have the final word in closing arguments.

Hobart Richards rose from his chair and walked over to the jury box. He spoke for approximately one hour. When he finished, Judge Chambers read the jury instructions that would oversee this case. "All people present in the courtroom are to remain seated until the jury has exited the courtroom."

The time was 12:20 p.m. The jury rose from their seats and in the custody of the sworn bailiff were taken to the deliberation room to consider their verdicts. Lunch would be served.

* * *

At 4:20 p.m. the jury foreman signaled the bailiff that all 12 jurists had reached a unanimous decision.

The defendants were brought back in from their holding cell at 4:28 p.m., and at 4:45 p.m. Judge Chambers read the jury's verdicts in open court.

Russell and Steven James were found guilty of the first-degree murder of Daniel Sycamore with the recommendation that the death penalty is imposed. They were found guilty as well of the armed robbery at the Texaco station.

After the verdicts were read, the judge polled the jury at the request of the defense counsel, and each juror affirmed their guilty verdict. Margaret James broke down in tears as she heard the verdicts read.

The judge gave the defense attorneys 30 days in which to file post-trial motions. Neither Russell nor his son showed any emotion when the verdicts were read.

Six deputies were in the courtroom and several others were in the hallway outside for security reasons, but neither father nor son put up any resistance. The deputies returned them to the Sturnus County jail to await their sentencing.

After most of the spectators left the courtroom, Margaret remained behind, devastated by the verdict. Through her sobs, she repeated "Oh no," over and over again.

* * *

On Monday, July 20, 1970, at 3:30 p.m., a hearing was held on aggravation and mitigation. The State placed into evidence the record of conviction of both father and son. Additionally, the prosecuting attorney asked to enter evidence of two prior convictions on Russell for theft exceeding $150 and for burglary in Sturnus County. The record of conviction in the Ryan's Jewelry Store robbery in Durham was proffered to the court as well.

The defense called the Reverend Gordon W. Edward, Pastor of St. Frances Xavier Cabrini Church. He had given instructions in July, 1962, to both Russell and his wife and in September of that year the couple entered the Catholic faith. He testified that Steven followed closely behind.

Russell took the stand to testify to all his hard work with the Khoury League in Starling. Steven spoke of his work record during and after high school before he entered military service. Both men had been in the military, and each had received an honorable discharge.

Judge Chambers asked the defendants if they had anything to say before he passed sentencing. The father and son stood up and declared their innocence.

Russell added, "I will continue to declare my innocence of this brutal murder until the day I die. I am innocent and I ask this court to do the right thing; set the wrongful conviction aside and send me home to my family."

After listening patiently to the indignant rantings of a guilty man, Judge Wilbur Chambers was ready for sentencing.

CHAPTER 39
On Ender's Shoulders
1996

Thursday, August 1, dawned with clanging thunder that shook the windows in the bedroom where Echo lay. Although the time was past 7 a.m., the sky remained dark and ominous.

She looked at the clock on the nightstand and threw back the floral-patterned sheet that covered her, swinging both legs to the floor as she sat on the edge of her bed.

She stretched and yawned and walked to the kitchen to start a pot of coffee, and made her way to the front porch to retrieve the newspaper. Fortunately, her industrious paperboy had placed it in a plastic bag so the rain was of no consequence to it.

The steaming hot coffee was doused with milk and a teaspoon of honey and carried to the dining room table where Echo spread out the newspaper for her perusal.

On page three her eyes fell upon the news story that she had been waiting weeks to learn of its conclusion. The headline out of Chicago read:

CLEMENCY DENIED TO SEVEN AGED INMATES

The article stated the governor had denied clemency for all seven of the murderers who sought release after spending decades in prison.

"The governor believes, after a thorough review of each case presented, that none of the seven prisoners were appropriate for clemency," Stuart Eglin, spokesman for the governor said without further explanation.

There was no mention that for one of the inmates, the Governor's decision didn't matter any longer. Time had already ran out for Heath Eggleston. The seventy-three-year-old convicted rapist and murderer succumbed to pneumonia just three days before the governor's decision was handed down. He was now free, receiving a sort of clemency after all.

Echo's thoughts immediately turned to Dallas and Addie Sycamore. They would certainly be pleased with the Governor's decision but the same couldn't be said for Geoff James.

His heart must have broken when he learned the news. Echo realized in the whole of time, that she would never feel the compassion for his father like she felt for Geoff. It is the same level of empathy she has for Dallas, Addie, Shari and Patrick; all victims of the father and son murdering team.

Echo hadn't heard from Geoff since the day of the hearing and now wondered if he, too, had learned of the decision through the newspaper. She realized how dreadfully awful it must be for him to have wanted something so badly, like having his father back home again, yet possessing no means to make it happen. There's just no rationality to be garnered from the abject cruelty that caused Geoff's predicament. It is, like the Vietnam debacle, a sort of hell that never had to be. "What a waste." Echo said, feeling melancholy for all the suffering humanity in this pitiful, painful saga.

CHAPTER 40
The Sentencing
1970

Judge Chambers sneezed into his handkerchief. He had been fighting a head cold unsuccessfully for a week. His throat was irritated and his voice was raspy.

"In all my years of growing up here and working in this county, as an attorney and judge, I have never heard of another case like this where a father and son were convicted of murder and the jury recommended their deaths."

"The relationship of the defendants was known by the jury and this court. Still, that didn't stop them from finding both guilty of murder and recommending death for each of them. They treated each defendant equally to the other."

"Russell James is forty-three years of age and Steven Wilbur James is over twenty-two years of age. In the eyes of the law, Steven James is an adult, and he shall be treated as such."

"Since both the father and son are adults, I cannot offer a greater degree of punishment for the father or a lesser degree for the son because of the relationship between the two."

"The defendants have been found guilty of murder in a trial where the case was based considerably on circumstantial evidence. Often, juries are hesitant to indorse the death penalty where there is no direct evidence. This jury, however, was obviously persuaded of the defendants' guilt as they recommended the sentence of death."

"As for me, before I would ever pass down a death sentence on any defendant, I would not only have to be certain of the defendant's guilt but the circumstances of the killing must warrant the death sentence."

"In this case, the court is convinced beyond any doubt the defendants murdered Daniel Sycamore. The analysis of the evidence leads to no other conclusion than the defendant's guilt. It was a cold-hearted, ruthless murder that need not have occurred. The defendants executed their victim."

"The defendants, used the very same gun two short weeks after the murder of Daniel Sycamore, to commit another armed robbery. It is my opinion that the defendants are cold and callous gunmen who will kill at their own discretion."

"In the manner and place prescribed by law, the defendants are hereby sentenced to death with the execution to occur on the first day of December 1970. A formal Order of Execution is being filed by the court at this time."

During the fifteen-minute reading of the sentence, Margaret James sobbed uncontrollably. Russell's mother held her in her arms, and the pair rocked back and forth in gut-wrenching sobs. Russell looked over at the devastated women and slowly shook his head. Steven leaned back in his chair on several occasions but made no noise.

As the jammed courtroom began to empty, Margaret emotionally blurted out, "They're innocent. They didn't do it!" Her outbursts fell on deaf ears.

Margaret's world had turned upside down. She tried desperately to understand how her life at one minute had been so peaceful and routine. Through no fault of her own, in the split second it took to pull a trigger, it imploded and would never return to normalcy again.

CHAPTER 41
Righting a Wrong
1996

Echo smiled at the prison guard pleasantly. "I'd like to see Russell James, please."

"Is he expecting you?"

"No, sir, I didn't know I was coming myself until an hour ago."

"Go ahead and have a seat while I check his visitor's list. Then, I'll track him down for you. Do you have your license?"

Echo handed it to the correctional officer and in just a few minutes, she was taken to the back where she removed her shoes and socks. When finished a female guard escorted her to the Visitor's Center.

Echo hoped Russell wouldn't balk at seeing her. She wasn't proud of the cruel things she said the last time they spoke. What she wanted now was the opportunity to apologize. She hoped he would receive it but her visit was intended for so much more than that. She wanted to share with him the experience of her recent epiphany concerning her brother.

Echo noticed Russell wasn't waiting for her as he always was before. An ominous feeling encircled her but was dispelled by the officer. "You can take a seat at one of the tables, and they'll bring him out in just a few minutes."

Echo sat down at the only table the two had ever shared.

When he entered the room, Russell had a big smile on his face as if he were pleased to see her. She stood to greet him and he extended his hand toward her, but she brushed it back and hugged him.

"It's good to see you again, Echo. I'm sorry you had to wait. Had I known you were coming; I would have arranged to be here upon your arrival."

"Oh, it was no wait at all. I hope I haven't caused a glitch in your schedule. I promise not to overstay my welcome."

"Are you kidding me? I'm laying insulation today and as chilly as it is outside, it's like a furnace up in the attic. So please, stay as long as you like."

The two smiled before Echo's countenance took on a more subdued expression. The room grew suddenly quiet.

"Russell, the reason I'm here today is to apologize, face to face, for the ugly manner in which I spoke to you the last time I was here."

"Nonsense, there is no apology necessary. All I want to hear are the details of Tia Marie's big day."

"Oh, I have so much to tell you concerning that, but there is something that I must say to you first."

He raised his hands and shrugged his shoulders in resignation and sat back quietly.

"I said hurtful things the last time I was here; things I didn't mean and had no right to say. I want you to know I am truly sorry. In all my shortcomings, I never meant to hurt you."

"There, now you've said it and I accept. I'm sorry too. So, let's move to a happier conversation, shall we?"

"Please, Russell, I must say what's on my heart right now. I'm not finished."

He acquiesced and leaned back in his chair.

"I desperately wanted to write a book. I thought the purpose of my coming here, as if it were something ordained from the beginning of time, was to write your story. I feel so foolish now."

"My drive was all consuming. Still, I had no right to expect the success of my dream to rise and set upon you. I put my personal desires ahead of yours and I was wrong to do that. I'm very sorry."

Russell reached over and gently patted Echo on the back. "Hush now, no more fretting. It's all right."

"You were right to call me out on Lyndon Johnson. I did loathe him for the deadly cost of his incompetence. I spoke to you of accountability, forgiveness and healing, when all the while I hadn't done that for myself."

"But something happened to me the day Tia Marie walked down the aisle. Her wedding was a wonderfully brutal experience that caused me to feel the entire gamut of my brother's loss so overwhelmingly strong. Ironically, it was the catalyst to lift my grief, remove the hatred and bring peace to fruition."

Russell looked confused and for a moment he appeared as if he didn't know what to say. Still, he couldn't help seeing a joy radiate from within Echo or recognize the infectious effect it had on him as well. Echo smiled. She put her hand on his and gently squeezed.

"I'm sure it must have been painful for you, feeling Tom's absence on that most special day for his only child; all grown now without him ever having known her."

"Yes. I cried bitter tears, so many that I didn't believe I would ever be composed again."

Russell smiled compassionately. "Well, at least with Tom being dead, you have Tia Marie to fill the void and your brother now lives through her."

"Oh no, Russell, that's not it at all! The epiphany is so much greater than that. You see, I believe Tom lives, more now than he ever did before. But not through his daughter. He lives an eternal life, and the euphoria this knowledge has given me no drug-induced ecstasy could compare."

"That's a powerful statement," Russell said.

"Yes, and powerfully shown to me as well!"

Russell genuinely wanted to understand. "How did you come to this?"

"You see, I re-read all of Tom's letters after the wedding and they spoke volumes. I found comfort in the ones from Vietnam; especially those written toward the end of his short life. They reflected his last known thoughts, his last written words."

"In them, I discovered through many tears that my brother suffered tremendous fear before his death. Learning of this was cruel but absolutely necessary. It was indeed, like a two-edged sword that broke my heart and healed it as well."

"You see, learning of his fear helped me to understand it was the thing that caused him to cry out to the only One who could save him. I know he did this because his last words to his family assured me of it. And for me, knowing this, I was finally able to heal."

"I cried out all the hurt, the loss, the ache and longing within me until my heart filled with hope in the promise of a better day when we're united to be divided nevermore!"

"I believe Tom is safe in heaven. Of this, I am persuaded beyond all earthly comprehension. I can embrace something other than the sorrow and pain of my family's loss. I found hope in spiritual promises on which to stand. I don't feel the sting of death anymore. I could shout for joy, but if I began, I don't think I'd be able to stop!"

"The peace I found in Tom's own words; no other human being was capable of conveying. The change they wrought within me is so much greater than any story I could ever write. I would never have thought so before, but I now believe the change that was effected in me is what this entire journey was all about."

"Echo, I don't think I've ever heard anything so beautiful. Thank you for sharing that with me. Now, I have hope, too, that I might see Tom again someday!"

Echo and Russell sat together; smiling through beautiful cleansing tears.

"Oh, my goodness, look at the time! It'll be dark before too long, and I'd like to be off the road before then. I really should be going."

"I have a feeling you're never coming back." Russell's tone was sad and downhearted. "I wish it wasn't so."

"But if you should ever need me, I'll be here. All you have to do is let me know. But I won't return with the aspiration to write your story. If there's a book out there for me to write, I won't look any further than my own experiences."

CHAPTER 42
With Fear and Trepidation
1970

Russell and Steven were handcuffed and taken back to the Sturnus County jail. On July 22, they were picked up by the Department of Corrections, placed in handcuffs and shackles and delivered by bus to the State Penitentiary-Stateville for processing into the system.

They were given their prisoner ID numbers, temporary jumpsuit clothing and a battery of medical examinations, both physical and psychological. The inmates were photographed and fingerprinted for identification purposes.

The father and son were required to provide a sample of blood or a saliva swab for the department's database. The samples were saved for any future identification purposes, including possible medical needs from inmate assaults.

But the Jameses needn't have worried about that. They'd be safe in their solitary cells, locked away where no one but the executioner might cause them harm.

In less than forty-eight hours, they were taken from the Reception and Classification Center and transferred to their new home in Chester.

Their tiny living quarters, the size of a parking space, was situated on the second floor at Menard Penitentiary in an alcove known as Death Row. The space contained no natural light but had Plexiglas windows in the door that looked out onto a hallway, lit with florescent bulbs. Meals were served through a slot in the cell door.

Their new digs consisted of a toilet, sink, shelf, and bed with little room for maneuvering. When allowed an hour of recreation out of doors, they remained alone and caged. Death row inmates are not allowed human contact. They would spend twenty-three hours out of a twenty-four-hour day in their cells.

If they didn't realize it when they first arrived, Russell and

Steven would soon come to recognize their existence as a sort of death before dying. Neither would have ever guessed their reprieve would come by way of the United States Supreme Court when the Justices ruled the death penalty unconstitutional on June 29, 1972.

Steven and Russell were brought back to Starling for re-sentencing on November 24. For the murder and armed robbery, Steven received an indeterminate term of not less than seventy-five years and a maximum of not more than one-hundred-twenty-five years. His father was sentenced to a minimum of not less than one-hundred years and not more than two-hundred years. Did the sentencing judge believe the father more culpable due to his position of authority over the son? One can only surmise.

No longer bearing their special inmate death classification, the Jameses became just like any other maximum-security prisoner. They were evaluated and moved to other top security facilities within the state. Steven was sent to Pontiac Correctional Center in Livingston County and Russell was shipped back to Menard.

After seven years removed from death row, Russell had a job in the prison commissary with a reputation as a good and trusted worker. He had a clean record and kept his nose in his own business. His boss was a thirty-five-year-old corrections' employee and Vietnam veteran named Brody Baylor, husband, and father of two daughters.

On the first day of March, 1982, Russell was assisting Baylor in stocking the shelves with a new shipment of products. They had been working for about half an hour on that Monday when Baylor was attacked from behind by Julius Copeland, an inmate serving twenty to thirty years for rape and aggravated sexual assault out of St. Clair County. Copeland later told authorities he wanted some cigarettes and didn't have the money to purchase them.

Baylor was grabbed around the neck from behind and wrestled to the ground where he was stabbed repeatedly in the abdomen with a homemade shank. One thrust of the weapon pierced his heart and caused the employee's death. An investigation was held to determine how the inmate was able to get into the commissary area without being detected.

Russell backed up and cowered in a corner. Copeland looked at him intently and started to approach with a raised hand gripping the bloody shank, but decided against further aggression. Now was not the time. Still, it wasn't over. "I'll deal with you later," he told Russell before reeling and running from the area.

Officers had no doubt Russell witnessed the murder but soon came to believe he didn't have any participation in it. Not one speck of blood was found on him or his clothing. He was taken to the Warden's office, shaking by every fiber within him. No one seemed to care.

"Karma coming back to bite him," one of the correctional officers later said. Russell was traumatized like Daniel must have been just moments before he and Steven raised their weapons and killed the station attendant.

Russell pleaded with the Warden. "You have to protect me. He's going to kill me. He said so. He said he'd deal with me later. So, I'll tell you who did it. I'll tell you everything. But you've got to get me out of here before he makes good on his promise!"

Warden Frankie Lawler had already examined the file and knew Russell was not a troublemaker; at least he never had been throughout the years of his entire incarceration. "You have a good record, and you've kept your nose clean. You tell us everything you know, hold back nothing, and we'll have you transferred out of here."

Julius Copeland received a minimum sentence of 250 years and not more than 350 years for the murder of Brody Baylor.

The warden kept his word. Transfer papers were prepared. And at 6:30 p.m., the next evening, a Department of Corrections transportation bus moved Russell and two boxes of his belongings to the Logan Correctional Center in Lincoln. Now his family, his mother, brother and children could visit more often and wouldn't have to travel so far to see him.

There was one family member that he, most likely, would never see again. The once-close father and son murdering duo have not seen one another since their resentencing. Chances are, at Russell's age, he will die in prison.

Steven may stand a chance of being released on parole one day. But he'll have to admit to the murder of Daniel Sycamore before that will ever happen.

THE END

EPILOG

Russell James was seventy-seven years of age in 2003 when, suffering with congestive heart failure, he developed a serious case of pneumonia. In August, he was taken in a Corrections van to Hope Memorial Hospital in Starling. He was placed in a private room in the cardiac intermediate care ward at the end of a long hallway, isolated from other patients. A Corrections guard stood watch just outside his door.

Russell was given antibiotics and a glucose intravenous for hydration but he didn't respond to treatment and slipped into a coma. His breathing became agonal, heavy and labored. A death rattle could be heard throughout the room.

Then at 5:35 a.m., on August 29, Russell drew his last breath and exhaled it. His fight was over. He was free once more.

The warden at Logan Correctional Center, Andre Philpot, was notified. He, in turn, notified the Starling Police Department and the Sturnus County Sheriff's Office of the death. The coroner was informed as well. Under State law, an autopsy must be performed on inmates who die in custody, regardless of the medical condition or age of the prisoner. Generally, that responsibility falls upon the local coroner's office.

Geoff was at his house preparing to rush back to the hospital after spending three days there. He arrived back home just a few hours earlier for a simple shower, a change of clothes and about an hour's worth of shut-eye.

Geoff later told Echo. "I knew his time was near, but not even the doctors expected it that soon, or else I would never have left him there to die alone. I was just about to head out the door on my way back to the hospital when the phone rang. It was the prison chaplain calling with his regrets."

Later that morning Geoff was contacted by Victim Services. Russell had $2.58 in his Inmate Trust Fund and $6.00 in wages that were due him. Those monies, Geoff was told, would be applied to the transportation of his father's body to a funeral parlor of the family's choosing. Kester and Evenly Funeral Home in Starling was decided upon and the body was transported there. The vast majority of the cost for the funeral and burial would come by way of public expenditure.

Steven was not allowed to attend his father's funeral. The two cohorts in crime would continue to be separated, at least while on the earth.

Geoff purchased a plot in the Pleasant Prairie Cemetery where his father would be buried. The gravesite is marked by a single flat granite plaque that bears Russell's name, birth and death dates.

Steven James remained in prison until 2014, some forty-four years after the conviction that sent him there. His final parole hearing was unlike any previous and was the catalyst that made way for his release on parole.

Six weeks before his scheduled parole hearing, Steven sent a message to the warden of the Pontiac Correctional Center where he spent his last twenty-five years. In it, he stated his desire to have Dallas Sycamore present at his parole hearing and asked the warden to make his wishes known.

"I have something I'd like to say concerning the murder of his brother. And I want him to feel free to ask me anything he wants to know."

Dallas agreed to travel to the center, approximately one-hundred-twenty miles northeast of his home in Downey. Addie refused to let him go alone.

The Sycamores were curious to hear what Steven had to say but there was more that drove Dallas to the prison that day. He was looking forward to some very specific answers to questions that had plagued him from the time his brother was murdered. The parole hearing lasted almost three hours that day.

Steven was ready to sing like a bird. And sing he did! He admitted his guilt in the role he played in Daniel's death, accompanied by his father. When he finished, there wasn't a dry eye in the room.

Mr. Calvin Garrett, the parole board member, asked Dallas if he'd like to make a statement or if he had any questions that he'd like for the inmate to address.

"Yes, if I may, sir." Dallas appeared apprehensive but determined. "First, I'm pleased you've taken responsibility for something we always knew you were guilty of. What I'd like to know from you today are the details of how the murder took place. Why did it happen? Was my brother made to suffer? Did Danny fight back? And most especially, what did he say before you pointed the gun at his head and pulled the trigger?"

Addie dabbed her eyes with the Kleenex she had in her hand. She rubbed her husband's knee to calm the anger and rage rising within him. Dallas took a few deep breaths to center and calm himself.

Garrett looked at the inmate but didn't speak. Steven was fully prepared to give Dallas the answers to every question he had. Tears streamed down Steven's face but he didn't hold back.

"We entered the station at approximately 2:20 a.m., with every intention of robbing it. My father had the revolver in his coat pocket. As soon as we crossed the station threshold, my dad hopped up and planted his butt on the desktop. Daniel, in a raised voice, told him firmly, "Get down off that desk right now!"

"My dad shot a surprised glance at me and said, "Are you going to let him talk to me that way?" And that's when he pulled the gun out of his coat pocket and handed it to me. Daniel's eyes grew huge with fear when he saw it."

Steven wiped his tears with his long-sleeve prison-issued shirt. He sniffled, and Garrett handed him a Kleenex.

"My father was a manipulator. He'd stir the pot, get things riled up and then expect me to handle the situation. He'd have all these scheming ideas but he didn't have the chutzpah to do the dirty work himself. I realize that now, but I didn't then. I used to think my old man was the greatest father on the face of the earth. I don't anymore."

Silence filled the room as Steven lowered his head and dabbed the Kleenex to his eyes before continuing. "So, that's when Daniel said, "What are you doing? Don't point that gun at me. Put it down before it goes off!"

"I told him to get in the back room and he complied. He was crying, pleading for his life. He begged us not to hurt him. He was shaking profusely. He kept saying, "Jesus, help me," over and over again."

"My father followed us into the storage room and as I kicked the door shut there was a shotgun that fell to the floor from behind the door and my father picked it up."

"That's when he pointed it at Daniel and fired it, hitting him in the right arm. I had no idea that was going to happen. I saw the buckshot force his arm into his chest like a rocket. I thought sure it must have come out of the socket. He screamed in pain as his body dropped to the floor and he began to cry more desperately. He appeared stunned and in shock; but I don't think the shot knocked him out temporarily or anything like that because in a matter of seconds he was moving."

"I told Daniel to stay down on the ground but he started to get back up again like he was going to defend himself and come at us."

"I remember thinking at the time that he must be a religious person, because he kept crying out to God for help. The last words I recall him saying were, "Don't shoot me. Oh God, please help me!"

"Everything was moving so fast now. I panicked and fired the revolver, but the bullet only grazed his forehead. Still, that shot seemed to knock him out momentarily. Before I could figure out what to do next, he began to moan and come around. He started to get back up and, in my fear and panic, I stepped closer to him, pointed the gun directly at him and I opened fire. This time I knew it was all over. I was sure he wouldn't be getting back up again."

Steven cried hysterically, on the verge of hyperventilating, while Dallas and Addie hung their heads, weeping in brutal contemplation. Calvin Garrett could feel the entire gamut all at once; the heartbreak of the victim's family, as well as the liberation from guilt and grief that was playing out before him.

It was after the hearing, outside the prisoner's presence, that Dallas informed the board he would never ask for Steven James' release but he was resigned to unconditionally accept the Board's decision without objection, if and when they deemed Steven James suitable for parole. Dallas was now truly free to move on.

He and Addie were grandparents to two boys and a girl. They moved to Danville to be closer to their grandkids, their daughter and son-in-law. Today, Dallas teaches a class in Information Technology at the Danville Area Community College. Don DeLario is a regular guest in the Sycamore home.

Steven was released from prison on December 3, 2014. He lives with his wife, a former high school classmate, whom he married three weeks after being freed. They live in rural Sturnus County with their dog, Bo, and two felines named Starsky and Hutch.

Steven reports to his parole officer on a weekly basis and must do so for the rest of his life. He is randomly drug-tested and has been clean and trouble-free since his release.

Don DeLario retired from the Sturnus County Sheriff's office in 1994 and went to work as an investigator for the Secretary of State Police. Lewis Morell followed him six months later. The two were partners once again. That is, until they both retired in 2002.

Don and Carla sold their home in Avery and moved to a retirement community in Starling. Carla passed away in 2014, and Echo visits Don regularly.

Echo never found her writing niche. Instead, she heard a call to join the Sturnus County Sheriff's office. She went back to school and obtained a bachelor's degree in criminal justice.

Don and Carla attended her graduation. On December 13, 1999, after passing the written examination, a physical agility test and having a valid driver's license, Echo entered the department.

After eight years she was promoted to detective in the Investigations Bureau. Five years later, she was promoted again. That day, she hopped in her car and drove to her mentor's apartment. She just had to talk to Don. He made coffee and they sat in his spacious living room.

"Don, I got the job; your old job. I'm now the Chief of Detectives for Sturnus County."

Don wrapped his arms around her in a bear hug. Yet, a knowing grin etched across his mouth as if he had known her secret all along. "Well, that's wonderful!"

She looked at him curiously. "You don't seem to be surprised by the news."

"Sorry Echo, I can't seem to keep a straight face. The truth is I had dinner with our new Sheriff Janson and his wife last night. And he, by way of knowing we're friends, let your promotion slip out of the bag. He told me he was going to offer you the job this morning. I told him he couldn't have picked a better person. Still, I think he felt bad for telling me before you had the chance to tell me yourself. So, he asked me not to say anything to you. I hope you're not angry?"

"No, I'm not angry. I'm much too happy to be angry right now. Besides, I know how you men in blue like to share information."

Don chuckled. "Ha-ha. I suppose you're right there. Still, I knew you could do it. You had that inquisitive mind from the very first time I met you. And now that the roles are reversed, maybe you'll help me on a book someday." Echo smiled warmly and took a sip from her cup of piping hot coffee.